Decoded

UNSOLVED MYSTERIES INVESTIGATIONS

THE EX-FILES

AMALIA ROSE

A Note from the Author

Dear Reader,

This novel is a work of factual dramatization, a narrative form that blends historical reality with fictional elements to create a compelling story. While inspired by the lives of real individuals and actual events, the characters and their experiences have been reimagined and embellished for dramatic effect.

The foundation of this novel rests upon extensive research, drawing from a rich tapestry of archival materials, including historical documents, academic papers, and news articles. These factual elements have been carefully woven into the fictional narrative, providing a sense of authenticity and grounding the story in the context of real-world events.

However, it is important to note that this novel does not purport to be a strictly factual account. Dialogue, certain characters, and specific scenes have been created or adapted to serve the story's narrative arc and themes. The inner thoughts, motivations, and relationships of the characters are products of my interpretation and imagination.

For readers interested in exploring the many factual underpinnings of this novel, a comprehensive historical timeline and a list of sources have been provided at the end of the book. These sections offer a glimpse into the real-world events, people, and documents that served as the inspiration for this work of factual dramatization.

While every effort has been made to remain true to the spirit of the historical record, this novel should be approached as a work of fiction, albeit one that is deeply rooted in the fascinating and often overlooked corners of our shared past.

My pen name is Amalia Rose, and this is my story. It's a tale of hope and heartbreak, of daring and discovery, and of the unbreakable bond between those who seek the truth. I may not have all the answers, but I've learned that sometimes, the only way to find them is to take a leap of faith and trust in the journey.

So, are you ready to join me?

Amalia Rose

Amalia Rose Publications
121-11-4 | 3-17-9 | 78-5-14
April 26, 2024
#TheExFiles
ko-fi.com/theexfiles

It was as if an entire civilization had undergone some self-inflicted brain surgery, and most of its memories, discoveries, ideas, and passions were extinguished irrevocably.

— CARL SAGAN

CHAPTER 1

The Blog Post

T hey say the truth will set you free, but in my experience, it's more likely to get you killed. My name is Amalia Rose, and I'm a journalist. At least, that's the name I'm using for this story. The real truth is, I'm undercover, and if the people I'm investigating ever find out who I really am, I'll be lucky to escape with my life. But I'm getting ahead of myself. Let me start at the beginning, with the blog post that changed everything.

It was a typical Tuesday morning, and I was scrolling through my favorite Reddit forums, looking for a lead on my next big story. I work for a major publication in New York, but I can't tell you which one. Let's just call it the City Rag. I was about to log off when a headline caught my eye: "Voynich Manuscript Decoded: The Shocking Truth about a Lost Matriarchal Civilization."

I clicked on the link, my curiosity piqued. The Voynich Manuscript[1] was a notorious historical enigma, a fifteenth-century codex written in an unknown script and filled with bizarre illustrations of plants, astrological diagrams, and bathing women. For centuries, the greatest minds in cryptography and linguistics had tried and failed to decipher its contents. And now, if this blog post was to be believed, the mystery had been solved by a lone computational linguist named Dr. Emily Hathaway.

As I read through the post, my skepticism gave way to a growing sense of excitement. Dr. Hathaway claimed to have used advanced AI techniques to crack the code, revealing the manuscript's true origins: a lost civilization of women who had achieved technological and social heights far beyond anything in recorded history. According to Hathaway, these women had lived in a utopian society free from the oppression and violence of men, using advanced herbal medicines and cosmological knowledge to guide their lives.

It was a stunning revelation, almost too good to be true. And as I scrolled through the comments section, I saw that I wasn't the only one who thought so. The post had gone viral, sparking a heated debate between those who hailed Hathaway as a visionary and those who dismissed her as a fraud. Some commenters demanded more proof, while others hurled insults and accusations. A few even made veiled threats, hinting at a conspiracy to suppress the truth.

I sat back in my chair, my mind reeling. If Dr. Hathaway was right, her discovery could rewrite history as we knew it. But if she was wrong, or if her claims were some kind of elaborate hoax, the fallout could be devastating. Either way, I knew I had to investigate further.

I was just about to start digging into Dr. Hathaway's background when my editor's name flashed on my phone screen. I picked up, already knowing what he was going to say.

"Amalia, have you seen this Voynich Manuscript story?" His voice was tense with excitement.

"I'm looking at it right now," I said. "What do you think?"

"I think it's either the biggest scoop of the decade or the

biggest load of bullshit I've ever seen. Either way, I want you on it. Drop whatever else you're working on and find out everything you can about this Dr. Hathaway character. If her claims are true, we need to be the first to break the story. If not, we need to expose her before this thing gets any more out of hand."

I hesitated for just a moment, weighing the risks and rewards of taking on such a high-profile investigation. But who was I kidding? I lived for this kind of story. The chance to uncover a world-changing truth, to solve a mystery that had baffled the experts for centuries? It was the reason I became a journalist in the first place.

"I'm on it," I said, my heart already racing with anticipation. "I'll start digging into Hathaway's background and see if I can track her down for an interview. But Boss, I've got a feeling this story is going to be bigger than anything we've tackled before. We need to be careful."

"Careful is for rookies," my editor barked. "You're one of the best investigative journalists in the game, Amalia. That's why I'm trusting you with this. Now get out there and bring me back a story that'll make the front page of every newspaper in the country."

He hung up before I could respond, leaving me alone with my thoughts and the weight of the task ahead. I took a deep breath and cracked my knuckles, ready to dive into the rabbit hole of the Voynich Manuscript and the enigmatic Dr. Emily Hathaway.

Little did I know that I was about to embark on a journey that would lead me to the darkest corners of history, the cutting edge of science, and the blurred lines between fact and fiction—a journey that would test my skills as a journalist, my loyalty to the truth, and my very understanding of reality itself.

But that's the thing about the truth. Once you start

chasing it, there's no going back. And as I began my investigation into the mystery of the Voynich Manuscript, I had no idea just how deep and dangerous the pursuit of truth could be.

CHAPTER 2

The Manuscript

As soon as I hung up with my editor, I knew I had to learn everything I could about the Voynich Manuscript. I'd heard of it in passing over the years, but I'd never really delved into the details of its history or the countless attempts to decipher it. If I was going to investigate Dr. Hathaway's claims, I needed to become an expert on the manuscript as quickly as possible.

I pulled up every reputable source I could find on the Voynich Manuscript and started reading. The more I learned, the more intrigued I became. The manuscript, it turned out, was a fifteenth-century codex written in an unknown script and filled with bizarre illustrations of unidentifiable plants, astrological diagrams, and naked women. It had been named after Wilfrid Voynich, the Polish book dealer who had acquired it in 1912, but its true origins remained a mystery.

As I dug deeper into the manuscript's history, I discovered a long line of brilliant minds who had become obsessed with its secrets. There was William Newbold, a philosopher who claimed to have deciphered the manuscript using a complex system of microscopic shorthand, only to have his theory debunked after his death. There were William and Elizebeth Friedman, the pioneering cryptologists who had tried and failed to crack the code during World War I. Even the National Security Agency had taken a crack at it during the Cold War, using the manuscript as a training exercise for its top code-breakers.

I read about Wilfried Voynich's own attempts to decipher the manuscript and the various theories that had been put forth over the years about its contents and purpose. Some believed it was a treatise on medieval medicine, others a work of alchemy or mysticism. A few even claimed it was a hoax, a clever forgery designed to fool collectors and scholars. But no one had ever been able to prove anything conclusively. The Voynich Manuscript remained one of the greatest unsolved mysteries in the history of cryptography—until now, if Dr. Hathaway was to be believed.

As I pored over the images of the manuscript's pages, I found myself drawn in by the strange beauty of its roughly sketched illustrations. The plants and flowers were unlike anything I'd ever seen before, with twisted stems and bulbous flowers that seemed to defy the laws of nature. It was as if they belonged to a different world entirely, a world where the rules of biology and botany held no sway. The cosmological charts, too, were filled with intricate symbols and diagrams that hinted at a deeper, hidden meaning, a cosmic significance that seemed to beckon me closer, daring me to unravel their secrets.

But it was the script itself that truly held me spellbound. The flowing, alien characters danced across the pages, their curves and lines as graceful and enigmatic as the movements of a serpent. I found myself tracing each symbol with my finger, as if by touch alone I could somehow absorb their meaning, could unlock the secrets that had been lost to time and history. It was a language that spoke to something deep within me, something primal and ancient, a whisper of a long-forgotten truth that seemed to hover just beyond the edge of my understanding.

And then, as I turned another page, I found them: the illustrations of naked women, their bodies natural and unadorned. These were not the idealized, sexualized figures I was used to seeing in art and media, but rather depictions of women in all their diverse, imperfect glory.

Some of the women—unfazed by shame or stigma—held phallic-shaped objects that pointed to their genitalia. Others were depicted bathing in pools or tubs, their bodies submerged in complex networks of pipes and conduits that seemed to suggest a deeper, more intricate system at work.

I was so engrossed in my research that I almost didn't hear my phone ringing. It was Jake, an old friend from college who now worked as a rare book dealer in New York. I'd reached out to him earlier in the day, hoping he might have some insider knowledge on the Voynich Manuscript or the people who had studied it over the years.

"Amalia, hey," he said when I picked up. "I got your message. What's this about the Voynich Manuscript?"

I filled him in on the basics of Dr. Hathaway's blog post and my editor's assignment. "I'm trying to learn as much as I can about the manuscript's history and the people who have tried to decipher it," I said. "I was hoping you might have some insights."

Jake was silent for a moment. "The Voynich Manuscript is a rabbit hole," he said finally. "I've seen a lot of people go down it over the years, and not many of them come back out again. It has a way of obsessing people, consuming them. I'd be careful if I were you, Amalia."

His words sent a chill down my spine, but I tried to play it off. "I'm a journalist, Jake. Chasing rabbit holes is kind of my job."

He sighed. "I know. Just . . . be careful, okay? The Voynich

Manuscript has a way of attracting some strange characters. And not all of them have the best intentions."

I promised him I would be careful, and we said our good-byes. But as I hung up the phone, I couldn't shake the sense of unease his words had stirred up in me. I had always prided myself on my ability to separate fact from fiction, to see through the hype and speculation to the truth at the core. But something about the Voynich Manuscript felt different. It was as if the manuscript itself was a living thing, with its own agenda and its own secrets to keep.

I pushed aside my doubts and went back to my research, determined to learn everything I could about the manuscript and the woman who claimed to have finally deciphered it. I reached out to every contact I had in the world of rare books and cryptography, hoping someone might have a lead on Dr. Hathaway or her work.

But the more I dug, the more elusive she seemed to become. No one in the academic community seemed to have known her well. It was as if she had appeared out of nowhere, dropping this bombshell revelation about the Voynich Manuscript and then vanishing back into obscurity.

As the hours ticked by and my emails and phone calls went unanswered, I began to feel a creeping sense of frustration. I was a seasoned investigative journalist, used to chasing down leads and unraveling complex mysteries. But Dr. Hathaway was proving to be a tougher nut to crack than any story I had ever pursued before.

I was just about to call it a night when a new email popped up in my inbox. The subject line made my heart skip a beat: "Dr. Hathaway and the Voynich Manuscript - Confidential Information."

I clicked on the email with trembling fingers, hardly daring to breathe. It was from an anonymous sender, but the contents were explosive:

Ms. Rose,

I have information about Dr. Emily Hathaway and her work on the Voynich Manuscript that I think you'll find very interesting. I can't say more over email, but if you're willing to meet in person, I can give you the details you need to blow this story wide open.

Meet me at the Rare Books Room of the New York Public Library tomorrow at 3:00 PM. Come alone and tell no one about this email. If you're not there, you'll never hear from me again.

The choice is yours.

I stared at the screen, my heart racing. I knew it could be a trap, that meeting with an anonymous source was a risky move for any journalist. But I also knew I couldn't ignore a lead like this. If this person really did have information about Dr. Hathaway and her work on the Voynich Manuscript, I had to follow the trail, no matter where it led.

I quickly typed out a reply, agreeing to the meeting and promising to keep it confidential. Then I leaned back in my chair, my mind spinning with possibilities. I had no idea what I was getting myself into, but one thing was clear: the mystery of the Voynich Manuscript was only just beginning to unravel, and I was going to be there every step of the way.

No matter how deep the rabbit hole went.

CHAPTER 3

The Linguist

As I stepped out of the taxi in front of the New York Public Library, I felt I was being watched. I glanced around, trying to catch a glimpse of anyone who might be paying a little too much attention to me, but the crowds of people hurrying by on the sidewalk seemed absorbed in their own worlds.

I shook off my unease and climbed the steps to the library's imposing entrance. I had more important things to worry about than phantom stalkers. I was here to meet with an anonymous source who claimed to have information about Dr. Emily Hathaway, the enigmatic linguist who had supposedly cracked the code of the Voynich Manuscript.

As I made my way through the library's cavernous lobby and up the stairs to the Rare Books Room, I couldn't stop thinking about the little I had managed to uncover about Dr. Hathaway so far. She was a brilliant but unconventional scholar, with a reputation for pushing the boundaries of linguistics and attracting controversy wherever she went.

Her work on the Voynich Manuscript, in particular, seemed to have become an obsession for her. From what I could gather from the fragments of information I had pieced together, she had spent years poring over the manuscript's strange illustrations and enigmatic script, convinced that it held the key to unlocking a lost history of women's power and knowledge.

The Voynich Manuscript's images of naked women, often depicted inside exaggerated or stylized reproductive organs, had apparently struck a chord with Dr. Hathaway's fierce feminist sensibilities. She seemed to believe that the manuscript was a codex created by and for women, a secret text that encoded ancient wisdom about the female body, sexuality, and spirituality.

I was intrigued by this idea, even as my journalistic skepticism warned me to be cautious. The Voynich Manuscript's illustrations—while unpolished—were certainly striking. But as fascinating as these images were, they hardly seemed like conclusive proof of a lost matriarchal civilization, as Dr. Hathaway had apparently claimed in her blog post. I knew I needed to keep an open mind, but I also couldn't let myself get swept up in what could very well be an elaborate hoax or delusion.

I pushed open the heavy wooden doors of the Rare Books Room and stepped inside, feeling the hush of centuries-old knowledge settling around me. The room was dimly lit and smelled faintly of old paper and leather. I made my way past rows of glass cases filled with ancient manuscripts and delicate, crumbling books, my footsteps echoing softly on the polished floor.

As I approached the back corner of the room, I noticed not one, but two women, in their sixties, sitting at a small table. The first, with deep brown skin and tight coils of black hair cropped close to her scalp, was engrossed in a book. Her high cheekbones and full lips were illuminated by the soft glow of the reading lamp, lending her face a regal quality. The second woman, with pale skin and long, white-blonde hair, sat a little further away, her hazel eyes darting between the first woman and me as I approached.

The woman with the book looked up as I drew near, her deep brown eyes bright with intelligence as she fixed me with an appraising gaze. "Ms. Rose, I presume," she said, her voice smooth and confident with a hint of a Harlem accent. "Glad you could make it."

I slid into the chair across from her, my heart hammering in my chest. "Thank you for reaching out," I said, trying to keep my voice steady. "I'm very interested in what you have to say about the Voynich Manuscript." I glanced at the blonde, who was still watching us intently. "I'm sorry, I didn't catch your name. And who's your friend over there?"

The woman leaned back in her chair, a faint smile playing at the corners of her mouth. "You can call me Regina, and that's Agnes. She's just keeping an eye out to make sure our conversation stays between us, if you catch my drift."

I nodded, my curiosity piqued by the mysterious circumstances. "I understand. So, what can you tell me about Emily Hathaway?"

Regina's smile widened. "Emily? She's more than just a brilliant linguist, Ms. Rose. She's a visionary, a trailblazer who's been working tirelessly to uncover the hidden history of women. And the Voynich Manuscript? That's the key to unlocking everything she's been searching for."

I leaned forward, intrigued. "Hidden history? What do you mean? What secrets does the manuscript hold?"

Regina glanced around the room, as if to make sure we weren't being overheard. "The Voynich Manuscript isn't just some ancient text full of women's wisdom," she said, her voice low and intense. "It's a testament to a time when women held the power of knowledge. We were the healers, the scholars, the guardians of life's mysteries. But more than that, it's evidence of a society that transcended the limitations men sought to place upon us."

She reached into her bag and pulled out a sheaf of papers, spreading them out on the table in front of me. I saw that they were photocopies of pages from the Voynich Manuscript, the strange, swirling script and the crudely drawn illustrations seeming to dance before my eyes.

"Take a look at these images," Regina said, pointing to a complex diagram of what looked like naked women inter-acting with enlarged plants and flowers shaped like reproductive organs. "This right here? It's a map of the female reproductive system, but it's encoded in the language of nature herself. But it's more than just a biological blueprint. It's a symbol of the power these women wielded to create life, to bring forth new generations without the need for men."

I stared at the images, trying to wrap my mind around the implications of what she was saying. "Are you suggesting that this manuscript describes a society where women could repro-duce without men?" I asked, my voice tinged with disbelief.

Regina nodded, a fierce light in her eyes. "That's precisely what I'm suggesting. We are convinced the text speaks of a civilization where women had unlocked the secrets of parthenogenesis, of virgin birth. They had discovered a way to combine their own genetic material, to create new life without the need for male fertilization."

She leaned forward, her voice dropping to a whisper. "Can you imagine the power that would give women? The freedom, the autonomy? No longer would we be dependent on men for our very existence. We could shape our own destinies, create our own societies, free from the oppression and violence that have plagued women throughout history."

"That's . . . a bit extreme, isn't it?" I felt a chill run down my spine, a mixture of awe, fear, and incredulity. The idea of a women-only civilization, one that had achieved such a radical level of self-sufficiency, was almost too incredible to believe. "But if this is true," I said, my mind racing with questions, "why has this knowledge been lost? Why has no one ever heard of this civilization before?"

"Because men, they have always feared the power of women," Agnes said, her Italian accent thick with bitterness. "They tried to control us, to keep us in our place, no? And when they couldn't control us, they tried to erase us from history, to destroy every record of what we achieved, of what we knew."

Regina pointed at the papers, her hands trembling slightly. "That's why the Voynich Manuscript is so important. It's not just a historical curiosity; it's a key to unlocking a hidden truth about the potential of women. And there are those who would stop at nothing to keep that truth buried."

I leaned back in my chair, my mind reeling with the implications of what she had told me. If what she was saying was true, then the Voynich Manuscript represented more than just a centuries-old mystery. For if the manuscript held such explosive secrets, then the forces arrayed against its decipherment must be powerful indeed.

I stared at the pages, trying to make sense of what I was seeing. The images were certainly striking, but I couldn't help but feel a sense of skepticism creeping in. "How do you know all of this?" I asked. "How can you be sure that this is what the manuscript really means?"

A hint of triumph emerged in Regina's smile. "Because Emily Hathaway and her . . . uhm . . . family have deciphered it, and she will prove us right. I'm sure of it," she said. "She's cracked the code, and what she's found will change everything we thought we knew about women's history and power."

I felt a thrill of excitement running through me, even as my journalistic instincts warned me to be cautious. "So, what happens now?" I asked. "What does Dr. Hathaway plan to do with this knowledge?"

Regina's smile faded, and a look of concern crossed her face. "That's where things get complicated," she said. "There are powerful people out there who don't want this knowledge to get out. People who will do whatever it takes to keep the Voynich Manuscript's secrets hidden."

She leaned closer, her voice dropping to a whisper. "Emily Hathaway is in danger," she said urgently. "And if we don't act fast, the secrets of the manuscript may be lost forever." She glanced at Agnes, who nodded almost imperceptibly. "We must leave now," she said, both of them rushing toward the wooden doors.

I felt a chill run down my spine, and suddenly the musty, shadowy room seemed filled with hidden menace.

As I gathered up the photocopied pages and prepared to leave, my mind was racing with questions and possibilities. I knew I had to find Dr. Hathaway, to learn the truth about her work and the forces that were trying to stop her. But I also knew that I was heading into uncharted territory, a place where the lines between science and mysticism, between fact and fiction, were beginning to blur.

I checked my phone for new messages and clicked on an email titled "Unlocking the Truth."

Amalia,

Your investigation into the Voynich Manuscript has not gone unnoticed. If you wish to uncover the secrets it holds, follow the path illuminated by the manuscript's history.

Seek the place where the sun sets behind the hills, where the vines grow heavy with fruit, and the ancient stones whisper tales of a forgotten past.

There, you will both find the answers you seek.
Come alone, and tell no one of your journey.

43.470336

Attached to the email was a series of cryptic numbers that seemed to hint at some hidden meaning. I stared at the screen, my mind racing with questions. "Both? What does it mean?"

I took a deep breath and stepped out of the Rare Books Room, into the bright, bustling world of the New York Public Library. The hunt for the secrets of the Voynich Manuscript was on, and I knew I wouldn't rest until I had uncovered the truth, no matter where it led me.

Little did I know just how deep and dark the rabbit hole would go, or how much it would change everything I thought I knew about the world and my place in it.

The Ex

A s I delved deeper into the mystery of Dr. Emily Hathaway and her surprising claims about the Voynich Manuscript, I found myself spending countless hours scouring the internet for any scrap of information that might lead me to her whereabouts. Late one night, as I was scrolling through a seemingly endless series of cryptography forums and conspiracy theory websites, a familiar name suddenly caught my eye: Bastian Ham.

My heart skipped a beat as I clicked on the link, already knowing what I would find. Sure enough, there was Bastian's smiling face, looking out at me from the thumbnail of his latest YouTube video. "The Voynich Manuscript Decoded: Uncovering the Secrets of a Lost Feminist Civilization," the title proclaimed in bold, sensationalistic letters.

I felt a rush of conflicting emotions as I stared at the screen. Bastian and I had a complicated history, to say the least. We had been partners, both professionally and personally, for years—the kind of passionate, tumultuous relationship that burned hot and bright before finally exploding in a supernova of anger and betrayal.

I still remembered the moment everything fell apart, the memory seared into my mind like a brand. I had been working on a major investigation into a powerful pharmaceutical company, chasing down leads and gathering evidence in secret for months. I was so close to breaking the story wide open, to exposing the corruption and greed that had led to the deaths of innocent people.

And then Bastian, in his relentless pursuit of views and subscribers, had stumbled upon my research. Without even bothering to ask me about it, he had promptly turned around and made a splashy, sensationalistic video about the story, complete with wild speculation and unverified claims. The video went viral, and within hours, my carefully cultivated sources had gone to ground, my leads had dried up, and the pharmaceutical company had lawyered up with the best crisis management team money could buy.

I was furious, heartbroken, and utterly betrayed. How could Bastian, the man I had trusted with my heart and my life's work, have so carelessly thrown it all away for a few cheap clicks? When I confronted him about it, he had the audacity to claim that he had found the story on his own, that he had no idea I was working on it. But I knew better. I had seen the guilty look in his eyes, the way he couldn't quite meet my gaze.

We fought bitterly, trading accusations and recriminations until we were both raw and exhausted. In the end, I walked away, determined never to let myself be so vulnerable, so trusting, ever again. But now, two years later, seeing Bastian's face on my screen, all those old feelings came rushing back—the anger, the hurt, the longing for what might have been.

I knew I should just close the browser window and forget I ever saw it. Bastian's involvement in the Voynich story could only complicate my investigation, dredging up painful memories and unresolved issues from our past. But I also knew that I couldn't afford to ignore him completely. Like it or not,

Bastian had a way of ferreting out information that no one else could, a nose for the strange and the mysterious that had served him well in his career as a YouTuber and paranormal investigator.

I sighed and clicked on the video, steeling myself for whatever wild theories and speculations Bastian was peddling this time. As I watched him gesticulate wildly, his boyish face alight with excitement as he described Dr. Hathaway's supposed discoveries, I felt a pang of nostalgia for the man I had once known—the man who could make me laugh until I cried, who could see the wonder and the mystery in the most mundane things.

But that man was gone now, replaced by the slick, polished persona of Bastian Ham, the self-styled "King of the Unexplained." As he prattled on about lost civilizations and ancient wisdom, I found myself growing increasingly irritated with his cavalier attitude, his willingness to treat the Voynich story as just another piece of clickbait.

I was just about to close the video in disgust when something Bastian said caught my attention. He was describing a mysterious email he had received, claiming to have information about Dr. Hathaway's whereabouts. My heart raced as I listened to him read out the contents of the email, which sounded eerily similar to the one I had received just a few days earlier.

Could it be a coincidence? Or was someone deliberately trying to play Bastian and me against each other, using our history and our mutual interest in the Voynich Manuscript to manipulate us? I didn't know, but I knew I couldn't afford to take any chances.

I noticed his email included a different set of numbers: 11.041777. It looked like some kind of code.

I laid out the numbers side by side, studying them closely. As I compared the patterns, a realization dawned on me. "I think these are coordinates," I said out loud, tracing my finger over the numbers. "Latitude and longitude, pointing to a specific location."

And based on the email's clues, it's likely somewhere in Italy, where the Voynich Manuscript is believed to have originated.

I cross-referenced the coordinates on Google Maps, and a specific region began to take shape: Tuscany, with its rolling hills, sprawling vineyards, and ancient towns steeped in history and mystery.

That's it, I breathed, my heart racing with excitement and trepidation. I'll follow these coordinates and unravel the secrets of the manuscript, no matter where they lead me.

But I also wondered if Bastian had more information than the one he was disclosing. Insights that could help me crack this code and navigate the challenges that lay ahead.

I reached for my phone and dialed Bastian's number before I could talk myself out of it. He picked up on the third ring, his voice as warm and familiar as ever. "Well, well, well," he said, a note of amusement in his tone. "If it isn't the lovely Amalia Rose. To what do I owe the pleasure?"

I rolled my eyes, even though he couldn't see me. "Cut the crap, Ham," I said, using the nickname I had given him back when we were still together. "I saw your latest video. What's this about an email from someone claiming to know where Dr. Hathaway is?"

There was a moment of silence on the other end of the line. "You saw that, huh?" Bastian said, his voice turning serious. "I don't know, Amalia. It could be a hoax, or it could be the real deal. But I'm not about to sit around and wait to find out. I'm going to follow up on this lead, see where it takes me."

I closed my eyes, knowing what I had to do. "You're coming with me," I said, my voice brooking no argument. "I received a similar email a few days ago. I have the coordinates. I know where to go. I think someone is trying to play us against each other, and I'll be damned if I'm going to let them get away with it."

Bastian let out a low whistle. "Well, damn," he said, a note of admiration in his voice. "The intrepid Amalia Rose, chasing down leads and taking names. Just like old times, huh?"

I felt a smile tug at the corners of my mouth, despite myself. "Don't get too excited, Ham," I said, falling back into our old pattern of banter and flirtation. "This is strictly business. I'm not letting you turn this into another one of your wild goose chases."

Bastian chuckled, the sound sending a shiver down my spine. "Wouldn't dream of it, Rosie," he said, using the pet name he knew I hated. "But you have to admit, we always did make a pretty good team. When we weren't at each other's throats, that is."

I sighed, knowing he was right. For all our differences and disagreements, Bastian and I had always had an undeniable chemistry, a spark that ignited whenever we were together. It was what had drawn us to each other in the first place, and what had made our partnership so dynamic and effective.

But it was also what had made our breakup so devastating, so impossible to move on from. We had both invested so much of ourselves in each other, in the work we did together, that when it all fell apart, it felt like losing a part of myself.

I pushed those thoughts aside, forcing myself to focus on the task at hand. "Meet me at JFK International tomorrow at 6 PM," I said, my voice crisp and businesslike. "We'll compare notes and come up with a plan. And Bastian?"

"Yeah?" he said, his voice soft and uncertain.

"Don't make me regret this," I said, my voice catching slightly. "I'm trusting you with this story, with my investigation. Don't let me down again."

There was a long pause on the other end of the line. "I won't, Amalia," Bastian said finally, his voice uncharacteristically serious. "I didn't—"

I hung up the phone, my heart racing with a mix of excitement and trepidation. I knew I was taking a risk, putting my trust in Bastian again after everything that had happened between us. But I also knew that I couldn't solve this mystery on my own, that I needed his intuition, his vast network of conspiracy theorists and underground sources, even if it meant opening myself up to the possibility of getting hurt again.

I lay in bed that night, staring up at the ceiling and trying to quiet my racing thoughts. Closing my eyes, I tried to push away the doubts and fears that swirled in my mind. Tomorrow, I would board a flight with Bastian Ham, my ex-lover and current rival, and together we would chase down the truth, no matter where it led us. It was a terrifying prospect, but also an exhilarating one—the kind of adventure I had always dreamed of, the kind of story that could make or break a journalist's career.

As I drifted off to sleep, my mind full of swirling images of cryptic symbols and lost civilizations, I wondered about what the future held, what secrets and revelations awaited me on this journey into the unknown. But one thing I knew for sure: with Bastian by my side, anything was possible—for better or for worse.

CHAPTER 5

Rendezvous

T he late afternoon chill clung to my bones as I made my way to the international terminal, my overnight bag slung over my shoulder and my heart heavy with trepidation. I had barely slept the night before, my mind racing with thoughts of Bastian, Dr. Hathaway, and the mysterious emails that had brought us all together.

As I stepped into Concourse A, I spotted Bastian almost immediately. He was leaning against a pillar, his signature leather jacket and tousled hair making him stand out from the crowd of bleary-eyed travelers. When he saw me approaching, he straightened up and flashed me a grin, his eyes sparkling with mischief.

"Hey gorgeous," he said, his voice low and teasing. "Look who decided to show up after all. I was starting to think you'd stood me up, Rosie."

I fought back a smile. "You know I hate it when you call me that, Ham," I said, falling into step beside him as we made our way to the platform. "And I wouldn't have proposed this little adventure if I didn't think it was important. So, let's skip the banter and get down to business, shall we?"

Bastian chuckled, but I could see a flicker of something else in his eyes—something like hurt, or regret. "All right, all right," he said, holding up his hands in mock surrender. "No need to get all serious on me. I'm just trying to lighten the mood a little, that's all."

We boarded the plane in silence, settling into our seats just before the engines rumbled to life. As the clouds began to roll by outside the window, I pulled out my laptop and opened up the email I had received, the one that had started this whole crazy journey.

"So," I said, turning to Bastian. "What do you make of all this? The emails, the mysterious instructions, the fact that we both received different pieces of the puzzle?"

Bastian leaned forward, his brow furrowed in concentration. "I don't know," he said, his voice low and troubled. "But I don't like it. It feels like someone is playing games with us, trying to manipulate us into doing their bidding."

I nodded, feeling a chill run down my spine. "I agree," I said. "But the question is, who? And why? What do they want with the Voynich Manuscript, and with Dr. Hathaway?"

We spent the next few hours poring over the emails, comparing notes and trying to piece together the clues. But the more we talked, the more questions we seemed to have. Who was behind the emails? What was the significance of the strange illustrations in the manuscript? And why had Dr. Hathaway disappeared?

As the plane wound its way through the Atlantic Ocean, the sun dipping low on the horizon, I found myself stealing glances at Bastian, watching the way the golden light played across his classical Hellenic features. Despite everything that had happened between us, I couldn't deny the magnetism that still existed between us—the crackle of electricity that seemed to fill the air whenever we were together.

But betrayal is a poison that lingers long after the wound

has healed, and I couldn't forget the pain he had caused me, the way he had abused my trust and shattered my heart. And so I forced myself to look away, to focus on the task at hand and the mystery that lay ahead.

We arrived at our destination late afternoon—a small, remote village nestled in the hills of Tuscany. Following the cryptic instructions in our emails, we made our way to the outskirts of town, to a decrepit, seemingly abandoned church that loomed like a shadow against the bright sky.

Bastian and I exchanged a wary glance as we approached the heavy wooden doors, our footsteps echoing in the stillness of the night. But as we pushed them open and stepped inside, we both froze in shock at the sight that greeted us.

The interior of the church had been transformed into a kind of makeshift laboratory, with ancient texts and artifacts scattered across every surface. In the center of the room stood a massive oak table, upon which lay a beautifully illuminated facsimile of the Voynich Manuscript, its pages glowing softly in the candlelight.

But it was the figure hunched over the manuscript that made my heart stop in my chest. As they looked up at us, their face obscured by a heavy hood, I realized with a jolt of recognition that it was none other than Dr. Emily Hathaway herself.

For a moment, we all just stared at each other, the air thick with tension and unspoken questions. Then, slowly, Dr. Hathaway lowered her hood and stepped forward, her eyes glittering with a strange, feverish intensity.

"Amalia Rose and Bastian Ham," she said, her voice soft but commanding. "I've been expecting you."

Bastian and I glanced at each other, our expressions mirroring the confusion and apprehension we both felt. "Dr. Hathaway," I said, my voice shaking slightly. "What is all this? What are you doing here?"

Dr. Hathaway smiled, a slight, enigmatic curve of her lips.

"I'm doing what I've always done," she said. "Seeking the truth. And the truth, my dear Amalia, is more incredible than you could ever imagine."

She gestured to the manuscript on the table, her fingers hovering reverently over the copies of ancient pages, now heavily annotated with fresh ink. "This manuscript is more than just a historical curiosity," she said. "It's a key—a key to unlocking the secrets of a lost civilization, a civilization that held women in the highest regard, that valued wisdom and knowledge above all else."

Bastian stepped forward, his eyes narrowed in skepticism. "And you expect us to believe that you, alone, have managed to decipher this manuscript?" he said. "After centuries of the greatest minds in the world trying and failing?"

Dr. Hathaway's smile widened, and she shook her head. "Not all of it, and not alone, no," she said. "But with the help of a powerful ally—an artificial intelligence that my family has been developing for decades, an AI that has the ability to see patterns and connections that the human mind could never perceive."

She turned to me, her gaze piercing and intense. "That's why I sent you those emails, Amalia," she said. "Because I needed someone with your skills, your dedication to the truth, to help me bring this knowledge to the world. And Bastian . . ." She glanced at him, her expression softening slightly. "You have a role to play, one that will be revealed at the right time."

Dr. Hathaway paused, her eyes darting nervously to the shadows that gathered in the corners of the room. "I fear I may have already said too much," she murmured, her voice low and urgent. "They are watching me, always watching as they used to watch my great-grandmother. I cannot stay in one place for too long, or they will find me."

"Great-grandmother?" Bastian asked, a hint of confusion present in his gaze.

She turned back to us, her gaze fierce and imploring. "You must understand, the knowledge I possess is dangerous. It pushed my great-grandfather into a serious depression for a while. There are those who would stop at nothing to contain it. I have taken great risks to bring you here, but I cannot linger."

I leaned in, my journalistic instincts demanding more evidence. "Listen, even if this ancient text is indeed decoded, how do you prove the authenticity of its tales? I'm sure, in a few millennia, some historian will read Harry Potter fan fiction and go on an expedition trying to find the Hogwarts School of Witchcraft and Wizardry."

Hathaway replied without hesitation, her voice filled with unwavering conviction. "We have proved it using technology, archeology, astronomy, and the scientific method. I have dedicated my life to this research, Ms. Rose. I wouldn't have contacted you if I wanted to peddle a hoax."

"I mean, you also called him," I said, tilting my head in Bastian's direction.

"Ouch, Rosie! You wound me!" Bastian clutched his heart dramatically, an impish grin tugged at the corners of his mouth. "Ease up on the barbs, will you?"

Dr. Hathaway turned to me, her gaze steady and challenging. "Ms. Rose, do what you do best and try to debunk my findings. And when you fail, come and celebrate with me and the women who hold up half the sky."

I felt a rush of emotion—fear, excitement, disbelief—all swirling together in my chest. Could it really be true? Could Dr. Hathaway have actually unlocked the secrets of the Voynich Manuscript, secrets that had eluded humanity for centuries?

But before I could voice my doubts, a sudden commotion erupted from outside the church. The sound of shouting voices and pounding footsteps grew louder, and Dr. Hathaway's face paled with fear.

"They've found us," she whispered, her voice trembling. "The ones who seek to steal my annotated copy of the manuscript, to use its knowledge for their own gain. We must go, now!"

Bastian and I exchanged a brief, knowing glance before springing into action. I snatched the manuscript from the table, its pages crackling softly beneath my fingers, as Bastian kicked over a nearby candelabra, plunging the room into darkness. Dr. Hathaway's silhouette darted through the shadows, leading us to a hidden door that seemed to materialize out of the stone wall.

The cool night air hit us like a shock as we burst out of the church, the sudden change in temperature sending a shiver down my spine. Behind us, the sound of splintering wood and angry shouts told us that our pursuers had discovered our escape route. My heart leapt into my throat as the first gunshot rang out, the sound as loud as a thunderclap in the quiet of the night.

We ran blindly, our feet pounding against the uneven cobblestones, each breath tearing at our lungs like shards of glass. The narrow streets of the village twisted and turned like a maze, the looming buildings on either side seeming to close in on us as we fled. The sharp crack of gunfire continued to echo behind us, each shot sending a fresh jolt of adrenaline surging through our veins.

"This way!" Bastian grabbed my hand, his fingers warm and strong against my clammy skin, and pulled me into a narrow alleyway. Dr. Hathaway followed us and we pressed ourselves against the rough stone wall, hardly daring to breathe as the sound of footsteps and shouted orders grew louder. For a moment, I was certain that they would find us, that our desperate bid for freedom had been in vain.

But then, as quickly as they had appeared, the sounds began to recede, our pursuers moving off in the wrong direction. We waited, hearts hammering, until the last echoes of their presence had faded into the night. Only then did we allow ourselves to move, slipping through the shadows like ghosts until the village was far behind us.

We walked for hours, the adrenaline slowly draining from our bodies, leaving us exhausted and trembling. The first light of dawn was just beginning to paint the sky in delicate shades of pink and gold when we finally stumbled into a secluded olive grove. The gnarled trunks of the ancient trees seemed to welcome us, offering shelter and concealment from prying eyes.

I sank to the ground, my legs no longer able to support me, and leaned my head back against the rough bark of a tree. Beside me, Bastian was a silent presence, his face unreadable in the half-light. Around us, the world was slowly coming awake, the first birdsongs mingling with the gentle rustling of leaves in the breeze.

Dr. Hathaway turned to us, her face drawn and her eyes haunted. "You must understand," she whispered hastily. "The knowledge contained within the Voynich Manuscript is powerful, more powerful than you can imagine."

She pressed the manuscript into my hands, her fingers cold and trembling. "I'm entrusting all my findings to you now," she said. "You must scrutinize my work. Uncover the truth behind the lost civilization, behind the secrets that have been hidden for so long. And above all, you must share it with the world at the right time. Not before. My life is at risk and I need to vanish for a while," she whispered, sprinting toward an old stone cottage. "Trust no one and don't search for me. I'll find you when the time comes."

I nodded, feeling the weight of the responsibility settling onto my shoulders. Beside me, Bastian's jaw was set in determination, his eyes gleaming with the thrill of the challenge ahead.

As we watched Dr. Hathaway disappear into the mist, her figure fading like a ghost into the morning light, I knew that this was only the beginning.

And so, as the sun rose over the Italian hills and the world began to awaken, we set out on our journey. We didn't know what lay ahead, what dangers and revelations awaited us. But one thing was certain, in the pursuit of truth, there are no shortcuts. Only long roads and dark alleys.

CHAPTER 6

The Hidden Code

I settled into a corner table at a café in Florence, just steps away from the Loggia dei Lanzi. The warm aroma of cappuccinos and cornetti enveloped me like a comforting embrace. Across from me, Bastian leaned back in his chair, a mischievous glint in his eye as he spread the annotated copy of the Voynich Manuscript on the worn wooden table between us.

As we began to discuss the manuscript, my gaze drifted to the nearby statue of "The Rape of the Sabines" by Giambologna. I couldn't take my eyes off the intricate details of the marble sculpture, the way the artist had captured the brutal scene with such haunting beauty. The intertwined figures, the anguished expressions, the palpable sense of violence and despair—it all seemed to come alive before me.

The sculpture reminded me of another masterpiece I had seen years ago, Bernini's "The Kidnapping of Persephone." The way Hades gripped Persephone's struggling form, his fingers digging into her flesh as he dragged her into the underworld . . . it was a disturbing yet mesmerizing portrayal of power, control, and the subjugation of the feminine.

I shook my head, trying to dispel the unsettling thoughts. Bastian, noticing my distraction, followed my gaze to the statue. "You okay, Rosie?" he asked, concern flickering in his eyes.

I forced a smile, turning my attention back to the matter at hand. "I'm fine," I said, tapping the manuscript. "Just lost in thought. Now, where were we?"

Bastian grinned, his fingers tracing the strange, swirling script on the pages before us. "I don't get it," he muttered, his brow furrowed in concentration. "These annotations . . . they're just as cryptic as the original manuscript. It's like she's added another layer of encryption on top of an already impenetrable text."

I leaned in closer, studying the dense, cramped handwriting that filled the margins of the pages and a couple of loose letters between the pages. He was right—Dr. Hathaway's notes were a jumble of numbers, with no discernible pattern or meaning.

"Wait a minute," I said, my eyes narrowing as I spotted a single line of English amidst the chaos. "'Family is key.' What do you think that means?"

Bastian's gaze snapped up to meet mine, a flicker of recognition dawning in his eyes. "Family . . . the Voynich family. That's it, Rosie. That's the piece we've been missing."

"Alright, Ham," I said, taking a sip of my coffee and savoring the creamy foam on my lips. "What's this big theory of yours?"

Bastian grinned, practically vibrating with excitement. "Prepare yourself, Rosie. I've been digging into the background of our friends Wilfrid Voynich and his wife Ethel, and I think I've uncovered the truth behind this whole manuscript mystery."

I raised an eyebrow, intrigued despite my skepticism. "Oh? Do tell."

"What if I told you," Bastian leaned forward conspiratorially, "that the Voynich Manuscript is nothing more than an elaborate hoax? A forgery created by none other than Wilfrid and Ethel themselves?"

I couldn't help but scoff at the idea. "A hoax? Come on, Bastian. I'm supposed to be the skeptic, remember? You can't be serious."

Bastian's grin only widened. "Oh, but I am. Think about it, Rosie. Wilfrid Voynich was a revolutionary, a man with a deep knowledge of languages and a history of fighting against the powers that be. He was arrested and exiled to Siberia for his activities against the Russian Empire. A man like that, with his skills and motivations? He'd be more than capable of creating a forgery like this."

As I listened to Bastian's theory, I had to admit it was intriguing. But something didn't quite fit. "Okay, let's say you're right," I said. "What about Ethel? What's her role in all of this?" I paused for a moment, remembering another crucial piece of information. "Let's not forget the letter she wrote before her death in 1960. In it, she attested to the manuscript's Jesuit origins, stating that Wilfrid had acquired it from a Jesuit college in Italy. If the Voyniches had created the manuscript themselves, why would Ethel lie about its provenance in her final years?"

Bastian's eyes lit up. "Ah, Ethel. The key to everything. You see, Ethel Voynich was a prominent figure in the women's suffrage movement. She was a member of the Women's Social and Political Union, a militant organization fighting for women's rights. And let's not forget her novel, 'The Gadfly,' which promoted revolutionary and socialist ideas."

He paused for effect, letting his words sink in. "Now, imagine this: a couple, both deeply committed to their political and social causes, deciding to create a manuscript that would advance their agenda. A manuscript that would tell the story of a lost feminist civilization, a society where women held the power and knowledge. It's the perfect way to spread their message and make some money in the process."

I shook my head, a small smile playing at the corners of my lips. "It's a fascinating theory, Bastian. But I'm not convinced. The carbon dating of the vellum places the manuscript in the early fifteenth century, long before the Voyniches were even born. And then there's the Collegium Romanum stamp on the first folio, suggesting the manuscript was once part of the Jesuit library in Rome. Not to mention the hidden text and erased names discovered through multispectral imaging. There's just too much evidence pointing to the manuscript's authenticity."

Bastian shrugged, unfazed by my counterarguments. "Evidence can be faked, Rosie. You of all people should know that."

I bristled at his words, a flicker of annoyance crossing my features. "Don't patronize me, Bastian Ham. I'm well aware of the possibilities. But I trust the experts, and something about this manuscript feels genuine."

As I spoke those words, my mind drifted back to our encounter with Dr. Hathaway in the dusty church in Italy. Her cryptic message about her family being the key to unlocking the secrets of the Voynich Manuscript had been gnawing at me ever since.

"Bastian," I murmured. "Remember what Dr. Hathaway said about her family? What if that's the missing piece we've been looking for?"

Bastian leaned forward, his eyes alight with intrigue. "You might be onto something, Rosie. But how do we even begin to unravel the mystery of Dr. Hathaway's family history?"

I pulled out my laptop, my fingers flying over the keys as I navigated to a popular genealogy website. "We start with what we know," I said, my brow furrowed in concentration. "Dr.

Hathaway's name, her age, her birthplace. Let's see if we can find any relatives or ancestors that might shed some light on this mystery."

We spent the next hour scouring the internet, combing through genealogy websites, digital archives, and social media profiles. Piece by piece, we began to construct a fragmented picture of Dr. Hathaway's family tree.

Suddenly, Bastian let out a low whistle, his eyes wide with surprise. "Rosie, check this out," he said, turning his laptop screen towards me. "I found an obituary for a Barbara Friedman Atchison, died 2010. It says here she was survived by her granddaughter, Dr. Emily Hathaway."

My heart skipped a beat as I read the words on the screen. "Friedman? As in, William and Elizebeth Friedman, the famous cryptographers?"

Bastian nodded, a grin spreading across his face. "Exactly what I was thinking. But we need to confirm the connection."

I opened a new tab and quickly pulled up the Wikipedia page for Elizebeth Friedman. My eyes scanned the article, searching for any mention of a daughter named Barbara. And there it was, a single line that made my heart race with excitement: "Elizebeth and William Friedman had two children, Barbara and John."

I turned to Bastian, my eyes wide with realization. "Bastian, this is it. Dr. Hathaway is the great-granddaughter of Elizebeth and William Friedman. The family connection she mentioned . . . it's been staring us in the face this whole time."

Bastian leaned back in his chair, his expression a mix of awe and disbelief. "Rosie, this changes everything. If Dr. Hathaway is related to the world's most famous cryptographers, it could explain her obsession with the Voynich Manuscript. And her reference to family being the key . . . what if she meant the Friedmans' cryptographic legacy?"

I felt a thrill of excitement course through my veins as the pieces began to fall into place. The Friedmans, their ground-breaking work in codebreaking, their daughter Barbara, and now their great-granddaughter Emily Hathaway . . . it was all connected, a web of secrets and mysteries spanning generations.

"Knowledge is power," I murmured, recalling the famous motto associated with the Friedmans' work.

Bastian's gaze snapped to mine, a flicker of recognition in his eyes. "You think the Friedmans' legacy could be the key to unlocking the secrets of the Voynich Manuscript?"

Pulling the annotated copy closer, I traced my fingers over the intricate illustrations. "Look at these drawings, Bastian. The detail, the complexity. The unidentified plants and cosmological diagrams. They're unlike anything I've ever seen before."

Bastian leaned in, his eyes following the path of my fingers. "I'll admit, they're enigmatic. But that doesn't mean they couldn't have been created by a wannabe artist with a vivid imagination."

My gaze was drawn to the pages depicting naked women bathing, their positions varied and deliberate. "And these women," I murmured, "the way they're posed, the differences in their orientations. It's almost as if they're trying to tell us something."

Bastian smirked, a teasing glint in his eye. "Maybe they're just enjoying a nice soak in the tub, Rosie. Not everything has to have a deeper meaning."

I shot him a withering look. "Funny. But I'm serious, Bastian. There's something more going on here."

Flipping through the pages, I stopped at a series of circular cosmological graphics. The intricate designs resembled clocks, with words and symbols arranged around the edges. I studied them intently, my brow furrowed in concentration.

Suddenly, my eyes widened, and I looked up at Bastian

with a smile. "The Friedmans," I said urgently. "What do you know about them?"

Bastian frowned, taken aback by my sudden change in topic. "The Friedmans? They were a husband-and-wife team, right? Worked on cracking codes during World War I and II. What?"

I felt a surge of excitement as the pieces began to fall into place. "There's a famous photograph of the Friedmans with a group of World War I cryptographers they trained. But what most people don't know is that there's a hidden message encoded in that photograph."

Bastian leaned forward, intrigued. "A hidden message? How so?"

I took a deep breath, gathering my thoughts before explaining the connection to Bastian. "In the photograph, the Friedmans used a clever technique called the Baconian cipher to encode a hidden message. The cryptographers in the photo were divided into five groups, each facing a different direction: some straight ahead, representing A, others to the sides, representing B. Together, each group made up the binary code for a letter in the Baconian cipher. AAAAA equals A and AABAA equals E, for example."

Bastian leaned in, his interest piqued. "I think I get it. Go on . . ."

"When you assign the groups to their corresponding letters and put it all together," I continued, "the message 'KNOWLEDGE IS POWER' is revealed. It's a simple yet effective way to hide information in plain sight."

I pointed to the circular graphics in the manuscript, my finger tracing the symbols along the outer edges. "Now, imagine if we applied a similar concept to these diagrams. What if the positions of the women in the bathing illustrations corresponded to specific symbols or words in the circular charts? Each woman's pose could point us to a different piece of the puzzle, forming a coherent message when combined."

Bastian blinked his eyes as he caught on to my train of thought. "So, you're saying the illustrations in the Voynich Manuscript could be hiding a message, just like the Friedmans' photograph? The bathing women and the circular charts working together to conceal and reveal information?"

I nodded, a sense of excitement building within me. "Precisely. The Friedmans' use of the Baconian cipher shows that hiding messages in plain sight is a tactic used by cryptographers. If we can decipher the connection between the women's positions and the symbols in the circular diagrams, we might finally be able to unravel the secrets of the Voynich Manuscript."

Bastian leaned back in his chair, a look of admiration on his face. "I've got to hand it to you, Rosie. You never cease to amaze me. But even if you're right, how do we go about cracking the code?"

"Well, for starters," I said, rolling my eyes playfully, "you can stop with your ridiculous hoax theory. I know it might be hard for you to accept the idea of a powerful matriarchal civilization, but that doesn't make it any less plausible."

Bastian raised his hands defensively, a smirk playing on his lips. "Hey now, let's not resort to personal attacks. I'm a firm believer in women's equality, both in the streets and between the sheets. I mean, have you seen my feminist rally attendance record? I just think it's important to consider all possibilities, that's all."

I shot him a teasing glare, the tension between us crackling like electricity. "Sure, Ham. Whatever you say."

"I mean, I've been chasing after a certain strong-willed, brilliant journalist for years now, haven't I?"

As we sat there, poring over the manuscript, our banter continued, the hours slipping away unnoticed. The café bustled around us, the clink of cups and the hum of conversation fading into the background as we lost ourselves in the thrill of the hunt.

The sun dipped lower in the sky, casting a warm, golden glow through the windows. Bastian and I, engrossed in our task, barely noticing the passing of time.

As the day drew to a close, we sat back, our eyelids heavy with fatigue but our hearts thrumming with anticipation. The Voynich Manuscript lay before us, its secrets tantalizingly close yet still out of reach.

I ran a hand through my hair, my mind buzzing with unanswered questions. The hidden code, the Friedmans' photograph, the Voynich couple's mysterious past . . . it was all connected somehow, I was sure of it.

But for now, the answers would have to wait. The café was emptying, the staff beginning their closing routines. Bastian and I gathered our notes, our minds still whirring with the day's revelations.

As we stepped out into the cool evening air, Bastian turned to me, a soft smile on his face. "You know, Rosie," he said, "I may not agree with all your theories, but I have to admit, working with you again . . . it feels good. Like old times."

I felt a familiar warmth stirring in my chest, a feeling I hadn't allowed myself to acknowledge in a long time. But as quickly as it appeared, I pushed it away, not ready to let my guard down just yet. "Don't get too sentimental on me now, Ham," I said, my tone light but guarded.

Bastian's smile faltered for a moment. "Me? Sentimental? I'll have you know I've never watched 'The Notebook' on repeat, wishing we had a love story like Noah and Allie's. Okay, maybe once or twice, but that's just because it's a classic." He quickly recovered, his eyes twinkling with mischief.

"Stop flirting with me Rosie, we've got a mystery to solve, remember?"

I nodded, grateful for the change in subject. As much as I enjoyed working with Bastian again, I couldn't afford to get caught up in old feelings and past history. We had a job to do, and I needed to stay focused on the task at hand.

As we made our way through the winding streets in the direction of the hotel to check out, the weight of our discoveries hung heavy in the air. The revelation of Dr. Hathaway's familial connection to the Friedmans and the potential key to unlocking the Voynich Manuscript's secrets had left us both exhilarated and unsettled.

But as we navigated the narrow alleys and cobblestone paths, a creeping sense of unease began to settle over me. It started as a prickling at the back of my neck, a feeling of being watched that I couldn't quite shake.

I glanced over my shoulder, scanning the shadows for any sign of movement. The streets were mostly deserted at this hour, with only the occasional flicker of a curtain or the distant sound of laughter echoing from a nearby tavern.

Beside me, Bastian seemed to sense my discomfort. He placed a hand on the small of my back, his touch warm and reassuring. "Everything okay, Rosie?" he asked, his voice low and concerned.

I shook my head, trying to dispel the sense of foreboding that had taken hold. "I don't know," I admitted. "I just can't shake the feeling that we're being followed."

Bastian's eyes narrowed, and he cast a furtive glance behind us. "I feel it too," he said, his voice tight with tension. "Like there's someone watching our every move."

We quickened our pace, our footsteps echoing off the ancient stone walls. The air seemed to grow colder as we walked, a chill that had nothing to do with the evening breeze.

Suddenly, a figure emerged from the shadows ahead of us,

their face obscured by a dark hood. I felt Bastian's hand tighten on my back, his body tensing as he prepared for a confrontation.

But as quickly as the figure had appeared, they vanished down a side street, melting into the darkness like a ghost.

I let out a shaky breath, my heart pounding in my chest. "Did you see that?" I asked, my voice barely above a whisper.

Bastian nodded grimly. "We need to get out of here," he said, his tone leaving no room for argument. "Whoever that was, they're not friendly."

We hurried inside the hotel, our eyes darting from side to side as we searched for any sign of pursuit. Every shadow seemed to hold a hidden threat, every rustling leaf a potential enemy.

Bastian nudged me with his elbow, a forced grin on his face. "Hey, look on the bright side. If we do get kidnapped by some nefarious organization, at least we'll have plenty of time to catch up on old times."

By the time we reached the airport, my nerves were frayed and my mind was racing with possibilities. Who was following us? What did they want with the Voynich Manuscript? And most importantly, how much did they know about our investigation?

As we boarded the plane back to New York, I knew in my bones that we were being watched. Even as we settled into our seats and the engines roared to life, I half-expected to see a hooded figure lurking in the shadows, their eyes fixed on us with malevolent intent.

Bastian must have sensed my unease, because he turned to me with a nervous grin. "You'll protect me, right, Rosie?" he asked, his voice cracking slightly. "I mean, you're the one with the black belt in investigative journalism. I'm just the pretty face."

I released an exasperated sigh, even as a smile tugged at the corners of my mouth. "Really, Ham?" I asked, raising an eyebrow. "You're going with damsel in distress?"

Bastian clutched his chest in mock offense. "Hey, I'll have you know I'm a proud feminist. I believe in equality, which means I'm equally terrified of mysterious figures lurking in the shadows."

I smiled, trying to relax. But as the plane lifted off into the night sky, I knew our journey was far from over.

As I stared out the window at the shrinking lights of Italy below, I knew that the real challenge was only just beginning. The secrets of the Voynich Manuscript were within our grasp, but the price of uncovering them might be higher than either of us had ever imagined.

CHAPTER 7

Road Trip

I t had been a week since Bastian and I returned from our whirlwind trip to Italy, and I was still reeling from the revelations Dr. Hathaway had shared with us. The Voynich Manuscript, a centuries-old enigma, was apparently the key to unlocking the secrets of a lost matriarchal civilization. And now, with an annotated copy of the manuscript in our possession, I felt like we were tantalizingly close to cracking the code.

But as I sat in my cramped New York apartment, poring over the strange illustrations and cryptic text, I felt something was off. Bastian had been uncharacteristically quiet since our return, and I had a sneaking suspicion that he was up to something.

My fears were confirmed when I received a notification from YouTube. Bastian had just uploaded a new video, titled "The Voynich Manuscript: Hoax or History?" I clicked on the link with a growing sense of dread.

There he was, in all his charming, infuriating glory, talking directly to the camera. "Hey, Hamsters!" he began, using the nickname for his devoted followers. "As you know, I've been investigating the Voynich Manuscript, and I've got some juicy updates for you."

I felt my blood pressure rising as he launched into a recap of our trip to Italy, casually mentioning his meeting with Dr. Hathaway as if it were just another day in the life of Bastian Ham, YouTube sensation. But it was what he said next that really made my blood boil.

"Now, I know a lot of you are convinced that the Voynich Manuscript holds the key to some ancient feminist utopia," he said, a smirk playing at the corners of his mouth. "But I've been doing some digging, and I'm starting to think that this whole thing might be a hoax."

I stared at the screen in disbelief as Bastian laid out his theory. He claimed that the manuscript was likely a forgery, cooked up by Wilfrid Voynich and his wife Ethel as a way to make a quick buck and push their politics. He even had the nerve to ask his viewers to help him debunk the carbon dating and other evidence that pointed to the manuscript's authenticity.

By the time the video ended, I was seeing red. How dare he? After everything we'd been through, after the incredible things we'd learned, he was just going to dismiss it all as a hoax? And worse, he was using his platform to spread misinformation and doubt, all for the sake of a few cheap clicks.

I grabbed my bag and stormed out of my apartment, determined to give Bastian a piece of my mind. I arrived at his door and pounded on it furiously, my anger rising with every passing second.

When he finally opened up, he looked surprised to see me. "Amalia!" he said, a grin spreading across his face. "Did you see my latest video? Did you see the animations of the bathing ladies in the manuscript? Pretty cool editing, right?"

I pushed past him into his apartment, barely noticing Scully—his cat—rubbing against my legs. "Cool editing?" I sputtered, my voice shaking with rage. "Bastian, what the hell were you thinking? You can't just go around claiming that the Voynich Manuscript is a hoax, not after everything we've learned!"

He had the nerve to look confused. "What's the big deal?" he asked, shrugging his shoulders. "It's just a harmless theory to get the bad guys off our tails. And besides, my viewers eat this stuff up. You should see the comments section."

I couldn't believe what I was hearing. "The big deal," I said, my voice rising with every word, "is that you're undermining the very thing we're trying to uncover. The truth about this lost civilization, about the power and wisdom of women."

He shrugged. "To keep us safe."

I waved away his excuses with a hair flick. "You're doing it all for the sake of your stupid YouTube channel."

Bastian's eyes narrowed, and I could see the defensiveness rising in him. "Hey, I was investigating this thing long before you came along," he said, his tone turning icy. "And in case you've forgotten, this YouTube channel is how I make my living. I can't just drop everything to chase after your feminist fantasy."

I felt like I'd been slapped. "Feminist fantasy?" I repeated, my voice low and dangerous. "Is that what you think this is?"

He threw his hands up in exasperation. "Let's be real. A lost civilization of women who had all the answers? It sounds a little far-fetched, don't you think?"

I stared at him, my heart sinking as I realized the truth. He couldn't bring himself to accept even the slightest possibility of a world where women held the power.

I turned to leave, my eyes stinging with tears of frustration. But as I reached for the door, Bastian called out to me. "Amalia, wait," Bastian said, his tone somewhere between exasperated and pleading. "It's not about men or women. It's about the idea of any ancient civilization having all the answers. I mean, think about it. If they were so enlightened, why did they disappear? Why aren't they still around today?"

I paused, my hand on the doorknob, but I didn't turn around. "You're going to Hamsplain ancient civilizations to me now? Please, enlighten me with your wisdom, oh great one." I scoffed, my voice dripping with sarcasm.

Bastian's eyes narrowed, and I could see the frustration simmering beneath the surface. "Don't twist my words, Amalia," he snapped. "All I'm saying is that we need to keep our minds open and our bullshit detectors on high alert. Or have you forgotten what happened the last time we got swept up in a wild theory?"

I flinched at the memory, the sting of his betrayal still fresh. "Oh, I remember," I said, my tone icy. "I remember you stabbing me in the back for a few thousand YouTube views. Forgive me if I'm not eager to take advice from the king of clickbait."

Bastian's eyes flashed with anger, his jaw clenching. "Oh, spare me the dramatics, Amalia," he sneered. "I had no idea you were working on that pharmaceutical story. Maybe if you'd actually talked to me instead of keeping secrets, we could've avoided this whole mess," he muttered.

I laughed, a harsh, bitter sound. "Right, like I didn't have the documents and photos spread all over my apartment."

For a long moment, we just stared at each other, the air crackling with tension. I could see the anger in his eyes, the stubborn set of his jaw. But there was something else there too —a flicker of uncertainty, of doubt.

There was a long silence, broken only by Scully's contented purring. Finally, he spoke again. "Let me make it up to you."

I turned to face him, my eyebrows raised skeptically. "How?"

He grinned, that familiar sparkle returning to his eyes. "By helping you crack this code, once and for all. And I think I know where we need to start."

He pulled out his phone and showed me a comment on his latest video. "One of my viewers mentioned that the Friedmans tried to decipher the Voynich Manuscript back in the day. And get this—their archives are kept at the Marshall Foundation Research Library, just a few hours' drive from here."

I felt a flicker of excitement despite myself. The Friedmans archives . . . of course. "Okay," I said, trying to keep my voice steady. "Let's go to the library. But Bastian, I swear—if you pull another stunt like that video, I'm done. No more chasing clicks. We do this my way, or not at all."

He held up his hands in surrender, his grin turning sheepish. "Partners in crime-solving, just like old times."

I laughed, even as I shook my head in exasperation. "Alright, Ham. Let's hit the road."

Bastian's face broke into a grin, and just like that, the tension between us evaporated. "You know it, Rosie. But fair warning—Scully calls shotgun."

I groaned; he knew all too well I was allergic to Scully. "Fine. But if I start sneezing, we're pulling over and you're walking the rest of the way."

We gathered our things and headed out to Bastian's car. I could feel my eyes starting to water as I popped an antihistamine, resigning myself to a long journey filled with sneezes and teasing banter.

As we merged onto the highway, I tried to call the Marshall Foundation to let them know we were coming. But to my surprise, the librarian who answered informed me that our request to view the Friedman archives had been denied— by the FBI, no less. "It's weird, because the Friedmans' official documents were declassified a few years ago."

I relayed the news to Bastian, who just shrugged. "Guess we'll have to go rogue," he said, a mischievous glint in his eyes. "Wouldn't be the first time."

I leaned back in my seat, my mind racing with possibilities. Why would the FBI block us from accessing declassified information? What secrets did the Friedmans archives hold?

But before I could ponder it further, I noticed a car in the rearview mirror, following behind us at a steady pace. I squinted, trying to make out the driver, and felt a jolt of recognition.

It was the two women from the New York Public Library: Regina and Agnes. The ones who had first told me about Dr. Hathaway's discovery. And they were definitely tailing us.

I nudged Bastian, pointing out the window. "Don't look now," I muttered, "but I think we've got company."

He glanced in the mirror, his eyebrows shooting up. "Well, well," he said, a slow smile spreading across his face. "Looks like this road trip just got a lot more interesting."

And as we sped down the highway, the city giving way to rolling green hills, I was certain we were hurtling towards something big—a truth that had been buried for far too long.

It was going to be one hell of a ride.

As Bastian and I pulled into the parking lot of the Marshall Foundation Research Library, we were sure we were being watched. The mysterious women from the New York Public Library had been tailing us the entire drive, and now they sat in their car a few spots away, their eyes fixed on the entrance.

We approached the librarian at the front desk, who greeted us with a polite but firm smile. "I'm sorry, but as I mentioned on the phone, your request to access the Friedman archives has been denied by the FBI. However, most of the information has been digitized and is available online."

My heart sank at the news, but before I could respond, Regina appeared at my side. "Amalia Rose and Bastian Ham?" she asked, her voice low and urgent.

"Who the hell are you?" Bastian asked.

"Regina Anderson, the third," she said. "Granddaughter of the greatest librarian in history. We need to talk."

Bastian and I exchanged a glance, but followed Regina outside, where she led us to a secluded bench near the library's entrance. "I trust your trip to Italy was productive," she said, her eyes darting around as if checking for eavesdroppers. "I have reason to believe that there's unreleased information in the Friedman room inside the vault. Information that the FBI doesn't want journalists like you to access."

I felt a surge of excitement at her words, but also a flicker of suspicion. "And why should we trust you?" I asked, my eyes narrowing.

Regina took a deep breath, as if steeling herself for what she was about to say. "Because I'm part of an ancient secret society of librarians and friends tasked with protecting the information contained in the Voynich Manuscript. Texts we can no longer decipher. We call ourselves the Order of the Nine Realms. Ethel Voynich, Elizebeth Friedman, and Dr. Emily Hathaway were all sisters, working to uncover the manuscript's secrets."

I could hardly believe what I was hearing. A secret society of librarians, dedicated to preserving and uncovering the truth about the Voynich Manuscript? It sounded like something out of a Dan Brown novel. But as I listened to Regina's story, the pieces began to fall into place.

"Why is the FBI blocking us?" Bastian asked.

"It all goes back to J. Edgar Hoover," she explained, her voice tight with anger. "When he was a young man, he worked as a clerk at the Library of Congress. He fell in love with a woman who was part of our Order and a prominent figure in the women's suffrage movement. But Hoover was vehemently against women's rights, and their relationship ended badly. He became obsessed with her, following her everywhere. That's how he discovered some of our society's secrets."

"Wasn't he the dude who took credit for Elizebeth Friedman's codebreaking work against the Nazis in WWII?" I asked.

Regina nodded, her eyes distant as if lost in thought. "Ever since then, a shadowy branch of the FBI created by Hoover has been trying to contain any information related to the manuscript, suppressing the truth about the lost matriarchal civilization it describes. But we've been fighting back, working in secret to decipher the manuscript's mysteries and share them with the world. Hoover is not the first man in history who has tried to suppress and even destroy our legacy. There have been many, for centuries. Too many sisters silenced, tortured, burned . . ."

I felt a chill run down my spine at the thought of a centuries-old war being waged in the shadows, with the Voynich Manuscript at its center. But I still had so many questions. "If what you're saying is true," I asked, "why come to us? Why reveal yourself now?"

Regina fixed me with a piercing gaze. "Because, like Dr. Hathaway, I believe you have the skills and the determination to help us unlock the manuscript's secrets. And because I think you deserve to know the truth about what you're up against."

She glanced at her watch, then stood abruptly. "Meet me back here after closing time tonight," she said, her voice urgent. "I'll get you inside the vault. But come alone, and tell no one what I've told you." And with that, she turned and ran toward her car.

Bastian and I sat in stunned silence for a moment, trying to process everything we had just heard. "I don't know if we can trust her," I said at last, my voice shaky. "But if there's even a chance that she's telling the truth . . ."

Bastian nodded, a grin spreading across his face. "Then we've got to check it out. I mean, secret societies? Hidden knowledge? This is the stuff of legends, Rosie."

I sighed. "Alright, Ham. Let's do this."

Hours later, under the cover of darkness, Bastian and I rendezvoused with Regina at the library's back entrance. Bastian had insisted on bringing his video equipment, and I couldn't help but roll my eyes as he adjusted the camera on his shoulder, Scully perched precariously on top of the lens.

"Ham, is that really necessary?" I hissed, glancing around to make sure no one had spotted us. "We're trying to be stealthy here, not film a documentary."

Bastian grinned, his teeth flashing white in the moonlight. "Come on, Rosie, this is the scoop of a lifetime. We've got to document every moment for posterity. And think of the views we'll get on YouTube!"

I groaned, but before I could argue further, Regina appeared at the door, her keycard in hand. She swiped it through the lock, and the door clicked open with a soft beep.

She scowled at Bastian. "Don't you dare film me."

As we slipped inside, I felt a twinge of annoyance as Bastian paused to take a photo of the darkened hallway, the flash illuminating the space like a lightning bolt.

"Bastian!" I said, grabbing his arm and dragging him forward. "We don't have time for this."

But Bastian just shrugged, his grin widening. "Relax, Rosie. With my keen eye for detail and your investigative skills, we'll crack this case wide open. And we'll look damn good doing it, too. Say cheese!"

I flashed a forced smile. Bastian's enthusiasm was infectious, even if it was sometimes misplaced.

Inside, the library was a different world. The musty smell of old books filled the air, and the dim emergency lighting cast eerie shadows on the stacks—the tall, imposing shelves that seemed to stretch on forever.

Regina led us through a maze of bookcases, her footsteps echoing in the emptiness. "The Friedmans first encountered extracts of a transcription of the Voynich Manuscript in the early 1920s through Professor John C. Manly. She and her husband William were working at Riverbank Laboratories under the eccentric tycoon George Fabyan."

"But they failed to decoded, right?" Bastian asked, tripping over a stack of books left on the floor.

"Decades later Elizebeth actually decoded a small part of the Voynich Manuscript," Regina explained as we walked, her voice hushed. "One of the methods she used was based on the illustrations."

My eyes widened as I remembered the photograph of the Friedmans and their World War I codebreaking team. "Wait," I said, stopping in my tracks. "Are you talking about the 'Knowledge is Power' Baconian cipher?"

Regina turned to me, a smile playing at the corners of her mouth. "Close. Emily Hathaway told me Elizebeth applied the same principle to the Voynich Manuscript, using the women's positions to unlock a hidden message."

I felt a rush of pride at having made the connection, and Bastian shot me an impressed grin. "Look at you, Rosie, cracking codes like a pro."

Regina smiled. "Elizebeth was hyped about what she found, you know? She wanted to share it with her crew, this group that William Friedman put together to study the manuscript. But as soon as they got to work, she started getting these shady letters, telling her to keep her 'feminine fantasies' to herself or her man would pay the price. Can you believe that? So Elizebeth had to put out these fake stories, saying the manuscript was impossible to decipher. 'The decipherer is doomed to utter frustration'—that's the quote everyone remembers, but it's a damn shame."

At last, we reached the vault. Regina typed in a code, and the heavy door swung open with a groan. Inside, the air was cool and dry, and the shelves were lined with boxes and books. We began searching through the materials, carefully examining each document and photograph for any mention of the Voynich Manuscript.

Time seemed to crawl by as we pored over the archives, the only sound the rustling of papers and the occasional meow from Scully. But just as I was starting to lose hope, Bastian let out a triumphant shout.

"I found something!" he called out, holding up a sheaf of papers. "An encrypted letter, addressed to Elizebeth from someone named Arthur Burton."

I felt a jolt of recognition at the name. "Arthur Burton? That's the protagonist of Ethel Voynich's novel. 'The Gadfly' was published in 1897 and became a bestseller in the Soviet Union. It was a hugely progressive book for its time, advocating for an end to oppression."

Regina peered over Bastian's shoulder, her eyes glued to the letter. "Okay, so check this out. Ethel? She was George Boole's daughter. You know, the guy who basically invented computer science and Boolean algebra? Yeah, that Boole. So, you know Ethel was no slouch when it came to ciphers." She paused, wheels turning in her head as she studied the letters. "I'm betting they used a book cipher. It was the go-to move back in the day. You take a specific book, right? And each set of numbers in the message points to a word or phrase in that book. Ain't no cracking that code unless you got the right edition."

I looked around at the hundreds of books lining the shelves, feeling a sense of despair wash over me. "But which book did they use?"

Suddenly, Scully leaped down from Bastian's shoulder and darted over to a dusty corner of the vault. She pawed at a stack of books until one tumbled to the floor, its pages splayed open. I picked it up, my heart racing as I read the title.

"The Gadfly, first edition," I breathed. "Scully, you brilliant little furball."

Bastian scooped up Scully and kissed her. "And that's why this hamster loves cats."

But before we could celebrate our discovery, an alarm pierced the air, and the vault was flooded with flashing red light. "We've been compromised!" Regina shouted over the noise. "Take the letter and the book. We need to go, now!"

We raced through the library, the sound of sirens growing louder with each passing second. My heart pounded in my chest as we burst through the back door and into the night. But as we reached the parking lot, I realized Scully was missing. Bastian turned to me, his eyes wide with panic. "Scully must have run back inside the vault!" he shouted. "I have to go back for her!"

Before I could stop him, Bastian sprinted back towards the library, disappearing into the shadows. I hesitated for a moment, torn between the need to help my friend and the fear of being captured myself. But Regina grabbed my arm, her voice urgent. "We can't wait for him, Amalia. We have to go, now!"

With a heavy heart, I followed Regina into the night, the sound of shouting and gunfire echoing behind us. We ran fast until my lungs burned and my legs ached, hiding in the shrubs until the darkness had swallowed us whole.

Finally, protected by the greenery, we collapsed against the side of a nearby building, gasping for breath. Regina turned to me, her eyes wide with fear and adrenaline. "We need to get out of here," she whispered urgently. "They'll be looking for us."

But all I could think about was Bastian and Scully. I peered around the corner, my heart in my throat, just in time to see Bastian emerging from the library, Scully clutched tightly in his arms.

But it was too late. As Bastian came out, a team of armed men in black tactical gear began running to block his path.

"Freeze!" one of them shouted, his weapon trained on Bastian's chest.

Bastian turned and ran, the sound of gunfire echoing in his wake. But as he rounded a corner toward me, I heard a sickening thud and a cry of pain.

I turned to see Bastian lying on the ground, clutching his leg. A dark stain was spreading across his jeans, and his face was twisted in agony. "Amalia, run!" he gasped. "Get the letters to safety! I'll be fine!"

Just as Regina and I hid in the shadows, a black van screeched to a halt beside Bastian, and armed men leaped out, their weapons trained on my friend. The men grabbed Bastian and hauled him into the van, slamming the door shut behind them.

I felt like my world was crumbling around me. Bastian, my partner, my friend, was wounded and captured by the sinister forces that sought to suppress the truth about the Voynich Manuscript and the lost civilization it promised. I knew I had to rescue him, no matter the cost.

The Letter

I burst into my apartment, my heart pounding and my mind reeling from the chaos of the night. Bastian's capture played on a loop in my head, the image of him lying wounded on the ground seared into my memory. I paced back and forth, my hands shaking as I reached for my phone. "I have to call the police," I said, my voice trembling. "We can't leave Bastian at the mercy of those bastards!" My eyes watered, and I wasn't sure if it was because of Bastian or the allergy to his cat now sprawled all over my sofa.

Regina's hand clamped down on my arm, her grip firm and unyielding. "Amalia, stop. Think about what you're doing. We can't trust the authorities, not now. The people trying to bury the Voynich secrets are too powerful. Going to the cops will only paint a target on our backs."

I yanked my arm away, glaring at her. "And why the hell should I trust you, huh? You and your super-secret librarian club waltz into my life out of the blue, and suddenly I'm supposed to believe every word you say? How did you even get access to that vault? And don't give me some cryptic bullshit —give me a straight answer!"

Regina's eyes flashed with impatience, but her voice remained infuriatingly calm. "The FBI doesn't give a rat's ass about Bastian. He's a pawn, a way to get to you, to stop you from digging deeper. It's a classic move, straight out of their playbook. They did the same thing to Ethel Voynich and Elizebeth Friedman—threatened their husbands, told them they'd end up in a shallow grave if they kept poking around."

She began to pace, her voice taking on a bitter edge. "Our sisters have been fighting this battle for centuries, Amalia. Passing down scraps of knowledge through coded manuscripts and ciphers, watching as time erased the keys to unlock them. But we never stopped searching for the truth, never stopped trying to keep it safe from those who'd bury it forever."

I threw up my hands in frustration. "Then I'll blow the lid off this whole thing! I'll go to the press, call out the FBI and their pet conspiracy. I'll make sure the whole world knows what they're trying to hide."

Regina let out a humorless laugh. "And who's going to believe you? Without hard evidence, they'll rip you to shreds. Paint you as some unhinged conspiracy nut, destroy everything you've worked for. And Bastian? He'll rot in some black site, never to be seen again. The only way to save him is to find the truth, to uncover proof that even the FBI can't deny."

I closed my eyes, my shoulders sagging under the weight of her words. As much as I hated to admit it, she was right. Going off half-cocked would only make things worse. I had to be smart, had to play the long game.

"Fine," I said, my voice barely above a whisper. "Where do we start?"

Regina swept a pile of papers off my dining table, replacing them with the encrypted letters and the battered copy of "The Gadfly." She ran a finger along the book's spine, her eyes alight with a newfound intensity.

"If Elizebeth and Ethel were half as clever as I think they

were, the key to cracking their code will be hidden in plain sight," she murmured. "We need to scour every page, look for anything that seems out of place or significant."

I nodded, already reaching for the letter. The handwriting was precise, almost mechanical, but the content was pure gibberish. It was going to be a long night.

I tried to make sense of the seemingly random series of numbers scattered across the page. Each set of numbers was separated by dashes, like a code waiting to be cracked.

As the minutes ticked by, the silence was broken only by the rustle of turning pages and the occasional muttered curse. My eyelids grew heavy, my mind dulled by the endless sea of meaningless symbols. But just as the first light of dawn began to creep through the curtains, I let out a gasp, my heart leaping into my throat. "The numbers," I said, my voice barely above a whisper. "They're not just random digits. They're referring to specific locations within the book."

Regina leaned in closer, her eyes scanning the page. "Indeed! I suspected it was a book cipher."

I grabbed a pencil and began to jot down notes, my mind racing with possibilities. "Look at the way the numbers are grouped. Three numbers separated by dashes. It's a common format for book ciphers. The first number could represent the page, the second the line on that page, and the third the position of the word on that line."

Regina's eyes widened with understanding. "So, if we have a set of numbers like '102-7-5,' it would mean . . ."

"Page 102, line 7, word 5," I finished, a grin spreading across my face. "Exactly. Elizabeth and Ethel used 'The Gadfly' as the key to encode their messages. Each set of numbers corresponds to a specific word within the book."

Regina nodded, a look of satisfaction crossing her features. "It's a simple yet effective way to hide sensitive information in plain sight. Only someone with access to the exact same edition of the book would be able to decipher the message."

I turned back to the letter, my finger tracing over the first set of numbers. "Let's give it a try. The first code is '12-20-2.' That would be page 12, line 20, word 2 in 'The Gadfly.'"

I flipped open the book, my heart pounding with anticipation. At that moment, two loose pages dropped from inside it. I quickly scanned them. One was in code, and the other was its translation. It was a letter addressed to Mrs. Friedman from a Ms. Money-Coutts at Bletchley Park. I folded and slid it back inside "The Gadfly," as it didn't seem relevant to our pursuits. Then, I scanned the designated page 12 and line 20. My finger landed on the second word, and I couldn't help but let out a gasp.

Regina looked at me, her eyebrows raised. "What does it say?"

I swallowed hard, my voice trembling slightly as I read aloud the first word of the decoded message. "'Dear,' it says 'dear.'" I glanced at Regina and smiled.

I turned back to the letter, my fingers trembling slightly as I began to decode the first line. As I worked my way through the text, the words began to take shape, revealing a message that had been hidden for decades.

My heart pounded in my chest as I read the first sentence, my eyes widening with shock and disbelief. I turned to Regina, my voice shaking. "You're not going to believe this," I said. "It's a letter from Ethel Voynich to Elizebeth Friedman, and it's all about the Voynich Manuscript. But that's not the craziest part. Listen to this . . ."

I took a deep breath and began to read aloud, my voice echoing in the sudden stillness of the room.

My dear Mrs. Friedman,

I hope this letter finds you in good health. I am writing to you at great personal risk to share a secret that I have long held close to my heart—a secret that, if revealed, could endanger both my life and that of my beloved husband.

My mother, Mary Boole, was a remarkable woman— a self-taught mathematician and passionate advocate for women's education. After my father's untimely passing in 1864, she returned to England and became a librarian at Queen's College. There, she was initiated into a clandestine sisterhood dedicated to preserving the knowledge of an ancient civilization.

From a young age, my mother told me stories of arcane manuscripts so powerful and transformative that men would go to unspeakable lengths to suppress them. These manuscripts, she said, held the key to a hidden realm of feminine light, abundance, and eternal virtue. But to reach this sacred place, one must undergo a purifying journey, traversing the river of life and partaking of sacred remedies that alter the very fabric of consciousness.

Fearing for her daughters' safety in a world where men sought to erase these secrets, my mother was forced to publicly denounce the suffragettes while tire-lessly advancing women's education behind the scenes. She often spoke of a vital force accessible only through moral living. Though she had not seen the manuscripts herself, she carried some of their ancient wisdom— pharmacopeia, passed down orally, through generations of sisters.

Central to this was an extract of a recipe for the kykeon, a sacred psychedelic elixir used in the ancient Greek Eleusinian mystery rites honoring Demeter and

Persephone. These revered rites were later condemned by Christians as they gained worldly power.

The makeshift kykeon, although incomplete, still had psychedelic properties and granted my mother a fleeting glimpse of the spirit realm. There she hallucinated images of ancient books, copies of even older texts, hidden away for millennia. Authorities, threatened by the idea of uniting science and spirituality, silenced these concepts and fired my mother from the library for daring to share even a fraction of these ideas in her writings. Yet she remained a sisterhood member until death, entrusting me to find the manuscripts she saw in her visions—a mission I have devotedly pursued.

I too have been chased by those fearing these secrets. Even before my husband and I found the manuscript, I caught the attention of Scotland Yard's Special Branch. During this time, I became entangled with the notorious "ace of spies" Sidney Reilly. To be frank, I was never sure if his interest in me was genuine or if he was spying on me for his superiors. Our passionate, intriguing affair peaked during a memorable encounter in Florence. While his true feelings remain unclear, I cherish our time together. He even inspired the protagonist of my book, "The Gadfly."

Years later, upon finding one of the fabled manuscripts, I felt compelled to share what I knew with a like-minded soul. Though I cannot decipher it myself, I believe the manuscript contains a kykeon recipe and a sacred realm-accessing process akin to the Eleusinian mysteries. The illustrations likely depict the life-giving river and purifying journey to reach the abundant realm where Persephone lives contentedly with her sisters.

But beware—this path is riddled with danger. Powerful forces will do anything to keep the manuscript's secrets hidden. Trust no one, not even those closest to you.

You are now an ally in the quest for knowledge and truth. I will support you however I can, but I implore you —keep this letter absolutely confidential. Use my same cipher and tell no one of our correspondence.

I await your reply eagerly. May ancient wisdom light your way.

Faithfully yours,
E. L. Voynich
5th of July, 1944

P.S. Please accept the accompanying copy of my book as a token of my esteem. I suspect you may find the spy motif rather diverting.

As I finished reading the deciphered letter, my heart raced with excitement and trepidation. I then turned my attention to the copy of "The Gadfly" that had accompanied the letter. I marveled at Ethel's ingenuity in using the book as a key to the cipher—a clever nod to her own work as a novelist and a subtle way of authenticating the letter's contents.

As I flipped through the pages of the novel, I felt a sense of kinship with Ethel—a woman who had risked everything to uncover the truth and preserve the legacy of her foremothers. I knew that I would have to be just as brave and just as resourceful if I hoped to follow in her footsteps and unlock the secrets of the Voynich Manuscript.

My mind buzzed with questions and possibilities. The idea of a hidden realm, accessible only through a purifying journey and a sacred elixir, was both thrilling and daunting. I glanced over at Regina, who was watching me intently, her eyes gleaming with a mix of excitement and apprehension.

"This is incredible," I breathed, my fingers tracing the edges of the letter. "But I still don't fully understand the connection between the Eleusinian Mysteries and the Voynich Manuscript."

Regina leaned forward, her voice low and urgent. "The Eleusinian Mysteries were a series of annual initiation ceremonies held in ancient Greece, in honor of the goddess Demeter and her daughter Persephone. According to the myth, Persephone was abducted by Hades, the god of the underworld. Demeter, in her grief and anger, withheld her blessings from the earth, causing crops to wither and die. Eventually, a compromise was reached, and Persephone was allowed to return to her mother for part of the year, bringing with her the renewal of spring."

I nodded, vaguely recalling the story from my high school mythology class. "And what does this have to do with the manuscript?" I asked, my brow furrowed in concentration.

"The initiates of the Eleusinian Mysteries believed that by participating in the rites, they could achieve a deeper understanding of the cycle of life, death, and rebirth," Regina explained. "Central to these rites was the consumption of a sacred elixir called the kykeon after fasting. Kykeon was believed to induce an altered state of consciousness, allowing initiates to access hidden knowledge and spiritual realms."

My eyes widened as I began to connect the dots. "So, Ethel believed the Herbal and Pharmaceutical folios in the Voynich Manuscript could contain recipes for similar psychedelic elixirs?"

"Precisely," Regina said, a smile tugging at the corners of her mouth. "And that's not all. Take a look at these Balneological folios."

I flipped through the pages, my gaze settling on the images of nude women bathing in interconnected pools, their bodies adorned with intricate headdresses. "What am I looking at here?" I asked, my fingers hovering over the strange, swirling designs.

"These images could represent the purifying journey mentioned in Ethel's letter," Regina explained, her voice trembling with excitement. "The water flowing from one folio to another could symbolize the river of life that must be traversed to reach the sacred realm."

As I studied the images more closely, I felt a shiver run down my spine. Suddenly, Scully leaped onto the table, startling me out of my reverie. I sneezed violently, my eyes watering as I tried to push the curious feline away from the pages of the manuscript. Regina chuckled softly, reaching out to scratch Scully behind the ears.

"Bless you," she said, her eyes twinkling with amusement. "It seems Scully is just as eager to unravel the mysteries of the manuscript as we are."

I smiled weakly, wiping my nose on the sleeve of my jacket. "Speaking of mysteries," I said, turning to the page that had caught my eye earlier. "What do you make of this? Nine connected realms, each with its own unique symbology and design. Is this not the name of your secret cult?"

Regina flashed a cryptic smile. "It's hard to say for certain, but it could represent the different stages or levels of the spiritual journey that Ethel alluded to in her letter. Perhaps each realm corresponds to a different aspect of the purifying process or a different level of consciousness that must be attained."

I felt a rush of excitement and trepidation as I considered the implications of Regina's words. If the Voynich Manuscript truly contained the key to unlocking a hidden realm, a feminist utopia where knowledge and power were guarded and preserved, then the stakes were higher than I ever could have imagined.

I became intrigued by the small clock face adorning one of

the corners of the page with the nine rosettes. I squinted my eyes in a hopeless attempt to decipher the glyphs around it.

"So, what do we do now?" I asked, my voice barely above a whisper. "How do we even begin to decipher the rest of the manuscript, to uncover the truth behind this lost civilization?"

As Regina and I pored over the cryptic illustrations, trying to make sense of the nine realms and their hidden meanings, a notification from YouTube jolted me out of my concentration. Bastian was streaming live. My heart leapt into my throat as a wave of conflicting emotions washed over me—concern for his well-being yet battling with the still-fresh sting of betrayal from our tumultuous past. With trembling fingers, I clicked on the link, bracing myself for whatever bombshell my erstwhile partner was about to drop.

CHAPTER 10

Betrayal

The video flickered to life, and there was Bastian, grinning at the camera from his sleek recording studio. The familiar backdrop of movie posters and paranormal paraphernalia seemed to mock me as he launched into his introduction.

"Hey there, Hamsters! Your favorite truth-seeker here, coming at you with a doozy of a revelation. Now, I know a lot of you have been following my investigation into the Voynich Manuscript and the whole lost feminist civilization theory. But what you don't know is the ugly truth behind this so-called groundbreaking discovery."

I gritted my teeth, my knuckles turning white as I gripped the edge of the table. Regina shot me a sympathetic look, her hand coming to rest on my shoulder in a gesture of solidarity.

"You see," Bastian continued, his voice dripping with self-satisfaction, "a few years back, I had the misfortune of getting involved with a certain pretentious journalist who fancied herself a regular Lois Lane. This woman—Amalia Rose—had a habit of looking down her nose at the hard work of dedicated researchers like myself and my loyal Hamsters. She thought her fancy degree and her cushy job at the City Rag made her better than the rest of us, that her methods were somehow more legitimate than the tireless efforts of citizen journalists and truth-seekers."

Scully let out a mournful meow, as if sensing the tension radiating from my rigid form. I barely registered Regina's murmured reassurances, my focus entirely consumed by the man on the screen and the bile rising in my throat.

"Well, I'm here to tell you that Ms. Rose is nothing but a fraud, a charlatan who will stop at nothing to push her feminist agenda, even if it means ignoring cold, hard facts. And that's exactly what she's doing with this Voynich Manuscript nonsense. I've been playing along, letting her think I'm on board with her little wild goose chase, all the while gathering evidence to expose her for the liar she is."

My mind reeled as Bastian's words sank in. Had our entire reunion been a ruse, a ploy to get close to me and sabotage my investigation?

Bastian rolled his eyes, "I bet soon Ms. Rose will be reporting that the likes of Taylor Swift and Ryan Gosling are part of a secret feminist society."

"Close, he forgot Greta," Regina said casually.

Confused, I ignored Regina. Bastian's betrayal made me sick to my stomach, even as a small voice in the back of my head whispered that something didn't add up.

As if reading my thoughts, Bastian reached up and fiddled with the medal hanging around his neck—a tiny golden "R" that glinted in the light of his studio. A wave of recognition crashed over me, followed by a surge of confusion. That medal, that token of our shared past . . . why would he wear it now, in the midst of this blistering attack on my character?

"I have proof," Bastian declared, his eyes glinting, "that Ms. Rose and her crackpot collaborator, Dr. Emily Hathaway, have been conspiring to fabricate evidence, to twist the truth to fit their narrative. Let me be clear, the Voynich is nothing else than a crude, encrypted copy of another medieval handbook mainly on health, herbs and venoms by Giovanni Cadamosto. Here, can you see the similarities?" His image was replaced by pages of a medieval manuscript showing plants and even a bathing scene. "And I'll be revealing all of it in my upcoming videos. So, stay tuned, Hamsters, and remember— don't believe a word these charlatans say. The truth will come out, and I'll be the one to bring it to you."

With that, the video froze, leaving me staring at Bastian's satisfied grin. Regina let out a low whistle, her eyes wide with disbelief. "Well," she said, her voice tight with anger, "I guess that settles it. No man can be trusted, not even the ones who claim to care about the truth. Bastian Ham is nothing but a lying, backstabbing, Joe Rogan wannabe. The carbon dating is clear, the Voynich Manuscript is older than Cadamosto's herbal."

I shook my head, my thoughts spinning like a kaleidoscope. Part of me wanted to believe Regina, to write Bastian off as just another man threatened by powerful women and their secrets. But something nagged at me, a persistent doubt that wouldn't let go.

"Maybe," I said, my voice barely above a whisper. "Or maybe there's more to this than meets the eye. That medal he was wearing . . . the R stands for Rosie; he bought it when we were together. A symbol of our partnership, our bond. Why would he put it on now, in the middle of all this? It doesn't make sense."

Regina snorted, her gaze hardening. "Girl, please. He's just trying to mess with your head, throw you off your game. Don't let that man and his fragile ego get to you, Amalia. We've got bigger fish to fry."

But before I could respond, my phone began to buzz insistently, the screen lighting up with my editor's name. With a sinking feeling, I lifted the phone to my ear, already knowing what was coming.

"Amalia, what the hell were you thinking?" My editor's voice was tight with barely contained fury. "Associating yourself with that hack Bastian Ham, letting yourself get dragged into his conspiracy theorist nonsense? Do you have any idea how much damage this could do to your credibility, to the credibility of this entire publication?"

I closed my eyes, suddenly feeling very small and very tired. "I . . . I can explain," I began, but my editor cut me off with a sharp bark of laughter.

"Explain? What is there to explain? You've let yourself get sucked into a world of pseudoscience and mysticism, and now you're paying the price. You have twenty-four hours, Amalia. Twenty-four hours to clear your name and prove that you're still the journalist I thought you were. Otherwise, you can consider yourself fired. Do I make myself clear?"

The line went dead before I could respond, the dial tone echoing in my ear like a condemnation. I slumped back in my chair, my head spinning with the weight of everything that had just happened.

Regina placed a gentle hand on my arm, her expression softening with sympathy. "Amalia," she said, her voice low and urgent, "I know this is a lot to process. But we can't let Bastian or your editor or anyone else stop us from uncovering the truth. We're on the brink of something incredible here, something that could change the world as we know it. Are you really going to let some man's lies and some bureaucrat's threats stand in your way?"

I took a deep breath, trying to steady myself. She was right, of course. I had come too far, risked too much, to back down now. But as I stared at the frozen image of Bastian's face on my laptop screen, I had the feeling that I was missing something, some crucial piece of the puzzle that would make everything fall into place.

CHAPTER 11

The Voynich Ninjas

Regina and I sat in my apartment, sipping our morning coffee as my mind reeled from the previous night's events. The silence was suddenly shattered by a sharp knock at the door, making me jump. Cautiously, I approached the door, my hand instinctively reaching for the pepper spray in my pocket. As I opened the door, I was greeted by an empty hallway. I was about to close it when a plain white envelope on the floor caught my eye.

With shaky hands, I picked up the envelope, my curiosity piqued. I tore it open and found a single sheet of paper inside, covered in a haphazard scrawl that looked like it belonged to a conspiracy theorist. My eyebrows climbed higher with each passing sentence as I began to read.

Dear Amalia,

I am an old-timer Hamster, one of Bastian's most loyal followers. I've been watching his YouTube channel since the very beginning, and I must say, his recent behavior has me and the other old-timers quite concerned for his and your safety.

You see, anyone who has followed Bastian for a long time knows that his recent messages don't make sense. We've watched him swoon over you countless times and speak proudly about your achievements. We also belong to a forum called Voynich.ninja, where multidisciplinary scholars and interested members of the public pore over all the details of the Voynich Manuscript.

While some people in the forum believe the Voynich is a copy of Cadamosto's herbal, there aren't many of them because of the carbon dating. Bastian would never record the last two videos because they don't align with the information he and the Hamsters have.

But it was Bastian touching his medal that set off the alarm. We still remember when he shared that he had bought it to surprise his girlfriend so she would know he always carried her close to his heart. We all made fun of him mercilessly—there were a lot of "man up" messages on the video post. But he never cared, and even when you two broke up, he was visibly sad.

So, it's clear that whoever is threatening him and forcing him to send those messages hasn't watched his old videos, which makes sense because Bastian has been going live twice a day for years.

Amalia, we Ninjas are here to support you. Go to the forum and check out the links to the digital copies of the Voynich archives held at the Beinecke Rare Book and Manuscript Library at Yale University. There, you'll find photos of Ethel Voynich's notebooks, letters, and other important artifacts.

Be warned, it's possible you are being watched. Avoid using digital or phone communication.

Stay safe,
   An Old-Timer Hamster

I let out a snort of laughter, the absurdity of the letter momentarily overshadowing my anxiety. "Hamsters? Ninjas? What kind of bizarre alternate reality have I stumbled into?" I muttered, crumpling the letter and tossing it aside.

But as I sat there, my mind began to wander. Bastian's recent behavior had been erratic, to say the least, and the image of him getting shot kept replaying in my mind, sending a chill down my spine. Could there be a grain of truth hidden in this ridiculous letter?

I smoothed out the crumpled paper and read it again, more carefully this time. Turning to Regina, who was watching me with a mixture of concern and curiosity, I asked, "Hey, Regina? Have you ever heard of a group called Voynich Ninjas?"

Regina nodded. "Yeah, I know them. They're legit—got scholars and experts from all over, been studying the Voynich Manuscript for years. That forum's the real deal."

My pulse quickened as I processed this information. If the forum was legitimate, then the letter's contents might hold more weight than I initially thought.

I decided to take another look at Bastian's video, specifically the part where he compared the Voynich Manuscript to Cadamosto's herbal. Pulling up the video, I paused it on the side-by-side comparison. At first glance, there were some similarities between the illustrations, but upon closer inspection, the similarities seemed cherry-picked.

Glancing at Scully, who was curled up on the couch, I was reminded of my complicated history with Bastian. "I need to confront him," I said to Regina, my voice filled with determination. "I'm going to return Scully and make it clear that I want nothing to do with him or anything that reminds me of him."

Regina nodded, understanding in her eyes. "Just be careful, Amalia. We don't know what kind of danger you might be walking into."

I scooped up Scully, ignoring the way my eyes began to water and my nose started to itch. With the cat securely in my arms, I headed out into the night, my mind racing with questions and possibilities.

The streets were eerily quiet at dawn, and every shadow seemed to hold a hidden threat as I made my way to Bastian's apartment. I quickened my pace, my grip on Scully tightening as I hurried towards my destination.

When I reached Bastian's building, I hesitated, suddenly unsure of what I would say or do when I saw him. But I knew I couldn't turn back now. I had to confront him, to demand answers and uncover the truth behind his bizarre behavior and the mysterious letter.

Taking a deep breath, I climbed the stairs to Bastian's apartment, Scully squirming in my arms. I knocked on the door, my heart pounding in my chest as I waited for him to answer.

Whatever secrets lay ahead, whatever dangers I might face, I was ready to face them head-on.

CHAPTER 12

The Baths

I burst into Bastian's apartment, Scully clutched tightly in my arms. The moment I laid eyes on him, I thrust the squirming feline into his chest. "Here's your furball back, Ham. I'm done playing cat-sitter for a lying, two-faced YouTuber."

Bastian stumbled backward, wincing as he caught Scully. I noticed he was favoring his left leg, a slight limp in his step. "Amalia, I can explain—"

"Oh, really?" I cut him off, jabbing my index finger against his chest. "Explain what? How you've been spreading lies about the Voynich Manuscript? How you've betrayed everything we've worked for?"

Bastian set Scully down and turned to face me, his expression a mix of defiance and something else I couldn't quite read. "I told you, Amalia, it's all a hoax. The Voynich Manuscript, the lost civilization, all of it. I was just trying to protect you from getting caught up in a wild goose chase."

I scoffed, shaking my head in disbelief. "Protect me? By lying to me? By going behind my back and making those videos? You've got a funny way of showing you care, Ham."

Bastian's eyes flashed with anger, and he took a step closer to me. "You don't understand, Amalia. There are things going on here that you don't know about."

I laughed bitterly. "Oh, spare me the cryptic bullshit, Bastian. If there's something going on, just tell me. Or have you forgotten what it means to be partners? Who were those guys? Did they offer you money to spread lies?"

Bastian's jaw clenched, and for a moment, I thought he might actually come clean. But then he shook his head, his voice rising in volume. "I stand by what I said in my video. The Voynich Manuscript is a hoax, and anyone who believes otherwise is delusional! You are delusional!"

I flinched at his words, feeling as if he'd slapped me. But as I studied his face, I noticed something odd. His eyes were wide, almost bulging, and his gestures were exaggerated, as if he were on stage performing for an invisible audience.

"Why are you shouting?" I asked, my voice low and suspicious. "And what's with the dramatic hand waving? You're acting like a bad actor in a high school play."

Bastian's expression shifted, and for a split second, I saw a flicker of fear in his eyes. I narrowed my eyes, studying his face. Something was off. Bastian's words were too emphatic, his gestures too exaggerated. It was as if he was putting on a performance, trying to convey a message he couldn't say outright.

Suddenly, a chill ran down my spine. The hairs on the back of my neck stood up, and I had the distinct feeling that we were being watched. I glanced around the apartment, half-expecting to see hidden cameras or listening devices.

Without warning, I grabbed Bastian's hand. "Come on, we're going on a little research trip. I'm going to prove to you once and for all that the bathing illustrations in the Voynich Manuscript have nothing to do with Cadamosto's herbal." I had to get him out of that flat.

Bastian protested weakly as I dragged him out of the apartment, leaving a confused Scully behind. He limped along beside me, struggling to keep up as I hailed a cab.

Once we were inside the taxi, Bastian turned to me, his brow furrowed. "Where are we going, Rosie?"

I scanned him up and down, taking in his disheveled appearance and the way he kept glancing nervously at his phone. A thought struck me: what if he was wired? What if someone was listening in on our every word?

I decided to keep our destination a secret, simply directing the driver to Brooklyn using gestures and half words. As we wound our way through the city streets, I felt a mix of suspicion and concern for Bastian. What had he gotten himself into?

Half an hour later, we arrived at a nondescript building in a quiet neighborhood. I paid the driver and led Bastian inside, ignoring his confused protests.

The interior was warm and humid, the air heavy with the scent of eucalyptus and steam. I had brought us to a bathhouse, a place where we could talk freely without fear of being overheard.

We made our separate ways to the changing rooms and then met at the sauna. There, I stared at the towel around Bastian's waist and commanded, "Strip!" My tone left no room for argument.

Bastian's eyes widened, and for a moment, I thought he might refuse. But then a smirk played at the corners of his mouth. "Wow, Rosie, if you wanted to see me naked, all you had to do was ask."

I fought back a blush. "Don't flatter yourself, Ham. I just need to make sure you're not wired."

Bastian chuckled and dropped his towel, his movements slow and deliberate. "All that matters is still down there," he said with a goofy grin. I tried not to stare, my eyes quickly scanning his skin, glistening in the low light.

I noticed a bandage wrapped around his left thigh, covering the spot where he'd been shot. A pang of guilt shot through me, but I pushed it aside.

When Bastian finally wrapped his towel around his waist again, I noticed something else: a glint of metal around his neck. It was the medal, the one he'd bought as a symbol of his love for me.

My breath caught in my throat. "Why are you wearing that?" I asked, my voice barely above a whisper. "Is this another one of your mind games?"

Bastian's expression softened, and he reached up to touch the medal. "I never took it off, Rosie. Not even after everything that's happened between us."

I stared at him, searching his face for any sign of deception. But all I saw was sincerity and a flicker of something else— fear.

"They threatened to kill you," Bastian spoke in a strained, hushed timbre. "They said if I didn't discredit the manuscript and your research, if I didn't make those videos, they'd end you."

My heart skipped a beat, and I felt a chill run through me despite the heat of the bathhouse. "Who? Who threatened me?"

Bastian shook his head, glancing around as if he expected someone to be listening in. "I don't know. Bad guys in dark suits. The FBI, maybe? But they're watching us, Rosie. Our homes, our phones, our computers . . . all under surveillance. We're not safe."

I let out a shaky breath, trying to process what he was telling me. If what Bastian was saying was true, then we were in even more danger than I'd realized. The people who wanted to suppress the truth about the Voynich Manuscript were willing to go to any lengths to keep their secrets hidden.

I stared at Bastian, my eyes searching his. "I hope you're telling the truth, Ham. Because if you're not . . ."

Bastian looked at me, his expression a mix of hurt and disbelief. "How could you doubt it, Rosie? After everything we've been through, you really think I'd betray you like that?"

I glanced down at his bandaged leg, guilt washing over me. "I'm sorry you got shot. I never meant for you to get hurt."

He shrugged, a lopsided grin spreading across his face. "It's alright, Rosie. But you know, I'd feel a lot better if you kissed me."

I ignored his flirtatious remark. "This is serious, Ham. If I don't come up with credible evidence to support my claims about the Voynich Manuscript, I'm going to get fired tomorrow. My editor's already breathing down my neck."

Bastian's expression sobered, and he nodded. "I know, Rosie. But we have to be careful. There are eyes everywhere, and we don't know who we can trust."

I remembered the strange letter from the "old-timer hamster" and the mention of the Voynich.ninja forum. "I might have some leads to chase," I said slowly, looking at Bastian. "I received a letter from someone claiming to be one of your longtime followers. They mentioned a forum called Voynich.ninja where scholars and enthusiasts discuss the manuscript. But we can't access it from our homes or offices. The FBI is probably monitoring everything."

Bastian's eyes lit up with understanding. "An internet cafe," he said. "Somewhere we can access the forum without being traced."

I nodded, a plan forming in my mind. "And we should bring Regina along. She knows more about the Voynich Manuscript than anyone else we know. Her knowledge could be invaluable. Let's get out of here before we turn into prunes."

As we made our way out of the sauna, Bastian leaned in close, his breath hot against my ear. "You know, Rosie, this isn't the first time we've been this hot and sweaty together."

I felt a blush creep up my neck at the memories, but I refused to let him see how much his words affected me.

Then he flashed an innocent smile and said, "Remember that stakeout in the middle of summer, when the air conditioning broke in the car?"

"Good times," I said dryly. "Now let's focus on the task at hand, shall we?"

We quickly got dressed and left the bathhouse, the cool early afternoon air a stark contrast to the steamy heat inside. As we flagged down another taxi, I felt a flicker of hope. Maybe, just maybe, we could unravel this mystery together and come out the other side stronger than ever.

Or maybe I was heading straight into the lion's den. Only time would tell, but one thing was certain: I wasn't going to back down without a fight.

CHAPTER 13

The Poppy Connection

We reunited in lower Manhattan, devoid of phones, computers, or anything else that could be used to track us. The dingy internet cafe buzzed with the hum of ancient computers and the chatter of patrons as Bastian, Regina, and I huddled around a flickering screen, scanning through photos of the Voyniches' correspondence. The air was thick with the stench of stale coffee and the acrid tang of sweat, but we barely noticed, our attention focused solely on the secrets unfolding before us.

Regina shot a disapproving glance at Bastian, then turned to me. "Amalia, I can't believe you're still trusting this guy after those videos he posted. He's clearly not on our side."

Bastian scoffed. "Oh, please. Like you're one to talk, Miss Mysterious. You come out of nowhere with your secret feminist cult, and we're supposed to just take your word for it?"

Regina's eyes narrowed. "It's not a cult; it's a society with a long and proud history. And I'm not the one spreading misinformation and conspiracy theories online."

Bastian leaned back in his chair, a smirk playing on his lips. "Conspiracy theories? I prefer to think of them as alternative facts. It's called playing to your audience, Regina. Something you and your little club might want to learn."

Regina's face flushed with anger. "Boy, please. You keep telling yourself that."

I held up my hands. "Enough, both of you. We're supposed to be working together, remember? Fighting amongst ourselves isn't going to get us any closer to the truth."

Bastian and Regina glared at each other for a moment longer, then grudgingly turned their attention back to the screen. I could feel the tension simmering between them, but for now, at least, they seemed willing to put their differences aside.

I could feel my brow furrowing as I navigated the labyrinthine threads of the Voynich forum, my frustration mounting with each passing minute. "I can't believe this," I muttered, my voice tight with annoyance. "I'm trying to report a credible story, and instead I'm getting wrapped up in YouTuber influencers, internet ninjas, secret societies, and psychedelics. It's like I've stumbled into a Joe Rogan podcast episode."

Bastian chuckled, his eyes shining with mirth. "I wish I had his subscriber numbers. Maybe this story will get me there, even if it does sound a bit far-fetched."

Regina shot a disapproving look at Bastian, then turned to me and spoke in a taut, muted tone. "Far-fetched or not, we can't ignore the evidence piling up. Look at this." She pointed to a digitized photograph of Ethel Voynich's notebook, where detailed notes of her research filled the yellowed pages. "Ethel, with the help of experts, identified both cannabis and poppy among the plants depicted in the manuscript. And the poppy, in particular, has a long history of use in religious and mystical traditions."

My eyes widened as I scanned the notebook, my journalistic instincts kicking into high gear. "Could the poppy be the psychoactive ingredient in the lost kykeon recipe? The Eleusinian Mysteries, the cults of Demeter and Persephone . . . they all have ties to the poppy. Could the Voynich Manuscript be a lost guide to these practices?"

Regina nodded, her face as serious as a heart attack. "It's definitely on the table. I mean, have you seen how many poppies are all over that manuscript? And the text, even though we haven't cracked most of it yet, keeps referencing 'prg'—that's Hebrew for poppy, according to some of the ninjas who've taken a swing at translating it."

Bastian leaned back in his chair, his brow furrowed in thought. "It's like a puzzle piece falling into place. The Friedmans suggested the Voynich language was an invented one, not simply an encrypted version of a known tongue. And that German AI researcher, Kondrak, found computational evidence pointing to Hebrew as a potential base language. If the Hebrew word for poppy really is all over those pages, as ninja Monica Yokubinas claimed, it could be a significant clue."

I sighed, massaging my temples as I tried to process the barrage of information. Seeking clarity, I reached for Hathaway's annotated copy of the Voynich Manuscript and began flipping through the pages, focusing on the enigmatic illustrations.

As I studied the images, a particular motif caught my eye: women holding what appeared to be poppy capsules. One illustration in particular reminded me of a Minoan signet ring I had come across during my research on the origins of Demeter. The ring depicted a Goddess holding three distinct poppy capsules, and the similarity to the Voynich image was striking. The Minoan Poppy Goddess was considered by some scholars to be a predecessor of Demeter.

Intrigued, I searched for Folio 66r, the page that Yokubinas had identified as mentioning the word "poppy" an astonishing thirty-seven times. As I located the folio, my gaze was drawn to a small, curious image tucked away among the text—a naked figure, either male or female, lying in a posture that suggested sedation or a trance-like state.

The pieces began to fall into place in my mind. The preponderance of poppy imagery, the mentions of the plant in the text, and the illustration of the sedated figure all pointed to a deeper connection between the Voynich Manuscript and the use of psychoactive substances in ancient religious and mystical practices.

I wondered if the manuscript was more than just a compendium of botanical and medical knowledge. Perhaps it served as a guide to the very rituals and ceremonies that formed the heart of the Eleusinian Mysteries and other ancient traditions centered around the transformative power of the poppy.

As I shared my thoughts with Bastian and Regina, I could see the excitement and realization dawning on their faces. We were unraveling a mystery that stretched back centuries, a secret history of altered states and hidden wisdom that had been carefully encoded in the pages of the Voynich Manuscript. I scanned Dr. Hathaway's annotations, wishing we knew how to decode them, and that's when a sudden realization struck me, my eyes widening with shock.

"Bastian, Regina . . . look at this." I laid the manuscript on the table, pointing to Hathaway's dense scrawl in the margins. "Hathaway's annotations . . . they look like they are encoded using the same type of book cipher as Ethel's letter to Elizebeth. Hathaway's family—the Friedmans—were indeed the key."

Regina gasped, her hand flying to her mouth. "My God, you're right. Hathaway must have used 'The Gadfly' to conceal her discoveries, just like Ethel and Elizebeth. Do you have the book with you?"

I did, but before I could respond, Bastian's head snapped up, his eyes narrowing as he peered out the grimy window of the internet cafe. "Uh, guys? I think we've got company." He gestured towards a pair of burly men in dark suits, their eyes hidden behind mirrored sunglasses as they loitered outside the entrance.

My heart raced as I quickly gathered up the manuscript and our notes, shoving them into my bag. "We need to get out of here, now. They must have tracked us somehow."

We made our way to the back of the cafe, slipping through a dingy hallway and out a rusted emergency exit. As we emerged into the alley behind the building, the weight of our discoveries hung heavy in the air.

My mind reeled with the implications. A lost manuscript, its secrets hidden in plain sight. A web of connections spanning centuries, from ancient mystery cults to the pioneering work of the Friedmans and the enigmatic Dr. Hathaway. And at the center of it all, the poppy—a flower with the power to unlock the doors of perception, to offer glimpses of a forgotten world.

We disappeared into the labyrinthine streets, the weight of the manuscript heavy in my bag.

CHAPTER 14

The Prison

I hurried after Regina through the streets, glancing over my shoulder to ensure we weren't being followed. Adrenaline coursed through my veins as we ducked into a side street and wove between the parked cars. Bastian was right beside me, his presence a reassuring constant in the chaos.

Suddenly, the sound of screeching tires filled the air. A dark sedan careened around the corner, its windows rolled down to reveal the glint of a gun barrel. Regina shouted, "Get down!" just as a shot rang out. I felt the heat of the bullet whizz past my ear as I dove for cover behind a dumpster.

Regina cried out in pain, clutching her arm as crimson blood seeped through her fingers. Bastian rushed to her side, his face etched with concern. "You're hit! We need to get you to a hospital."

Regina shook her head, gritting her teeth against the pain. "No hospitals. They'll be watching. I know a place we can go, but we need to move."

Bastian and I exchanged a worried glance, but I trusted

Regina. We helped her to her feet, supporting her weight as we fled down the alley.

The roar of engines grew louder behind us. Another car had joined the pursuit, their headlights glaring like predatory eyes. Bastian risked a glance over his shoulder. "They're gaining on us!"

Regina pointed to a narrow side street. "This way! Quickly!"

We stumbled down the alley, the cars screeching to a halt behind us. I heard the sound of doors slamming and feet pounding on the pavement. Our pursuers were closing in.

Just as I thought we were done for, Regina pulled aside a rusted metal grate, revealing a dark, gaping hole in the ground. "Get in!" she hissed, ushering us forward.

Bastian wrinkled his nose as we descended into the dank, musty tunnels. "Ugh, it smells like something died down here."

Regina let out a grim laugh, then winced as her injured arm moved. "Wouldn't be surprised if something did. These tunnels? They've got stories, and most of 'em ain't pretty. Lots of death and pain down here."

I shot Bastian a quelling look, then turned to Regina. "Where are we going? How do you know about these tunnels?"

Regina's face was pale in the dim light filtering through the grates above, but her eyes glinted with a fierce determination. "We're heading to a place where no one will think to look for us. No nice girls go there."

Bastian snorted. "Well, that rules you out, Rosie. You're the nicest girl I know." Leave it to Bastian to crack jokes in the middle of a life-or-death situation.

We trudged through the damp, echoing tunnels, the only light coming from the occasional grate overhead. The air was thick with the stench of mold and decay, and I had to fight the urge to gag. Just as I thought we were lost, Regina paused before a rusted metal door. "We're here."

Bastian and I exchanged uncertain looks as Regina pushed the door open, the creak echoing eerily in the cool tunnels.

"The Jefferson Market Library," Regina said, striding into an antique brick-vaulted chamber filled with leather-bound books. "It was once a women's courthouse and prison that saw plenty of death and suffering."

Blood continued to bloom across Regina's blouse, where the bullet grazed the back of her arm.

"Here, let me help," I said, guiding Regina to a musty velvet sofa. I tore a strip of fabric from my own shirt to bandage the wound.

Regina grimaced but continued. "In 1911, a fire broke out in the Triangle Shirtwaist Factory, just a block away from here. The factory was notorious for its poor working conditions and labor disputes. In fact, just a few years earlier, the factory workers, mostly young immigrant women, had gone on strike to protest low wages, long hours, and oppressive rules.

"During the strike, many of these brave women were imprisoned here where we stand. They were tried in Night Court, a tactic meant to intimidate them by associating them with the prostitutes whose cases were usually heard there at night. As one striker put it, 'No nice girls go there.'

"But the women remained undaunted, and their strike led to some improvements in working conditions. Tragically, it wasn't enough. When the fire broke out in 1911, 146 garment workers, mostly young women and girls, were killed. Some died in the flames, while others jumped to their deaths from the high windows, with no other means of escape. The fire was a turning point in labor history."

A solemnity descended on the library chamber as she spoke of the disaster. "The prison closed and was reborn as a library. The perfect secret headquarters for the Order of the Nine Realms."

Bastian wandered the dim chamber, taking in the exposed brick archways. "So you're saying in a city with thousands of skyscrapers, the creepy feminist Illuminati gathers in an old prison basement?"

Regina scowled at his jibe. "I'll have you know our society traces its roots back to the Library of Alexandria in Egypt, founded in the 3rd century BCE. It was the largest and most significant library of the ancient world."

"Seems like wherever your little cult goes, fire ensues," Bastian barked back.

Regina leaned forward on the sofa, eyes blazing despite her wound. "Scholars from all over the Mediterranean came to study and conduct research at the Library of Alexandria. But what few people know is that the library also housed a collection of ancient texts from even older civilizations."

My heart quickened as I started to connect the dots.

"The library," Regina continued, "housed a group of nine scrolls, fragments from an ancient library, said to have travelled from the port of Kommos in Crete. These artifacts contained cryptic information about nine realms and goddesses, touching on the intersection of science, spirituality, and mathematics."

I felt a shiver run down my spine. Could these be the origins of the Voynich Manuscript's mysterious content?

"We believe so," Regina said. "However, when the scholar and poet Callimachus created the Pinakes, the first library catalog, he struggled with how to categorize the 'nine realms' scrolls, as they defied easy classification."

Bastian chuckled. "Typical. They couldn't handle anything that didn't fit into their narrow little boxes."

Regina smiled wryly. "It's a familiar story, isn't it? Those scholars, the ones all about that secular learning? They straight up ignored the 'nine realms' scrolls. Brushed 'em off as some religious cult nonsense."

"But some librarians must have recognized the importance of the scrolls, right?" I asked, already knowing the answer.

Regina nodded. "According to our lore, a few did. And although we don't know their names, we know they took it upon themselves to preserve and protect this knowledge. Centuries later, the Library of Alexandria began to decline and the city was embroiled in political turmoil. Luckily, during the siege and fires of Alexandria, they smuggled the 'nine realms' scrolls to the Library of Serapeum. There, a group of scribe apprentices worked tirelessly to transcribe the scrolls into nine codices, the historical ancestors of the modern book."

I leaned forward, hanging onto Regina's every word. "And what happened to the books after that?"

"They remained in the Serapeum for several centuries," Regina continued. "Until the library was destroyed by Roman Christians. Fortunately, the books were rescued by Hypatia and her father in their efforts to preserve seminal mathematical books."

Bastian's eyes widened. "Hypatia?"

Regina nodded. "Yes, Hypatia was a remarkable woman. She was renowned for her teachings in mathematics, astronomy, and philosophy. When she learned of the nine codices, she became fascinated by their contents. She gathered a group of her most trusted students and colleagues to study the books in secret, hoping to unravel their mysteries."

I felt a chill run down my spine. "But Hypatia was killed by a Christian mob, wasn't she? Because of her pagan beliefs and her teachings?"

Regina's expression turned stormy. "It wasn't just that. Hypatia was into those nine books, with all their wild ideas about women's power and ancient goddess-worshipping cultures. That made her a target. The Christian establishment, they were on the rise, and they saw her as a threat to their boys' club."

"So, they silenced her," Bastian said, his voice heavy with anger and sorrow.

Regina nodded, her expression grim. "One of the first documented witch-hunts in history. But Hypatia and her crew, they had a plan to keep those books safe. They knew the knowledge in those pages was too valuable, too risky, to let it disappear."

"What did they do?" I asked, almost afraid to hear the answer.

"They divided the books among themselves and fled Alexandria, each taking a different path to avoid detection. They scattered across the globe, some as far as Constantinople and Baghdad, each tasked with safeguarding their portion of the knowledge. They committed to reproducing them once every couple of centuries as the materials aged. We lost track of all of the books, until now."

I felt a swell of admiration for these brave men and women, risking everything to preserve the legacy of a civilization that the world was determined to forget. "And the Order of the Nine Realms? Is that when it was formed?"

Regina shook her head. "Not officially. But the seeds were planted then, in the hearts and minds of Hypatia's followers." She stood up, her injured arm cradled against her chest. "It wasn't until centuries later, in medieval times, that the Society formally came together. Scholars, artists, healers, and mystics from across Europe, each holding a small piece of the puzzle, united in their quest to rediscover the lost wisdom of the nine realms."

Bastian smirked. "So, is Tay Tay in on this? I mean, she's all about squads and secret societies, right?"

I glared at him, gently adjusting the makeshift bandage on

Regina's arm. "Is this really the time for snark? Regina is hurt, we were almost killed, and you're making pop culture jokes?"

Regina hauled herself up, eyes fierce even though she was hurting. "Bastian's not too far off, you know. We've only got one rule for joining: one must not be orthodox in her opinion. We've got pop stars, athletes, politicians—all kinds of powerful women, hiding right under everyone's noses."

Bastian let out a low whistle. "And now, here we are. Two humble journalists stumbling headlong into a centuries-old conspiracy."

I shot him a wry smile. "Humble? Journalist? You?"

He grinned, and for a moment, the tension in the room lifted. But then Regina stepped forward, her expression grave.

"Amalia, you have a choice to make. You can walk away now, forget everything you've learned, and go back to your normal life. Or you can join us, and help us find the lost books and the truth they hold."

Wasn't that why I became a journalist in the first place? To uncover the truth, no matter how deep it was buried or how dangerous the pursuit?

Revelations

The chill of the basement seeped into my bones as Bastian, Regina, and I huddled around the table, the flickering light of the fireplace casting eerie shadows on the walls. Regina had lit the fire to ward off the cold, but the warmth did little to ease the tension that hung heavy in the air.

We each focused on our assigned tasks, determined to unravel the secrets hidden within Dr. Hathaway's annotated copy of the Voynich Manuscript. I concentrated on decoding a letter tucked inside the pages, while Regina worked on deciphering Hathaway's side notes on the herbal pages. Bastian, meanwhile, scrutinized a folded letter stuck inside the front cover of the manuscript.

As I carefully applied the decoding method using "The Gadfly,"[1] the words began to take shape, revealing a correspondence between two remarkable women. My heart raced as I read the letter, realizing it was Elizebeth Friedman's response to Ethel Voynich:

Dear Mrs. Voynich,

I hope this letter finds you in good spirits. I wanted to take a moment to express my sincerest gratitude for sharing your invaluable insights and research on the Voynich Manuscript. Your letter has been a guiding light to unravel the secrets hidden within this enigmatic text.

Our study group has been diligently working on the manuscript, and we believe it is likely written in an invented language, rather than a simple substitution cipher of an existing language. We also note there are no mistakes in the manuscript, a clear indication that it is copied from an older version.

As for my own secret efforts, after carefully studying the manuscript and considering the information you provided, I believe I may have made a significant break-through.

Using the labels close to images of plants and stars, I transcribed some of the glyphs to ancient Hebrew, due to similarities, and then to English. This is not an exact science as both Voynichese and ancient Hebrew combine root words into new compound words. To bring the challenge to life, 'bookworm' could be interpreted as a 'worm in a book' for someone not familiar with English.

An insight came from your letter and from the poppy, which is very present throughout the manuscript. I tested our hypothesis of whether all or part of the manuscript could, in fact, be related to the myths of Demeter and Persephone and rites that date as far back as the Minoan Bronze Age civilization. I got an astonish-ingly high success rate.

At this stage, I am going to refrain from sharing complete paragraphs, mostly because some are nonsensical, while others leave significant room for interpretation, but I attach some of the words, phrases, and themes. I would like to warn you that the Voynich covers issues related to women's medicine such as fertility, termination of pregnancy, sexuality etc. that may be disturbing to sensitive minds.

Finally, the Manuscript may seem disjointed and fragmented at first glance, but there is an underlying structure. It appears that the circular diagram in folio 57v, the bathing women in the Balneological section, and the Herbal and Pharmaceutical folios may work together to encode a hidden recipe.

The circular diagram, with its concentric rings of symbols, bears a striking resemblance to the combinatorial wheels of Ramon Llull's Ars Combinatoria. Each ring seems to represent a key concept, while the position and orientation of the bathing women in the Balneological folios act as pointers, guiding the reader through the diagram to generate a specific permutation.

This permutation, in turn, references specific Herbal and Pharmaceutical folios, which provide the necessary components for the recipe. The all-text folios at the end of the manuscript likely contain the final instructions for preparation.

It is difficult to say with certainty whether this ingenious system was devised in the medieval period when the present copy was made, perhaps as a means to protect the knowledge from the scrutiny of the Inquisition, or if it was present in the original source material. Albert Rehm's research on the Antikythera Mechanism, an ancient Greek astronomical computer, suggests that complex encoding systems were not beyond the capabilities of earlier civilizations.

My husband and I will continue to work with scholars and experts from different fields to gain a better understanding of the manuscript's content and context.

However, I can't help but notice a growing interest in the Manuscript from certain quarters. J. Edgar Hoover, in particular, has taken a somewhat obsessive interest in the activities of our research group. I must admit some recent anonymous threats give me pause. I assure you that I will maintain the utmost secrecy regarding my findings, as I understand the sensitive nature of this knowledge.

I will write to you again as my work progresses, and I look forward to any further insights or suggestions you may have. Once again, I cannot thank you enough for your invaluable contributions to this field of study.

Very truly yours,
Elizebeth Friedman
5th of January, 1945

As I finished reading the letter aloud, Regina leapt to her feet with excitement. "I've got it!" she exclaimed, waving her notes in the air. "According to Hathaway's annotations, Elizebeth managed to translate a partial recipe for an elixir using the approach outlined in her letter, with the circular diagram as a guide."

Regina clutched the notes to her chest, kissing them feverishly. "This is it," she whispered, her voice trembling with emotion. "The key to heaven itself." She carefully folded the paper and tucked it into her pocket, her hand lingering there as if to reassure herself of its safety.

Bastian and I exchanged a glance, then I turned our attention to him, eager to hear what he had discovered. He stared at Regina, his eyes narrowed with suspicion, before finally speaking.

"Hathaway's letter suggests that once her great-grandmother understood the manuscript's structure, she realized it was a multidimensional tapestry of interwoven knowledge, a complex system of wheels and words and images, each element positioned with deliberate care to point to a greater truth," he said, his voice low and measured. "It's like a cosmic dance, a symphony of secrets hidden in plain sight."

He paused, his eyes distant, as if lost in thought. "Imagine a vast, intricate machine, not unlike gears and cogs, but of pages and ink. Each folio, a delicate component, precisely placed to guide the initiated through a labyrinth of meaning. The bathing women, the herbal drawings, the cosmological charts—all working in harmony to unlock the doors of perception, to guide the seeker on a journey through the very fabric of reality itself."

Bastian's words hung in the air, painting a vivid picture of the manuscript's complex beauty. I found myself entranced, drawn into the vision of a world where ancient wisdom lay hidden, waiting to be discovered.

"But Elizebeth knew she was dealing with a system far beyond her time," Bastian continued, his brow furrowed in concentration. "She realized that to truly decipher all its secrets, she would need the help of machines that could think, that could process multidimensional, multimodal information with a speed and complexity far beyond the human mind."

He smiled wryly, shaking his head. "It was the 1950s, the dawn of the computer age. The ENIAC and the UNIVAC, the first general-purpose computers, had just been unveiled. But even these marvels of technology were primitive compared to what Elizebeth envisioned. She knew that the true key to unlocking the Voynich Manuscript lay in the future, in the hands of a new generation of codebreakers."

Bastian fell silent, his expression darkening. Regina and I leaned forward, hanging on his every word.

"There's much more, passages I won't share," he said finally, his voice heavy with uncertainty. "Hathaway's letter ends with a warning. She says she initially trusted all members of the Order of the Nine Realms, but later realized a few radicals within their ranks were committed not just to smashing the patriarchy, but to destroying all men."

Regina scoffed, her eyes blazing. "Look, we've all got plenty of reasons to be mad at men. But why the hell would we go and ruin everything our sisters have been working for all these years? My grandmother's work? We're not about to become the thing we're trying to crush."

"See?" Bastian looked at me. "They're trying to crush us."

"That's ridiculous!" Regina snapped, her voice rising in pitch. "Emily would never say such things about us. You're lying, Bastian Ham. You're an agent of the FBI, of the patriarchy, trying to sow distrust and chaos."

Bastian's face reddened, his jaw clenching with barely controlled rage. "I'm telling you what I read," he said, his voice shaking with emotion. "There's more in this letter, things I won't share with you. Hathaway is on the run, unsure of who to trust. She's warning us to be careful."

"Oh, really?" Regina sneered, her lips curling into a mocking smile. "And why should we trust you, Bastian? You, who've been spreading lies and misinformation about the manuscript, about Amalia's work? How do we know you're not the one trying to lead us astray? Give me that letter."

Bastian slammed his fist on the table, making me jump. "Damn it, Regina! I'm trying to protect Amalia, to keep her safe from whatever dangerous game you and your little cult are playing."

Regina laughed, a harsh, biting sound. "Protect her? By undermining her at every turn? By making her doubt herself, doubt the very truth she's fighting to uncover? You're nothing but a traitor, Bastian Ham. A liar and a fraud."

The tension in the room was palpable as Regina and Bastian faced off, their words laced with accusation and suspicion. I felt torn, unsure of who to believe. They both seemed so certain, so convinced of their own truths.

In a flash, Regina lunged for Bastian, her hands grasping for the letter. They grappled for control, their voices rising in a cacophony of anger and frustration. I watched in horror as the letter slipped from their fingers, fluttering into the fireplace, where it was quickly consumed by the flames. Whatever claims were laid out in it, I could no longer verify them.

Bastian turned to me, his eyes wide with urgency. "Amalia, we need to go," he said, his voice low and insistent. "Hathaway was clear about what we need to do next. We can't stay here."

I hesitated, glancing between Bastian and Regina, my heart racing with uncertainty. Regina's warning echoed in my mind, urging me to be cautious, to question Bastian's motives. I had reasons to doubt him . . . But as I looked into his eyes, I saw a flicker of sincerity, a desperation that seemed all too real.

I made my decision. Gathering up the manuscript and all the notes, I turned to follow Bastian, my steps heavy with the weight of my choice. Regina's voice rang out behind me, pleading, warning, but I didn't look back. I couldn't afford to second-guess myself, not now.

As Bastian and I fled into the streets, the cold air stinging my face, I felt a sense of unease settle over me. The truth lay somewhere ahead, buried in the pages of the manuscript and the secrets of the past. But with each step, I was being pulled deeper into a web of lies and betrayal, unsure of who to trust or where to turn.

The path forward wasn't clear. I could only hope that my instincts would guide me, that the light of truth would pierce the darkness before it was too late.

"Where are we going?" I asked.

YIAYIA
Greek word. Used often in VMS
Modern meaning: Grandmother
Ancient meaning: Woman
Priestess

Predominance of the
Hebrew word for poppy and
poppy images!

r1

A woman is taken.
Her mother wants the
village to rise up because
the woman is innocent.

? Persephone abduction ?

"Arrogant toward
the bull" 40v

"how long until end of sexual
misconduct, emasculation by
crushing a broken man"

Vitex Agnus-Castus,
stifles sexual urges

16r

"Life of women to have value now"

"make a search of the forest"

"mother makes her wine to infiltrate mystic realm"

"Woman famished"

"Pomegranate"

? Hymn to Demeter and Persephone ?

8r

Last Paragraph: ? Gaza ?

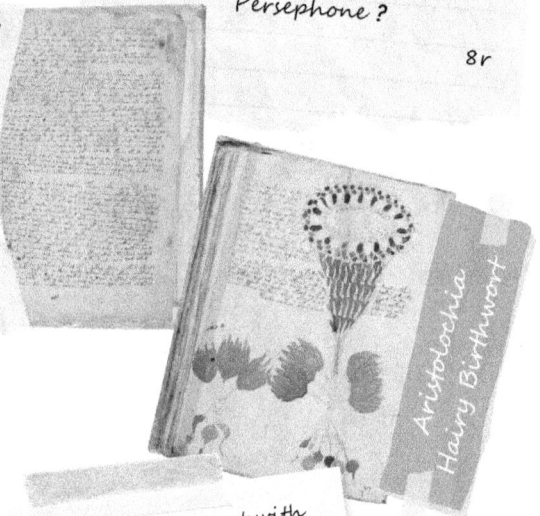

Aristolochia
Hairy Birthwort

"So not to become pregnant with fetus"

"To seize the Lord of the fetus"

"Dead body from the womb and she is grieving"

? A guide for abortion ?

40v

CHAPTER 16

Broken Statues

The adrenaline was still pumping through my veins as Bastian and I hurried down the bustling streets of Manhattan. We needed to get off the grid, and fast.

"They can't be tracking us; we don't have any devices on us," I said, glancing over my shoulder.

Bastian nodded, limping beside me. "Let's withdraw a lot of cash, pick up a couple of burner phones from the electronics store up ahead, and get out of here before they pinpoint the ATM," he said, his eyes scanning the storefronts.

A few minutes later, we emerged with two new iPhones and a handful of change. It wasn't much, but it would have to do.

"Where to now?" Bastian asked, pocketing his new phone.

I thought for a moment. "The library. The Stephen A. Schwarzman Building. It's big, public, and easy to blend in. We can access the internet and do some research there."

"Aren't we on the run from librarians?"

I shrugged. "I mean, they're not the ones trying to kill us."

Bastian sighed heavily. "No, they are just trying to annihilate all men." Then, he bowed dramatically. "Okay, lead the way."

As we approached the imposing marble facade of the library, I felt a sense of awe. The Beaux-Arts architecture was breathtaking, with its grand arches, intricate sculptures, and the iconic lion statues guarding the entrance. For a moment, I forgot about the danger we were in and allowed myself to be swept up in the grandeur of it all.

Inside, we made our way to the Rose Main Reading Room, a grandiose space with long oak tables and ornate chandeliers. The room was quiet, save for the occasional turning of a page or the soft footsteps of the librarians. We found a secluded spot in the corner and huddled around one of the old desktop computers.

As Bastian searched the library's catalogue, I pulled out the Voynich and the Gadfly and began to decipher Hathaway's notes on the elixir recipe. "Listen to this," I whispered. "The recipe contains a potent mix of psychedelics, including poppies for opium, ergot fungi which grows on barley and has compounds similar to LSD, and a bunch of other herbs I've never heard of."

Bastian's eyes widened. "Whoa, a concoction worthy of Pablo Escobar."

As I continued working on the translation, Bastian pulled up a search engine and started digging for information. "Hey, check this out," he said, pointing to the screen. "A study from 2019 by some guy named Griffiths of Johns Hopkins University. It says that people who took psychedelics reported encounters with 'benevolent, intelligent, sacred, eternal and all-knowing' entities. Half of them even described it as a 'mystical' experience."

I rolled my eyes. "Of course, they saw God. I bet they also saw the Wicked Witch of the West. They were tripping on a cocktail of dangerous hallucinogens. It's not exactly a reliable source of information, is it?"

Bastian shrugged. "I don't know, Rosie. Maybe there's more to it than that."

I sighed, rubbing my temples. "This whole thing is a career-killer. If my editor finds out I'm chasing down some ancient psychedelic recipe, I'm finished."

Bastian put a hand on my shoulder. "Hey, don't think like that. This is a real story. In fact, it might be the story of a lifetime."

I gave him a small smile, then turned my attention back to the computer. Something about the recipe tickled at the back of my mind. "Poppies . . . opium . . . It's all connected . . ." Then I remembered the Minoan Poppy Goddess, the idol of a Bronze Age civilization that thrived on the island of Crete over three thousand years ago.

A quick search through the library catalogues and we requested every book on the subject. "Bastian, look at this," I said, pointing to a series of photos of colorful Minoan frescoes from Knossos in one of the books. "The women are depicted in positions of power, while the men are shown serving on them, wearing these bizarre codpieces and jewelry."

Bastian leaned in, a grin spreading across his face. "Hah! It's like the Chippendales. I don't know if I could pull off that look."

I stifled a laugh and kept turning the pages. Something caught my attention and I squinted my eyes, trying to figure it out. One of the servers wore something on his wrist, a round object that could be a clock face or something. I shook my head, discarding the idea. It was probably just a piece of jewelry.

Then, as I turned the page, I saw it—a statue of a bare-breasted goddess, her arms outstretched, two serpents in her grasp.

"The Snake Goddess," I breathed. "Apparently, she was a major deity in the Minoan pantheon, often depicted holding snakes, which were symbols of wisdom and renewal."

As I read on, my excitement grew. The Minoans had a remarkably advanced society for their time, with a strong focus on women in religious and political roles. But maybe there was a darker side to their culture as well.

"Amalia, listen to this," Bastian said, his voice trembling slightly as he read from another book. "Archaeologists found thousands of clay figurines at peak sanctuaries around Crete—mostly animals and male figures that had been deliberately broken and smashed. They think it might have been part of some kind of ritual." Bastian's face paled. "That's messed up. Why would they do that?"

I shrugged. "I don't know, but Elizebeth's notes seem to allude to it."

"But there's more. They found this statue called the Palaikastro Kouros. It was a young male figure, burned and mutilated, with its genitals removed. Two holes in his crotch left to tell the tale." Bastian shuddered. "I'm telling you, Rosie, this is starting to sound like some kind of man-hating religious cult. We need to be careful."

"Oh dear, a statue broken and burned. What a crime!" I mocked. "Don't jump to conclusions. We don't have all the facts yet."

Just then, a flicker of movement caught my eye. A man was browsing the shelves nearby, his gaze lingering just a little too long in our direction. I felt a prickle of unease run down my spine.

"Bastian," I whispered, nodding towards the man. "I think we're being watched."

He glanced over, then back at me. "Okay, don't panic. Just keep researching. We need to figure out our next move."

I took a deep breath and turned back to the pile of books.

As I scanned my eyes through the images of ancient frescoes and shattered figurines, I couldn't shake the feeling that we were on the brink of something huge.

"Hey, look at this," I said. It was a photo of a terracotta sculpture of Ceres, the Roman counterpart of Demeter. In her hands, she held a bundle of wheat and poppies, with serpents twining around her arms. "Ceres, Demeter, the Minoan Poppy and Snake Goddesses, they all lead to some kind of hallucinogenic sacrament."

Bastian's eyes widened. "A man bashing ritual."

I ignored his antics. "I'm certain the Eleusinian Mysteries were a continuation of the matriarchal Minoan tradition. The Snake Goddess, the poppy seeds, the focus on powerful female figures . . . it's all there."

Bastian ran a hand through his hair. "Okay, so we've got an ancient cult that used psychedelic drugs to commune with their gods."

"But that doesn't prove the existence of a super advanced matriarchal society capable of parthenogenesis," I added.

"Partawhat?"

"Virgin birth," I replied. "Regina mentioned it when we first met."

"See? They are trying to end us," Bastian said, gesturing dramatically. "In her letter, Dr. Hathaway quoted the accounts of Plutarco and some other dude called, uhm . . . Elio, I think. I remember the quotes mentioned words like 'most atrocious and luminous' and 'terrible things, panic, shivers and sweat.' These were men describing the said mysteries."

I chewed my lip, thinking. "Was there any other information in Hathaway's letter?"

Suddenly, Bastian snapped his fingers. "The coordinates! I just remembered—in Hathaway's letter, she mentioned the coordinates of where she was heading next. The longitude was 23.525, and the latitude was, uhm, somewhere in the 30s."

I pulled up Google Maps on the computer and started entering the numbers. "23.525 longitude, that's easy enough. But the latitude . . . let's scan the map and see what comes up."

As I hit enter, the map zoomed in on the Aegean Sea. Then, I made an educated guess and clicked on Elefsina, where the Eleusis Archaeological Site is located. "Checkmate! Eleusis is precisely located at that longitude," I breathed. "Of course. That's where the Mysteries were held."

Bastian leaned in, excitement sparking in his eyes. "That's it, Rosie. That's where Hathaway is heading. We need to get there."

Just then, a loud bang echoed through the reading room. Bastian and I jumped, our hearts racing. A group of men in suits burst through the doors, weapons badly concealed.

Panic surged through me. They had found us. But how?

Bastian grabbed my hand, his face set with determination. "Rosie, do you trust me?"

I nodded weakly, my throat too tight to speak.

"Then follow my lead."

He reached into his pocket and pulled out his new phone, typing madly.

"Don't login with your credentials, you fool," I warned. "They'll track us." I quickly realized the pointlessness of my words. They were onto us despite every precaution.

Seconds later, he held it up with one hand while keeping a firm grip on me with the other.

"Hey there, my loyal Hamsters!" he said, his voice ringing out through the library. "Bastian Ham here, coming to you live from the New York Public Library. I'm here with the lovely and talented Amalia Rose, and boy, do we have a story for you!"

I stared at him in disbelief. He was live-streaming? Now, of all times?

The men hesitated, confused by this sudden turn of events. Bastian took advantage of their momentary distraction and pulled me towards the exit.

"That's right, folks," he continued, his voice echoing off the walls. "We're investigating the groundbreaking findings of Dr. Emily Hathaway, and let me tell you, it's a doozy. Ancient man-hating societies, crazy drug-fueled parties, and a secret cabal trying to keep it all under wraps."

I stumbled along behind him, my mind reeling. "Bastian, what are you doing?" I hissed.

He grinned, the camera still trained on his face. "Saving our skins, Rosie. If the FBI wants to come after us, they'll have to do it in front of a quarter of a million witnesses."

I glanced down at the screen and saw that he was right— the viewer count was climbing rapidly, with comments and questions flooding in from all over the world.

"Now, I know what you're thinking," Bastian continued, his tone turning serious. "This all sounds like some kind of crazy conspiracy theory. But trust me, my friends, the truth is stranger than fiction. Amalia and I have seen the evidence with our own eyes, and let me tell you, it's enough to blow your mind."

I finally found my voice, pushing my face in front of the camera. "What Bastian means," I interjected, "is that we've uncovered some fascinating historical records that suggest the existence of advanced prehistoric societies with a strong emphasis on women in positions of power. It's a remarkable discovery, but we need to be cautious about drawing conclusions without further research."

Bastian flashed an enormous smile. "Always the skeptic, eh Rosie? But that's what I love about you. You keep me honest."

I felt my cheeks flush, and I was suddenly very aware of the hundreds of thousands of eyes watching us.

"The point is," Bastian said, turning back to the camera, "Ms. Rose and I are committed to following this story wherever it leads. And if something happens to us, well . . . let's just say it won't be an accident. We've been hunted and shot at, no kidding! The FBI, the feminist Illuminati—whoever's behind this, they can't stop the truth from coming out."

He paused for effect, then winked at the camera. "Oh, and if friends watching this happen to be in New York, could you swing by my place and check on my cat? I left her some food, but you know how needy she can be."

"Bastian!" I snapped, yanking him towards the door. "Focus!"

He laughed, letting me pull him along. "Alright, alright. Anyway, you heard it here first, folks. The Voynich Mysteries decoded, coming soon to a library near you. Bastian Ham, signing off!"

With that, he ended the stream and pocketed his phone, just as we burst out of the library and into the crisp evening air.

I whirled on him, my heart still pounding. "Are you insane? You could have gotten us killed back there!"

Bastian shrugged, that infuriating grin still plastered across his face. "But I didn't, did I? Come on, Rosie, you have to admit that was pretty badass."

I opened my mouth to argue, but something stopped me. He was right—as reckless and foolhardy as it was, his impromptu live stream had bought us the time we needed to escape. And with the eyes of the world now watching, the FBI would have to think twice before making any overt moves against us.

"Fine," I said, trying to keep the reluctant admiration out of my voice. "You've still got a lot to answer for. Feminist Illuminati? Are you kidding me? For all I know, you could be working for the FBI, planting misinformation."

"I mean, as we learned today, they have reasons to worry about what the Voynich Manuscript will uncover," Bastian said. "I'm still pretty shaken about that castrated statue . . ."

I looked straight into his eyes and asked, "Are you working with them? With the FBI?"

He released an exasperated sigh. "How can you even ask that?" he said, throwing his hands in the air quite dramatically.

I nodded, pushing aside my doubts. We had come too far together, for better or worse.

A deep, authoritative voice cut through the air. "Ms. Rose."

We spun around, coming face to face with a tall, broad-shouldered man in his sixties. His steely blue eyes, framed by a shock of silver-blond hair, locked onto mine with an intensity that sent a chill down my spine. He took a deliberate step forward, his imposing presence forcing me to crane my neck to meet his gaze.

Bastian, sensing the man's threatening demeanor, swiftly positioned himself between us, his arm outstretched to maintain a safe distance. "Back off, buddy," he warned, his voice low and firm.

The man barely acknowledged Bastian's presence, his piercing gaze never wavering from my face. "You have no idea what you're meddling with," he said, his words measured and cold. "We have the power to destroy your credibility, to turn your Hyperborea misinformation campaign into a laughing-stock. You'll be lucky to find work writing tabloid horoscopes."

He leaned in closer, his voice dropping to a whisper that was somehow more menacing than a shout. "Consider this your final warning. Drop the story, or we'll make sure you rue the day you set your eyes on the Voynich."

"Who the hell are you? FBI? Neo-Nazi cult leader?" Bastian asked.

"Why choose one?" With that, the man turned on his heel and strode away, his tailored suit jacket flapping in the breeze. Bastian and I stood frozen, watching his retreating figure until he disappeared around a corner.

I let out a shaky breath, my heart pounding in my chest. Bastian turned to me, his eyes wide with concern. "Hyperborea?" he asked, his voice tinged with both anger and fear. "That's the Nazi version of Atlantis. The myth that served as a pretext for their ideological platform and genocidal tendencies. How is that related to the Voynich?"

I shook my head, trying to process what had just happened. "I don't know," I admitted, my voice trembling slightly. "But whatever it is, we must be getting close to something big. Something they desperately want to keep hidden."

Bastian nodded grimly, his jaw set with determination. "Then we keep digging," he said, placing a reassuring hand on my shoulder.

I managed a small smile, drawing strength from his unwavering support. "Damn straight," I said, squaring my shoulders. "Let's get back to work."

As we flagged down a cab and sped off to the airport, I was certain we were heading into something more dangerous than either of us could possibly imagine.

CHAPTER 17

Here's to Hypatia!

As we approached the sprawling ruins of Eleusis, the feeling of unease crept up my spine. The ancient site, once home to the famous Eleusinian Mysteries, loomed before us, its crumbling columns and weathered stones a testament to the passage of time.

Bastian, who had been uncharacteristically quiet for most of the journey, suddenly spoke up. "You know, my grandma used to tell us stories about our Greek ancestry. Yiayia always said our family line could be traced back to ancient rituals, probably like the ones that took place here."

I raised an eyebrow, intrigued by this unexpected revelation. "Really? I never took you for the type to put much stock in family legends."

He shrugged, a wistful smile playing on his lips. "Honestly, it's part of the reason I got into investigating unsolved mysteries in the first place. I guess I always hoped that maybe, someday, I'd find the connection, you know? Uncover the truth behind the stories."

I couldn't help but chuckle. "Well, look at you, Bastian

Ham, secret descendant of ancient Greek mystics. I suppose that explains your flair for the dramatic."

He grinned, the familiar sparkle returning to his eyes. "Hey, don't knock it till you've tried it, Rosie. Might come in handy during this little adventure of ours."

As we drew closer to the ruins, I glanced at Bastian, his brow furrowed in concentration as he studied the map in his hands. "The entrance to the Telesterion should be just ahead," he said, pointing to a large, rectangular shape in the distance.

I nodded, my heart pounding with anticipation and a touch of fear. The Telesterion was the central hall where the secret rituals of the Mysteries took place, a place where only the initiated were allowed to enter. As we drew closer, I noticed something strange—a flickering light emanating from the right side of the courtyard.

"Bastian, look!" I gasped, grabbing his arm. "Is that . . . a fire?"

He followed my gaze, his eyes widening in surprise. "It can't be. The sacrificial pit hasn't been lit in centuries."

We quickened our pace, the sound of our footsteps echoing off the ancient stones. As we approached the pit, the smell of smoke assaulted my nostrils. The fire was indeed lit, its flames licking the night sky, casting eerie shadows on the crumbling walls.

Bastian and I exchanged a worried glance. Someone was here, someone who may be attempting to reenact the Mysteries. We scanned the area, looking for any sign of Hathaway or her pursuers. That's when we heard it—a faint moan coming from the direction of the Kallichoron Well.

The well, I knew, was where the maidens of Eleusis used to perform dances, which formed part of the sacred rites in honor of the goddess. Two concentric stone rings formed the well's mouth, serving as steps to stand on and draw water, but also as seats where maidens chanted hymns to the goddess.

Bastian and I raced over to the well, the moans growing louder with each step. As we peered over the edge, my heart leapt into my throat. There, at the bottom of the dry well filled with debris, lay Regina, her hair matted with blood.

"Regina!" I cried out, my voice echoing off the stone walls. "We're here; we're going to get you out!"

Bastian looked around frantically, searching for anything that could help us. "The well is too deep, and we don't have a rope. I'll have to lower you down by your arms, and Regina will need to grab onto your legs."

I swallowed hard, realizing the risk we were about to take. The well was quite deep, and one slip could mean serious injury or worse. But we had no choice—Regina needed our help.

I nodded, steeling myself for what was to come. "Let's do it."

Bastian kneeled on the outer rim of the well, bracing his uninjured quad muscle against the ancient stones. I sat down, dangling my legs over the edge with Bastian behind me. I lifted my hands and gripped his forearms tightly.

"Ready?" he asked, his gaze locked on mine.

I took a deep breath and nodded. Slowly, Bastian began to lower me down, leaning over the rim of the well, his muscles straining with the effort. The rough stone walls scraped against my back as I descended, the darkness enveloping me. I braced my feet and back against the wall on opposite sides of the well, taking the pressure off Bastian for a second.

"Regina!" I called out, my voice echoing in the confined space. "I'm coming down. When I get close enough, I need you to jump, grab onto my legs, and hold on tight."

I heard her labored breathing, punctuated by whimpers of pain. "Okay," she managed to croak, her voice weak.

The descent seemed to take an eternity, my arms burning

with the strain of supporting my weight. Finally, I felt Regina's hands grasp my ankles, her grip weak but desperate.

As Bastian started to haul us up, I felt Regina shift her grip on my legs. "Regina, try to brace your feet and back against the walls of the well," I called down to her, my voice strained with effort. "It'll help ease the weight on us and give you some leverage."

"I'll try. I've sprained my ankle, and it hurts," she replied, her voice thin but determined. As Bastian pulled, I could feel Regina pushing against the walls, using the friction to inch her way up. Each time she moved, she whimpered in pain, but it took a bit of the strain off my arms and legs, and I knew Bastian must have felt the difference too.

Inch by inch, we made our way up the narrow shaft, the rough stone scraping against my skin. Regina's movements became more coordinated, her good foot finding purchase on the smooth walls. She grunted with exertion each time she pushed upward, the sound echoing in the confined space.

As we neared the top, I held onto the edge of the rim as Bastian reached down with one hand and grabbed Regina's arm, helping to pull her over the edge. I felt a rush of relief as the weight lifted from my body, and a moment later, Bastian was hauling me up and over the lip of the well.

"I gotcha," he said, hugging me tightly.

We collapsed onto the stone, gasping for breath. Regina lay curled on her side, her face pale and streaked with blood. I knelt beside her, my heart pounding with fear and adrenaline.

"Regina, what happened?" I asked, inspecting the bruise by her hairline. "How did you end up inside the well?"

"I . . . I don't remember. I think she drugged me."

"Who did this to you?" I pressed.

She blinked slowly, as if trying to focus through a haze of pain. "Agnes," she croaked, her voice barely above a whisper. "She took the recipe."

Bastian and I exchanged a confused glance. "Agnes?" he repeated, his brow furrowed.

"A dear sister of the Order of the Nine Realms and the head librarian at Biblioteca Medicea Laurenziana. Agnes is our representative for all the women—past and present—targeted in witch trials. She's a direct descendant of Matteuccia de Francesco, an expert of herbs and the first woman in Europe to be burned at the stake for witchcraft."

"Dear sister?" Bastian crossed his arms in front of his chest and shot me a dirty look. "See! I told you. They are man-haters with a millennia-old grudge."

"Zip it, Ham!" I warned before I turned to Regina. "Agnes has the kykeon recipe?"

Regina nodded weakly. "She prepared it: wine, honey, barley, cheese . . . mixed with psychoactive substances. Opium, cannabis, henbane . . ." She paused, her breathing labored. "And ergot . . ."

My mind reeled, trying to make sense of Regina's words. Surely Agnes was smart enough not to consume such an explosive mix of drugs.

Regina's eyes fluttered closed, her head lolling to the side. "She's going to die," she whispered, her voice fading. "Convulsions, spasms, vomiting . . . mania and psychosis."

Bastian grabbed Regina's shoulders, his eyes wide with urgency. "Regina, where is she?"

But Regina had already slipped into unconsciousness, her breathing shallow and uneven. I checked her pulse, my own heart racing with fear. "We need to get her to a hospital," I said, my voice shaking.

Bastian nodded, already pulling out his phone to call for help. But before he could dial, a piercing shriek split the night air. We froze, our eyes locked on the flames soaring over the sacrificial pit.

"What the hell was that?" Bastian whispered, his face pale.

I swallowed hard, my mouth suddenly dry. "It sounded like . . . an animal. Like it was in pain."

We looked at each other, the same thought passing between us. We couldn't leave Regina, but we couldn't ignore the sound either. Bastian grabbed his backpack, pulling out a small first-aid kit.

"Stay with her," I said, my voice tight. "I'll go check it out."

Bastian called out, "Rosie! Please be careful."

My heart pounded as I made my way towards the Telesterion, walking through the front porch where Demeter's statues once stood. The sound had come from Hades's and Persephone's caves to the right.

The caves—representing the underworld—were dark, lit only by flickering torches lining the walls. I moved slowly, my eyes straining to see in the dim light. The sound of my footsteps echoed off the stone floor, mingling with the eerie silence.

And then I saw it—a figure hunched over a stone altar, their back to me. As I got closer, I saw the lifeless body of a piglet, its throat slit, blood pooling on the stone.

I must have made a sound, because the figure whirled around, their face hidden beneath a dark hood. In their hand, they clutched a golden chalice.

"What have you done to the poor creature?" I shouted, my voice shaking.

The figure lifted their head, and I caught a glimpse of their face in the torchlight. It was the woman I'd met at the New York Public Library, her eyes wild, her skin damp with sweat.

"Amalia Rose," she said, her voice a hoarse whisper. "Thank you for your help, cara."

I took a step forward, my heart pounding. "What is going on? What are you doing here?"

She smiled, a manic twist of her lips. "I'm fulfilling nostro destino," she said, her voice rising with fervor. "Don't you see?"

"You don't know what you're doing," I warned, attempting to use arguments she'd buy. "The mysteries, the kykeon, the traditions . . . they must be performed by the initiated."

She lifted the chalice to her lips, and I caught a whiff of the pungent liquid inside. It smelled like death and madness, like something that should never be consumed.

"Stop!" I cried, lunging forward. "That concoction is dangerous; you'll die!"

But Agnes was too quick. She danced out of my reach, her laughter echoing off the cave walls. "You don't understand," she said, her eyes gleaming in the torchlight. "The kykeon is the key to everything. To the regni beyond, to the knowledge of the ancients."

She began to circle the cave, her movements jerky and uncoordinated. "For millennia, women were sacerdotesse, goddesses, fair rulers. We guarded the passage to other regni, through secret rituals and sacred pharmacopeia passed down from generation to generation."

I watched in horror as she lifted the chalice again, her hands shaking. "But men, they appropriated our power, our knowledge. They twisted it, corrupted it, like the drinking of Cristo's blood, uno eco of our secret rituals." Her voice was rising, becoming more frantic. "And then they stamped us out, burned us, crushed us beneath their boots."

Bastian burst into the cave, his eyes wide with fear. "Amalia, what's going on? I heard shouting."

I held up a hand, my eyes never leaving Agnes. "Agnes, please, think about what you're doing. The elixir, it's not meant to be abused like this."

She shook her head, her laughter turning to sobs. "You don't understand. I need this. I need to unlock the secrets of the virgin birth, the power to crush the patriarchy once and for all."

"Agnes, no!" I cried.

But Agnes was beyond reason. Her gaze glinted with a fervor that bordered on madness as she raised the chalice in a defiant toast. "Here's to Hypatia, to the witches, to the sisters who came before us, and to the power they knew was our birthright!"

With those words, she brought the chalice to her lips and drank deeply, the dark liquid spilling down her chin. For a moment, she stood tall and triumphant, a priestess of a forbidden rite. Then, her eyes rolled back in her head, and she crumpled to the ground, her body convulsing as the chalice clattered to the floor beside her.

"No!" I screamed, rushing forward. But it was too late. Agnes collapsed to the ground, her body wracked with spasms, foam flecking her lips. Bastian and I watched in horror as she twitched and writhed, her breathing becoming more and more labored.

It seemed to go on forever, the agony of watching a life slip away before our eyes.

"Il meccanismo," she screamed, using her last breath.

Finally, Agnes stilled, her eyes staring sightlessly at the ceiling.

I sank to my knees, tears streaming down my face. Bastian wrapped his arms around me, holding me as I sobbed. The weight of what we had just witnessed crashed over me like a tidal wave, threatening to pull me under.

Behind us, I heard a soft moan. I turned to see Regina, leaning heavily against the stone wall, her face streaked with tears. "She's gone," she whispered, her voice thick with grief. "My sister, my friend . . . she's gone."

I pulled away from Bastian, crossing the damp space to

wrap Regina in an embrace. She clung to me, her body shaking with sobs.

"I tried to stop her," she cried, her voice muffled against my shoulder. "I tried to make her see reason, but she wouldn't listen. I didn't know . . . I didn't know of her plans."

I stroked her hair, murmuring words of comfort that felt hollow even to my own ears. There was nothing I could say that would ease the pain of this moment, nothing that could bring back the woman who had been so consumed by her quest to vindicate all women accused of witchcraft. Sisters who endured the most violent and punishing of deaths.

As the night wore on, we sat huddled together in the Telesterion, surrounded by the ghosts of the past and the weight of the present.

"How did you find me?" Regina asked, her voice weak and filled with despair.

"Dr. Hathaway's letter, the one that went up in flames," Bastian explained. "It had a set of coordinates hinting at her location. I couldn't remember all of it, but the longitude was 23.525, and the latitude was in the 30s."

"We figured she wanted us to come here," I added.

Regina smiled grimly, a flicker of realization in her eyes. "No," she whispered, her voice gaining a touch of strength. "Like Agnes, you didn't go back far enough. You settled for the shadow of the shadow of the birthplace of the mysteries."

Her words sent a jolt through me, a sudden understanding dawning. "Oh!" I gasped, yanking my phone from my pocket and pulling up the maps app. "I know where she is!"

Regina nodded, her face etched with pain and determination. "We must help her."

"Care to enlighten me?" Bastian asked.

CHAPTER 18

To the Sea!

A s I stood on the deck of the fisherman's traditional kaiki, the salty sea breeze whipped through my hair, and I watched the rugged Greek coastline unfold before me. The boat's pointed bow rose sharply from the water, its old wooden hull painted in vibrant hues of blue and white. Beside me, Bastian and Regina gazed out at the azure expanse, their faces etched with a mixture of anticipation and trepidation.

We were sailing south on our way to Crete's Elafonissi peninsula, the only place in Crete that matched Hathaway's coordinates. To our right, we could see the Laconian Gulf, an inverted U-shaped gulf whose tips separate the Mediterranean and Aegean Seas.

The old sailor, his face weathered by years under the sun, leaned over, his eyes brimming with the wisdom of a lifetime spent on the waves. "You know," Kostas said, his weathered face crinkling into a smile, "the Laconian Gulf, with its shape like a horseshoe, has been a signpost for us sailors in these waters since time out of mind. The old folk, they used to call the tips of the gulf the Pillars of Heracles, like they marked the edge of the world."

Bastian's eyebrows shot up, recognition dawning on his face. "Hold on," he said, turning to Regina and me, his voice tinged with excitement. "Didn't Plato mention something about the Pillars of Heracles when he was talking about Atlantis?"

Regina nodded, her gaze distant as she recalled the passage. "'For in front of the mouth which you Greeks call, 'the pillars of Heracles,' there lay Atlantis . . .'" she recited, her voice soft and reverent.

I gasped, my heart skipping a beat as the pieces fell into place. "And in front of the mouth of the Laconian Gulf lies . . ."

"Crete," Bastian finished, his voice trembling with the weight of the realization. "Rosie, do you think . . . ?"

I held up a hand, my mind racing with the implications. "The FBI seemed quite worried about what we could reveal about Atlantis . . ."

Regina leaned in, her face alight with wonder. "You know, there's an old legend that says the heart of Atlantis was Thera, the island we now call Santorini," she said, her voice low and conspiratorial. "What if the Minoans were the ones who built that legendary civilization?"

Kostas nodded, his eyes squinting against the glare of the sun on the waves. "The whole of this place, with Santorini's caldera sitting there like a giant's bowl, it all changed when Thera blew its top and the sea came rushing in," he said, his voice raspy from years of shouting over the wind. "Back then, it was a ring of islands, with channels between 'em wide enough for ships to sail through to Thera's heart. And Crete, well, it was believed to be part of the outer ring."

Regina's eyes widened, a breath escaping her lips. "And

now, much of it lies underwater, its brilliance lost beneath the volcanic ash . . ."

"The old stories, they talk about the Keftiu. That's what they called themselves, not Minoans," Kostas continued, his rough hands gesturing to the sea around us. "They lived on the seven islands in this very stretch of water, islands sacred to Persephone herself."

He paused, taking a moment to let the weight of his words sink in. "The Keftiu were known to have befriended the great Egyptian queens, Queen Ty and Pharaoh Hatshepsut. Both visionary leaders who sought to forge peaceful trade with foreign lands."

Bastian and I exchanged a meaningful glance at the mention of Persephone and female pharaohs. It seemed that every thread we had been following was slowly weaving together into a tapestry of truth.

I stood by the helm. "We need to change course," I declared, my voice filled with unwavering resolve. "Set sail for Santorini."

Regina stepped forward, her eyes gleaming with excitement. "Yes, to Akrotiri and the Prehistoric Thera Museum in Fira, to be precise. If we're going to find the answers we seek, that's where we must begin our search."

Kostas nodded in agreement. "We'll make a stopover at Milos for the night," he said, his weathered hands already adjusting the ship's course. "It's a beautiful island, and it will give us a chance to rest and restock our supplies."

At dawn, as the boat charted a new path across the shimmering sea towards the Santorini caldera, I felt a thrill of anticipation running through my veins. The salty spray stung my cheeks, and the sun beat down upon the deck, but I barely noticed the discomfort. My mind was racing with the possibilities of what we might uncover in the ruins of Akrotiri and the museum's ancient artifacts.

Reaching for my phone, I hesitated, my finger hovering over the login screen. The temptation to use my credentials and check my messages, to see what new challenges or threats awaited me, was nearly overwhelming.

The FBI's ominous warning and my editor's looming ultimatum hung like a dark cloud over my thoughts, a constant presence that I couldn't quite shake. But as I glanced at Bastian and Regina, their faces alight with the thrill of discovery, I made a choice. Whatever problems were brewing in the outside world, whatever consequences I might face, they could wait.

For now, I needed to focus on the task at hand. With a deep breath, I slipped my phone back into my pocket, pushing aside my worries and doubts. The real world could wait. The truth couldn't.

CHAPTER 19

Cataclysmic Eruption

We finally approached the crescent-shaped island, its towering cliffs rising from the turquoise waters like the walls of a fortress. The whitewashed buildings of Fira, perched precariously atop the caldera's edge, gleamed in the afternoon sun, a stark contrast to the black volcanic sands that lined the shores.

Upon arriving, we were greeted by a treasure trove of Minoan artifacts and frescoes, each one more stunning than the last. The vibrant colors and intricate designs of the "Minoan Lady" and the "Fisherman" Frescos took my breath away, their beauty and sophistication a testament to the skill and artistry of the ancient civilization.

But it was the excavation of the "House of the Thrania" that truly captured our attention. The collection of 3,600-year-old ritual artifacts, including a clay chest containing a marble figurine of a goddess, sent a shiver down my spine.

Regina, her eyes wide with wonder, turned to Bastian and me. "What's amazing about the Minoan archaeological discoveries," she said, her voice hushed with reverence, "is the lack of fortifications and the infrequency of weapons. Their art and records focus on agriculture, trade, and beauty, a clear sign of a society where women were at least equal to men."

I nodded, my mind whirling with the implications. "The statues in the temple areas are exclusively female," I mused.

Bastian, his eyes scanning the exhibits with rapt attention, chimed in. "I'd like to point out that if an alien visits the Virgin Mary sanctuaries of Fatima or Lourdes, they may assume the Catholic Church was dedicated to women's empowerment."

I conceded, "Sure, but the lack of depictions of weapons and combat points to a peaceful society. It's a stark contrast to the militaristic focus of other ancient civilizations."

"And yet, there are hints that the Minoans controlled trade in the eastern Mediterranean," he said. "But perhaps they used diplomacy and commerce rather than brute force."

As we wandered through the museum and archaeological site, each new discovery fueling our excitement and curiosity, I knew we were on the cusp of something extraordinary. The pieces of the puzzle were falling into place, revealing a picture of a lost civilization that challenged everything we thought we knew about the ancient world. But even as I reveled in the thrill of discovery, a nagging sense of unease tugged at the back of my mind.

With trembling fingers, I pulled out my phone and finally mustered the courage to check my messages. My heart sank as I scrolled through the notifications, each one hitting me like a punch to the gut. Friends and family expressed their concern, sending me links to a barrage of articles that had surfaced about me. Tabloids had twisted fragments of my past, painting me as a call girl based on nothing more than a pole dancing class I had taken years ago. I felt violated, exposed, and utterly betrayed by the media's relentless desire for sensationalism.

But it wasn't just the tabloids. Mainstream news outlets had jumped on the bandwagon, giving a platform to so-called academics who eagerly supported Bastian's claims that the Voynich Manuscript was a hoax. They questioned the carbon dating, casting doubt on the very foundations of our investigation. I was watching my credibility crumble before my eyes, helpless to stop the onslaught of misinformation.

And then there was the City Rag, the publication I had once trusted with my livelihood. They had released a series of articles discrediting Dr. Hathaway, interviewing colleagues who claimed she had a history of peddling pseudoscience in her lectures. It was a blatant attempt to undermine her reputation and, by extension, the legitimacy of our entire investigation. I felt sick to my stomach, betrayed by the institution I had devoted my career to.

Bastian, sensing my distress, began to surf the net, his eyes widening with each passing moment. "Rosie, you won't believe this," he said, his voice a mix of amusement and disbelief. "In the last 24 hours, YouTube has been flooded with videos discrediting Sir Arthur Evans and other archaeologists who worked on uncovering the Minoan artifacts. They're accusing them of projecting their Eurocentric perspective, of being myth makers instead of myth finders, all for the sake of fame and fortune."

He let out a bitter laugh, shaking his head. "The number of videos from stuffy male Oxford experts is ridiculous. One of them is even analyzing the frescoes of Minoan men jumping bulls, claiming it's clear proof of aggression and a male-centric society. It's absurd."

But even as Bastian tried to inject some levity into the situation, I could feel the weight of the disinformation campaign crushing me. The sheer scale of the effort to discredit our work, to bury the truth before it could even see the light of day, was staggering. I felt like I was fighting a losing battle against an enemy with endless resources and no scruples.

"Hey, you okay?" Bastian asked, placing my hand in between his.

And in that very moment, I wanted to trust him, to bury my face in his chest and sob. I wanted to let him spoil me with kisses and little nothings that meant the world to me. But regardless of his intentions, he had started the disinformation campaign. He was as terrified of this world of powerful goddesses and matriarchal societies as the rest of them.

"Rosie, you're trembling. Come here," he said, pulling me closer.

I couldn't find the right words, so I just stepped away and stood there, lost in my thoughts. I noticed Regina speaking to a woman who had approached her. They seemed to know each other, and Bastian's eyes widened in recognition. "Is that Bettany Hughes?" he whispered, his voice tinged with awe.

"Who is Bettany Hughes?" I asked.

"Seriously, Rosie. She's only the most important Bronze Age historian and broadcaster. A real goddess." He blinked his eyes adoringly.

Regina, noticing our curiosity, intervened. "We maintain the discretion when it comes to the identities of our members," she said, a hint of warning in her tone.

Bastian gasped. "Bettany is in the Order?"

But the other woman, undeterred, spoke directly to me. Her voice was warm and calming, with a British accent that lent her words an air of authority. "Amalia, I saw the news," she said, her eyes filled with understanding and empathy. "You can call me Bremusa. I want you to know you're not alone in this fight. We've seen it all before—the pushback, the attempts to silence and discredit. But you can't let them win."

She paused, her gaze distant as if lost in thought. "The Minoans . . . We don't know the way it was, and we may never will. But we can try to grope our way towards the truth. For too long, the tales spun from every archaeological find, every relic of the past, have been filtered through the lens of men. Their perspective, their prejudices, their heavy-handed interpretations have shaped the myths that color our understanding of history and limit our vision of what could be. It's time for us to behold these treasures with fresh eyes, to trust our instincts and bring our own wisdom to bear."

Her words struck a chord deep within me, resonating with the very reason I had become a journalist in the first place. To uncover the truth, to give voice to the voiceless, to challenge the dominant narratives that had held sway for far too long.

"Evans was far from perfect," Bremusa continued, her voice firm and resolute. "Consider Harriet Boyd, a pioneering American archaeologist who was present with Evans when they uncovered the throne at Knossos. In her journal, she wrote that Evans initially believed the throne might have belonged to a priestess, based on its shape and size."

Bremusa paused for a moment, gathering her thoughts. "However, at that crucial moment, Evans was influenced by the myths of Theseus—tales created many centuries after the fall of this great civilization. Myths carefully designed to promote Athens and crush foreign women and their mysterious rituals. In these tales, Theseus dominates the Amazons, the King of Eleusis, and the Marathon bull. Propaganda to promote modern Athens' supremacy over ancient Crete."

She took a deep breath before continuing, "Evans changed his tune and boldly proclaimed to the world that he had found the throne of King Minos. With that single decision, the Keftiu became known as the Minoans, and the disinformation campaigns designed by Athens effectively reframed an entire culture."

And all I could think about were the parallels between history's disinformation campaigns against women and my own current drama. I shook off my self-pity party and stood tall.

Bastian shot Bremusa a skeptical look. "But bulls are everywhere in Minoan art. Isn't that proof of the existence of King Minos?"

Regina sighed dismissively. "Healthy initiation ceremonies; unarmed boys leaping bulls into manhood," she said, then leaned forward, her gaze scintillating with admiration. "Harriet was one of us, a true ally. Her accounts give us a glimpse of what might have been, if only the world had been ready to listen."

Bremusa nodded, her expression grave. "Yet, the strength of the scrutiny pushed towards Evans, and not so many other archaeologists, tells us more about the power these 'Minoan' artifacts have to disrupt the status quo and unlock future possibilities than about Evans himself. Because when a child reads a history book, she's not contemplating the past, she's dreaming the future."

As I grappled with the weight of the woman's words, Bastian's voice cut through my thoughts like a knife. "Holy guacamole, Rosie, you've got to see this!" he exclaimed, his eyes wide with a mixture of excitement and horror. "I found a new article about a place called Anemospilia, the 'Cave of the Winds,' where the Minoans supposedly performed human sacrifices of young boys." He turned to Bremusa. "Is this true?"

The woman's smile was as enigmatic as Mona Lisa's. "It depends who you ask. But the eruption around 1600 BCE and the events that preceded it . . . It changed things. It was the beginning of the collapse of this great civilization. Scared and starved, they were now at the mercy of the Mycenaean Greeks. The age of the Mother Goddess was ending. Poseidon—the earth shaker—had arrived with a bang. Minoan refugees scared across the seas using the few vessels they had left. Their archaeological vestiges found in Philistine settlements as far as Gaza. Pottery fragments and goddess figures, similar to the one in the House of Thrania."

I took a deep breath, pushing aside the creeping sense of doubt and frustration. Turning to Bremusa, I voiced the thoughts that had been nagging at the back of my mind. "This is all fascinating, but according to Dr. Hathaway's interpretation of the Voynich, we are looking for evidence of a far more advanced society. A lost matriarchal civilization who had mastered technology, biology, and perhaps even quantum physics to travel to different realms. But are we on the right track? Or are we, as my critics suggest, veering dangerously close to the realm of pseudoscience?"

"Technology?" Bremusa smiled, a glint in her eyes. "I'll take you to some friends who have a track record of innovation. They can help you separate fiction from fact," she said, in a low, fevered pitch. "They've been waiting for you."

As we followed Bremusa out of the museum, I felt a flicker of hope amidst the crushing weight of doubt and frustration. Perhaps, with the help of these mysterious allies, we could rewrite history, not as it had been told, but as it truly was.

The focus on technology made me recall the Minoan fresco's "watch" at the library. I asked Bremusa about it, and she laughed wholeheartedly.

"It's a Minoan seal," she said. "There are many types: rings, carved knobs, others worn around the neck or wrist on a string."

"I see." I felt a rush of heat rise to my cheeks as I realized I had jumped to wild speculation.

"The seal impressions tell us that an object belongs to the owner of the seal. Some symbols are combined for more complex recordings." Bremusa narrowed her eyes with a renewed intensity, and then, she whispered, "There's an archaeological site called Monastiraki where they found three archives with hundreds of Minoan seals, and vestiges of parchment and ink on the backs of seal-impressed clay nodules."

"Hey Bettany," Bastian cleared his voice. "I was wondering if you were up for a livestream with an up-and-coming YouTube channel about . . . uhm . . . history and such." The elbow Regina projected into his ribs made him gasp for air.

Bremusa turned to me and winked. "Don't worry, you'll find your 'watches' in no time . . ."

I cringed, still ashamed of my unfounded conclusion. It was so tempting to dream up history from small fragments of ancient plaster.

And so, with a deep breath and a determined stride, I stepped out into the bright Santorini sun, ready to face whatever challenges lay ahead. The truth was waiting, and I would not rest until I had claimed it as my own.

CHAPTER 20

The Calypso

As I stepped aboard the Calypso II, I was struck by the sleek, futuristic design of the sailing yacht. The ship's crew, a group of women ranging in age from their twenties to their eighties, moved about the deck with a sense of purpose, their red beanie hats standing out against the deep blue of the Aegean Sea.

Bastian, ever the curious one, turned to Regina. "Hey, are they related to Jacques Cousteau, the famous undersea explorer?"

Regina shot him a warning look. "Let's focus on the task at hand."

As we waved goodbye to Bremusa, trepidation washed over me. Who were these women, and where were we heading?

A striking blonde woman in her mid-forties approached us, her eyes alight with intelligence. "Welcome aboard the Calypso II. I'm Alcippe," she said, her voice carrying easily over the hum of the ship's engines.

Bastian flashed the biggest grin. "Alcippe? Sure you are."

Alcippe winked at him, flicking her hair to one side. "I hope you're ready for a journey like no other."

I watched as the crew prepared the boat for departure, their movements precise and efficient. The deck of the Calypso II was a marvel of modern engineering, with gleaming white surfaces and sleek, aerodynamic curves.

"Solar-Hydro-Sail technology! Harnesses sun, wind, and waves to propel the vessel. Our family has a long tradition of innovation," Alcippe said as we followed her toward the helm, a raised platform at the rear of the ship. It was equipped with an array of high-tech screens and controls that looked like something out of a science fiction movie. I couldn't quite believe the sheer scale and sophistication of the vessel.

"Bremusa told us you'd help us find an advanced matriarchal civilization," I said, flashing a cheeky smile at Alcippe.

I found my gaze drifting toward Bastian. He was at the center of a group of young sailors, all of whom seemed delighted by his stories. Bastian gestured enthusiastically, his face flushed with excitement as he regaled them with tales of our adventures.

As if sensing my gaze, Bastian glanced over at me, his eyes meeting mine across the deck. He flashed me a grin, his face lighting up with a warmth that made my heart skip a beat.

"Back to work, girls. Stop flirting with the handsome devil," Alcippe ordered. "Let's meet Celaeno. She's our Captain," she said, as we approached an intriguing figure sporting a magnificent mustache with tips curled skyward.

Celaeno approached me with an infectious smile, her eyes sparkling with mischief. "So, you're the journalist who's been stirring up trouble with our resident YouTube sensation," she said, her French accent, rich and melodic, delivered in a smooth baritone range.

I couldn't help but return her smile. "Guilty as charged," I replied, extending my hand. "Amalia Rose. It's a pleasure to meet you, Captain."

Celaeno grasped my hand firmly, her grip strong and

confident. "The pleasure is all mine, Amalia. I've heard great things about your work. It takes a lot of courage to pursue the truth, no matter where it leads."

I felt a rush of pride at her words, mixed with a twinge of uncertainty. "I just hope I'm doing the right thing," I confessed, my gaze drifting back to Bastian.

Celaeno followed my gaze, her expression softening. "Trust your instincts, Amalia. And don't be too hard on yourself, or on him. We all have our own paths to follow, and sometimes they lead us to unexpected places."

Bastian took a step toward her. "Get to meet you. Before we embark on this journey, do you think we could grab a bite to eat? I don't know about you ladies, but I'm starving."

He was right; I too was in need of some sustenance.

Alcippe's gaze snapped to Bastian, her eyes narrowing with a sudden intensity. "I'm afraid there's no food available on this journey we're taking," she said, her voice firm and unyielding. Then she turned to me and said, "To find your advanced civilization, we need to travel to the past. 205 BCE to be precise."

As we pulled away from the dock, the hum of the engines intensified, sending vibrations through the deck beneath my feet. Seagulls wheeled overhead, their cries mingling with the splash of the waves against the hull.

"We're totally ready," I replied, eager to know more, even as my gut growled with hunger. "But I have to ask, what's the significance of the year 205 BCE? How does it tie into the Voynich Manuscript and the lost civilization we're chasing?"

Alcippe leaned against the railing, the wind tousling her hair. "That year, the Romans were in a state of panic. They had witnessed two suns in the skies over South Italy, and at night, there had been an eerie light that lingered for a time. Showers of stones shot across the heavens from east to west, all of which were seen as omens of impending doom, especially after their losses against Hannibal and the Carthaginians."

I listened intently, trying to piece together the puzzle in my mind. In the distance, I could see the rugged coastline of Santorini receding, its whitewashed buildings and blue-roofed churches growing smaller with each passing moment.

Alcippe continued, "The Romans consulted the Sibylline books, which predicted that they would defeat the foreign foe if the Great Mother from Ida was brought to Rome. A delegation was sent to the Oracle of Delphi to interpret this prophecy, and that's where we believe they made a critical error."

My curiosity piqued. "What kind of error?"

"We are convinced that Apollo's priestess, Pythia, misunderstood the prediction of the Sibylline books. It was an honest mistake. You see, years earlier, the books had rightly foretold the fall of a meteor in Pergamum, now Turkey, where the Magna Mater was worshipped. The meteor was kept in her temple on Mount Ida in Pergamum and was itself worshipped as the goddess. So the Roman ambassadors, acting on the advice of the Oracle of Delphi, went to Pergamum and retrieved the black stone."

As Alcippe spoke, I noticed the captain hunched over a sonar screen, her brow furrowed in concentration.

"Is everything okay, Celaeno?" Alcippe asked.

"Give her all she's got!" Celaeno ordered, her voice cutting through the wind. "We've got company."

My heart raced as I realized we were being pursued by an unidentified object beneath the waves. The Calypso surged forward, its engines roaring to life as we tried to outrun our mysterious follower.

Despite the growing tension, Alcippe remained focused on her story. "The Magna Mater was brought to Rome in the Navis Salvia in April, 204 BCE. This event marked a turning point in Roman history as they went on to defeat the Carthaginians and establish themselves as a dominant empire. However, the true wisdom and power of the Goddess, which could have led them down a different path, was never truly attained."

I struggled to keep my balance as the ship pitched and rolled, the mysterious object still in pursuit. Bastian, his face pale, turned to Alcippe. "So the stone wasn't the good omen the Sibylline books were speaking of?"

She shook her head, a hint of sadness in her eyes. "The key to a different future was kept elsewhere. A future guided by knowledge and cultivation rather than force and domination."

She paused, her gaze distant as if lost in thought. "Centuries later, early Christian writers painted a horrible picture of the rituals related to the Magna Mater, projecting their own values and insecurities onto the practices. They wrote of blood baths, incest, emasculation, self-castration, and orgies, accounts that led to the great Roman witch hunts and the erasure of paganism. St. Peter's Basilica on Vatican Hill now stands atop the Magna Mater's shrines."

I shook my head, trying to wrap my mind around the implications of her words. "So, if it wasn't for Delphi's mistake, things would have been different."

Alcippe smiled, a flicker of wistfulness in her gaze. "As Arthur C. Clarke, the science fiction writer, once said, if the gift had been found and understood, 'by this time we would not merely have sent a few men to the Moon, we would have colonized all the stars visible to the naked eye.' Instead, the gift was lost to the ages."

Regina shot Alcippe a disapproving look. "We don't need to colonize anything. We've done enough of that!"

As the Calypso raced through the turbulent waves, the tension on deck was palpable. I gripped the railing tightly, my knuckles turning white as the mysterious object pursuing us crashed against the hull with a sickening thud. The ship shuddered under the impact, and for a moment, I feared we might capsize.

Celaeno, her face a mask of grim determination, barked orders to the crew. "Deploy the Crabs!" she shouted over the roar of the engines. "And get ready to launch the counter-measures!"

I watched in awe as some of the crew jumped into four sleek, oval-shaped submersibles, just before they detached from the Calypso II and plunged into the churning waters. The Cyber Crabs, as they were called, were a marvel of modern engineering—highly maneuverable underwater vehicles equipped with advanced AI, sensors, and manipulators.

As the Cyber Crabs sped towards the unidentified object, I caught a glimpse of it on one of the monitors—a sinister-looking submersible bristling with cameras and other sensors. It moved with an eerie, almost alien grace, its movements too precise and calculated to be human.

The Crabs quickly surrounded the hostile submersible, their powerful lights piercing the murky depths. They began to probe and prod at its hull with their articulated manipulators, searching for weaknesses.

Suddenly, the enemy submersible lashed out, a pair of razor-sharp, scythe-like appendages emerging from its sides. It spun and twisted, trying to eviscerate the Crabs with its deadly blades.

I watched in horror as one of the Crabs was caught in the submersible's grasp. The noise was almost deafening.

Celaeno gasped. "The Crab's carbon nanotube shell is groaning under the immense pressure."

But just as I thought it would be crushed, the Crab twisted free, leaving a jagged gash in the enemy's hull.

The battle raged on, our Crabs working in perfect unison to outmaneuver and outfight their opponent. They used their advanced sensors to anticipate the submersible's moves, dodging and weaving through the water with incredible agility.

But the enemy was relentless, its movements becoming more erratic and desperate as it sought to break free from the Crabs' grasp. It slammed into the Calypso's hull again and again, each impact sending shockwaves through the ship.

I stumbled and nearly fell, catching myself on the railing at the last moment. That's when I heard a scream pierce through the chaos. My heart stopped as I saw Regina lose her balance and tumble overboard, plunging into the turbulent waters below.

"Regina!" I cried out, my voice barely audible over the roar of the battle. I watched helplessly as she struggled to stay afloat, the violent churning caused by the clashing submersibles threatening to pull her under at any moment.

Bastian, without hesitation, leaped into action. He grabbed a life preserver and dove into the water, swimming towards Regina with powerful strokes. The waves crashed over him, but he pressed on, determined to reach her.

I held my breath, my heart pounding in my chest as I watched Bastian battle the currents. He managed to reach Regina, wrapping an arm around her waist and pulling her close. Together, they fought against the pull of the water, slowly making their way back to the Calypso.

The crew sprang into action, throwing a rope ladder over the side of the ship. Bastian helped Regina grab hold, and they began the arduous climb back to safety. I rushed to the railing, my hands outstretched, ready to help pull them aboard.

As soon as they were within reach, I grasped Regina's arm, hauling her over the railing and onto the deck. She collapsed, coughing and sputtering, her body shaking from the ordeal. I quickly wrapped a towel around her shoulders, trying to provide some warmth and comfort.

Bastian clambered over the railing, his clothes dripping and his hair plastered to his forehead. He flashed a lopsided grin, his chest heaving as he caught his breath.

"Well, that was refreshing," he quipped, his voice hoarse from the salty water. "I'll add flotation device to my CV."

Around me, the crew struggled to maintain their footing, their faces etched with fear and determination.

Alcippe, who had been watching the battle on the monitors, suddenly leapt into action. "The submersible is being controlled remotely!" she shouted. "We need to jam its communication signal!"

Celaeno raced to one of the control panels and began typing furiously, her fingers a blur on the keys. Moments later, the Crabs attacked anything on the submersible that looked like a comms device.

The effect was immediate. The enemy submersible faltered, its movements becoming sluggish and uncoordinated. The Crabs pressed their advantage, swarming over the crippled vessel like a pack of hungry predators, all together sinking fast away from the Calypso.

"Well done, gals!" Celaeno said, standing proudly.

With a final, wrenching motion, the Crabs tore open the submersible's hull, exposing its inner workings to the cold, crushing depths. The vessel imploded, crumpling in on itself like a discarded soda can.

As the debris settled and the adrenaline began to fade, I realized I had been holding my breath. I exhaled slowly, my heart hammering in my chest.

The crew of the Calypso II erupted in cheers and applause, their relief and elation palpable.

"Let's clean up the debris, gals. No trash left behind," Celaeno ordered.

As the excitement died down, I turned to Celaeno, my curiosity getting the better of me. "Who are they?" I asked, gesturing towards the debris of the mysterious object that had pursued us. "And why were they trying to stop us?"

Alcippe's expression grew somber, her blue eyes darkening as she met my gaze. "These waters have been at the center of an archaeological battle for a long time," she explained, her voice low and serious. "A recent international expedition suffered significant upheaval from right-wing businessmen and politicians, including a local mayor. They see our work as a threat to their power and their control over the narratives of the past."

She paused, glancing out over the waves as if searching for the right words. "Officially, we are only able to work on environmental restoration in these waters because of the history and the global clout of our family's organization."

I nodded slowly, trying to wrap my mind around the implications of her words.

"But because they can't stop us publicly," Celaeno continued, her voice taking on a harder edge, "they try to destroy our equipment, to sabotage our efforts in any way they can."

I felt a chill run down my spine at the thought of the powerful forces arrayed against us. I wanted to learn more as fast as humanly possible. "So what was the error made by the Oracle of Delphi?"

Alcippe smiled. "What Delphi didn't know was that there were two Mount Idas, both sacred to the Mother Goddess. One in Turkey and one in Crete. On the slopes of Mount Ida in Crete was the Amari Valley, home to ancient settlements and the birthplace of the Minoan written language at Phaistos and Monastiraki."

Regina, who had been listening intently, spoke up. "Our stories say that men first received the 'nine realms' scrolls from the goddess on the slopes of Mount Ida."

Alcippe nodded, her gaze heavy with the weight of history. "The Amari Valley was a region of such strategic importance that it was illegally excavated by the Germans during World

War II. They attempted to crush any proof that contradicted their Atlantis and Aryan race myths. The valley was known as a center of resistance to the Germans during the Battle of Crete and the subsequent occupation."

Regina sighed, her voice tinged with bitterness. "Romans and Nazis alike, stealing the gifts of the goddess for their own self-interest."

My head was spinning with all the information. "I still don't understand how this all connects to the Voynich Manuscript and the lost civilization we're seeking."

Alcippe blinked her sparkling eyes. "We will show you how it connects when we arrive at our destination."

"And where exactly are we going?" I asked, my heart pounding in anticipation.

"Antikythera," Alcippe replied, the name hanging in the air like a prophecy. "A small island halfway between Kythera and Crete."

"Whoa! Where they found that ancient computer?" Bastian spoke with the excitement of a five-year-old in a candy shop.

Celaeno lifted the lid of a storage chest, pulling out several diving suits and handing them around.

The Calypso II pressed on, its sleek form cutting through the waves like a knife. I took a deep breath of the salty air, letting it fill my lungs and clear my mind.

Whatever secrets Antikythera held, whatever dangers we might face, I was ready.

CHAPTER 21

Cyberwar

As the Calypso II sliced through the shimmering Aegean waters, bound for Antikythera, I retreated to a quiet corner of the deck to check my messages. In the distance, a dark line of clouds hugged the horizon, a subtle warning of the brewing storm. The air felt heavy and charged, as if nature itself was holding its breath in anticipation of the coming tempest. I tried to ignore the feeling that the ominous weather was a harbinger of the challenges that lay ahead. I unlocked my phone with cold fingers, bracing myself for the inevitable barrage of notifications.

Amid the sea of concerned messages from friends and family, one email caught my eye. It was from my editor at the City Rag. My heart raced as I opened it, expecting the worst.

"Amalia," it read, "I've had a change of heart. The Voynich controversy is blowing up online, and our shareholders want a piece of the action. I'm giving you the green light to run with your story. Go as wild as you want with your theories—the crazier, the better. But remember, we want the scoop. Stay away from Bastian Ham's YouTube channel. The Rag needs to be first to publish."

I stared at the screen, a mix of relief and disbelief washing over me. After all the threats and ultimatums, my editor was suddenly on board? A world-renowned publication, famous for its unbiased reporting and journalistic credibility, was willing to sell out for traffic and ad dollars.

Bastian, who had been watching me with concern, leaned in close. "What is it, Rosie? More bad news?"

I shook my head, a wry smile tugging at the corners of my mouth. "Quite the opposite, actually. My editor wants me to run with the story. Apparently, the Voynich controversy is good for business."

Bastian snorted, his eyes narrowing. "Of course it is. Those vultures will do anything for eyeballs." He placed a hand on my shoulder, his touch warm and reassuring. "Rosie, listen to me. Drop that scumbag and his dirty rag. Partner with me instead. I'll share the profits, fifty-fifty. The mainstream media is broken, controlled by self-interested moguls and political agendas. The future is indie—creators taking control of their own narratives."

I hesitated, torn between the security of my job and the allure of freedom. Regina, who had been listening in, chimed in with a scoff. "And what, become hamsters running on a wheel, chasing clicks? It's just another form of toxic misinformation, fueling the algorithms' thirst for controversy."

Bastian shrugged, unfazed. "As an indie creator, you get to choose how you behave. Sure, clickability and retention are key if you want to make a living. But it's on you to find the balance between truth and sensationalism."

He turned back to me, his gaze intense. "Amalia, whatever you decide, you need to take control of the narrative. Call out the smear campaign. Set the record straight."

I mulled over his words, the weight of the decision heavy on my shoulders. Finally, I nodded. "I won't commit to a partnership, and it's not time to share our findings, but I want to address the misinformation."

Bastian grinned, already pulling out his phone. "Atta girl, Rosie. The Hamsters are going to love this."

We set up on the deck, the stunning backdrop of the Aegean Sea stretching out behind us. Bastian hit record, his signature charm turned up to eleven. "Hamsters! Bastian here, coming at you live from an undisclosed location. I'm here with the brilliant Amalia Rose, and boy, do we have some bomb-shells to drop on you today."

He paused for effect, his eyes twinkling with mischief. "First things first, we're still alive and kicking, despite the best efforts of some very nefarious characters. We've been shot at, engaged in deadly sea battles, and are currently hanging out with the coolest, prettiest feminist illuminati you'll ever meet."

Regina rolled her eyes but couldn't hide a small smile. I jumped in, my tone measured and serious. "We're thoroughly investigating historical artifacts with the help of experts to fully decode the Voynich Manuscript. But there's a coordi-nated disinformation campaign targeting our efforts, attempting to undermine our credibility with false claims and personal attacks."

I stared directly into the camera, my eyes flashing with defiance. "And to those cowards hiding behind their keyboards, leading this vicious smear campaign—if you really want to damage my reputation, you shouldn't hint at the world's oldest profession." I stood tall, my voice ringing out with conviction. "No, if you want to sling some stinky mud at me, call me a politician or a media mogul. That's where you'll find the real dirt."

Bastian nodded, his face uncharacteristically somber. "Hamsters, don't believe a word they say about us. The powers that be are running scared, and they'll stop at nothing to bury the truth. Trust only the information that comes directly from Amalia and me."

I took a deep breath, meeting the camera's gaze head-on. "We ask for your patience and support as we continue our investigation. Don't fall for the sensationalism or the smear tactics. Focus on the facts, and wait for our findings. Together, we'll uncover the truth behind the Voynich Manuscript and the lost civilization it points to."

As Bastian wrapped up the livestream with his signature sign-off, I felt a flicker of hope amidst the chaos. Maybe, just maybe, we could beat the disinformation machine at its own game.

But that hope was short-lived. Seconds after ending the broadcast, Bastian's face paled as he stared at his phone in horror. "Rosie... you need to see this."

I leaned over his shoulder, my heart plummeting as I took in the sight before me. Bastian's YouTube feed was filled with video thumbnails bearing my face, each more outrageous than the last. In one, I was ranting about debunked conspiracy theories like crystal skulls. In another, I appeared to be chanting Nazi propaganda. And then there were other deep-fakes—explicit videos with my face crudely plastered onto the bodies of adult film actresses, or were these generated from scratch?

I felt sick to my stomach, violated and exposed in the most heinous way imaginable. I stood up quickly, leaning over the railing to throw up. Bastian scrolled through the feed, his expression a mix of rage and disbelief. "They've hacked into the accounts of some of the biggest YouTube channels," he said, his voice shaking with anger. "It's a coordinated attack, using AI-generated deepfakes to spread disinformation and destroy your reputation."

Regina shook her head, her eyes filled with weary know-ing. "I tried to warn you, Amalia. You can't win this fight using their tools. It's like wrestling in the mud and expecting to come out clean."

Bastian shot her a dirty look. "Please, do go on and on with the I-told-you-so's. It's not like I've saved your life once or twice."

I barely registered their bickering, my mind reeling from the vicious attack on my character and my privacy. How could I possibly combat a machine that could generate an infinite stream of lies and twisted half-truths?

As if sensing my despair, Bastian placed a gentle hand on my shoulder. "We'll find a way, Rosie. We always do. These bastards picked the wrong journalist to mess with."

I managed a weak smile, drawing strength, even as I resented the swamp of anonymous, unaccountable misinformation he represented. Still, he was right—I couldn't let them win. Not when the truth was so close I could almost taste it.

As the Calypso pressed onward, the island of Antikythera looming on the horizon, I went online and emailed all my contacts, addressing the deepfakes and the smear campaign. The disinformation machine may have fired its opening salvo, but this war was far from over.

CHAPTER 22

The Descent

As we approached the small island of Antikythera, the sky darkened ominously. Menacing clouds gathered on the horizon, looming like silent sentinels. The wind whipped the waves into a frenzied dance, rocking our vessel with increasing intensity. In the distance, the low rumble of thunder echoed across the water, a deep, unsettling sound that warned of the impending storm.

Amidst the growing turbulence, an unexpected sight caught my eye. Above us, two large circles began to unfold out of one of the masts, their sleek, metallic surfaces glinting in the fading light. Hundreds of interlocking blades moved with fluid, almost organic grace, rotating and shifting until they transformed into two massive platforms that flipped horizontally over our heads. The surface of the platforms was covered in what appeared to be solar panels, their dark, glossy surfaces absorbing the meager sunlight that managed to penetrate the gathering clouds.

Bastian furrowed his brow, his eyes fixed on the strange apparatus above us. "Solar panels? In this weather? Seems like an odd choice."

Alcippe shook her head, a knowing smile playing at the corners of her mouth. "Not quite," she explained, her voice barely audible over the rising wind. "The solar panels double as a camouflage system, designed to shield us from prying eyes as we transfer to the Squid."

As the panels locked into place, creating a nearly seamless canopy above us, the churning waters ahead began to bubble and froth. Slowly, a sleek, metallic shape emerged from the depths, its smooth, curved lines glistening with seawater. It was a submersible, but unlike any I had ever seen before.

"Meet the Squid, our ride to the Antikythera wreck," Alcippe said, her voice tinged with excitement.

As the Calypso II maneuvered alongside the waiting Squid, Alcippe gestured for us to gather our gear and prepare for the transfer. "Time to go," she announced.

I took one last look at the gathering storm, the wind whipping my hair around my face and the first fat drops of rain beginning to fall. With a deep breath and a silent prayer for the safety of our mission, I followed Alcippe and the others.

As we descended into the depths, the Squid's innovative propulsion system allowed us to glide effortlessly through the water. The dim light filtering through the portholes cast an eerie glow on our faces as we huddled together, our anticipation growing with each passing moment.

Alcippe broke the silence, her voice low and serious. "Let's get back to our story," she said, her eyes intense. "Legend has it there were originally nine Sibylline books, a number familiar to our Order. Throughout history, some books were burned, and by 205 BCE, only three of the nine books remained. Very little of the original content was left, but some things ring true of their utterances."

Bastian raised an eyebrow, his curiosity piqued. "You're part of the Order too?" he asked. "I thought only librarians were part of the Order, and others were just allies."

Alcippe chuckled, shaking her head. "Historians, cryptanalysts, and archaeologists, including us sea archaeologists, are librarians too," she said. "We find and catalogue information, stories in different shapes and formats, like the ones I'll show you today. But I'm getting ahead of myself."

She paused, gathering her thoughts before continuing. "You see, the Sibylline books revealed their origins quite early when, in 496 BCE, they advised the introduction into worship of the Eleusinian triad gods: Demeter, Persephone, and Triptolemus."

Regina leaned forward, staring at Bastian intently. "Triptolemus was healed by Demeter and then taught the art of agriculture."

Alcippe nodded. "Precisely. Myth has it that Demeter helped him complete his mission of educating the whole of Greece in the art of agriculture. He's briefly mentioned as one of the original priests of Demeter, one of the first men to learn the secret rites of the Eleusinian Mysteries."

Bastian snorted, his snark evident. "Wait, what? There are good guys in this cult?"

Regina and Alcippe exchanged cryptic looks. "We'll find out if there are still good guys in this cult real soon," Regina said, her tone somber.

Alcippe pressed on, her expression serious. "The Mother Goddess had more to share with men than just agriculture. In 205 BCE, the Sibylline books once again offered guidance, pointing men towards Mount Ida and a gift that would unlock the age of knowledge, away from empire-building by force."

Bastian chuckled, a hint of mischief on his expression. "For the record, I don't spend all my time thinking about the Roman Empire. I mean, sure, I might have posted a video or two about it, but it's not like I'm obsessed or anything."

He leaned in conspiratorially, lowering his voice. "Now, if

you want to talk about my true passion, let me tell you about the time I investigated the haunted porta-potty at the annual Chili Cook-Off. I swear, that thing had a mind of its own! I even caught a ghostly apparition on camera, but it turned out to be just a reflection of my own face after trying the extra-spicy 'Diablo's Revenge' chili."

Ignoring Bastian's antics, I couldn't help but interject as my journalistic instincts kicked in. I crossed my arms in front of my chest and turned to Alcippe. "Why are you relying on oracular utterances that sound like tabloid daily horoscopes?"

Alcippe acknowledged my skepticism with a nod. "Indeed, the science behind the Sibylline books did turn into esoteric pseudoscience over time. If the gift had been unveiled in 205 BCE, it would have shed light on our books' true meaning and purpose."

"Which is?" I pressed, leaning forward eagerly.

"To spread science and the scientific method across the world. To teach agriculture, medicine, astronomy . . ." Alcippe's words flowed like a song, her passion evident in every syllable.

As we descended further into the depths, the Squid's powerful lights illuminated the dark, seemingly endless abyss that surrounded us. The occasional flicker of bioluminescent creatures provided a brief respite from the all-encompassing darkness, their eerie glow casting ghostly shadows across our faces.

Alcippe's voice was steady as she continued to reveal the ancient connections between the Library of Alexandria, the Sibylline books, and the Minoans. "In the second century BCE, some scholars at the Library of Alexandria started paying attention to the 'nine realms' scrolls and learning the knowledge they contained. After visiting the Library, Archimedes went on to build two planetariums and write manuscripts on the construction of these devices," she explained, her eyes beaming with excitement.

"Similarly, the Sibylline books, which were extracts of the 'nine realm' scrolls, made predictions about astronomical positions and eclipses decades in advance. They described the movement of the sun, moon, and planets, as well as eclipses, solstices, and everything else we needed to engage in agriculture and astronomy."

Bastian leaned forward, his interest piqued. "How did the scrolls communicate these complex predictions?" he asked, his voice tinged with curiosity.

Alcippe smiled, clearly enjoying the opportunity to share her knowledge. "They did it in terms people could understand at that time, using Greek zodiac signs, Egyptian month names, and an observer-centric perspective on the astronomical movements. These predictions, written in the Sibylline books, indicated celestial events that were perceived by people to be good or bad omens. The word 'disaster,' of French origin, actually means 'bad star.' As a result, texts of science evolved into almanacs, pseudoscientific tools hinting at a shadow of a shadow of their original truth."

Something still nagged at the back of my mind. "You said the scrolls originated from Crete," I prompted, hoping to steer the conversation back to the Minoan connection.

Alcippe nodded, her expression growing more serious. "Yes, as far back as 1800 BCE, the Minoans at the slopes of Mount Ida were tracking and predicting astronomical events."

As Alcippe spoke, the Squid's lights flickered, casting shadows across her face. She carefully reached into a padded case and retrieved a clay disk. As she held it up, the intricate spiral of symbols seemed to dance in the dim light of the submersible.

"This is a replica of the Phaistos Disk, a Minoan artifact from that time. Look," Alcippe said, her voice trembling with excitement as she pointed to groups of tokens stamped on the clay, "here, here, and here. Six words refer to 'light' and six to 'sunset.'" She turned the disk around, her eyes wide with revelation. "And this side," she paused for dramatic effect, "this side tracks eclipses from that time as validated against NASA information."

Bastian and Regina gasped in unison, their eyes locked on the ancient artifact. "That's incredible," Bastian whispered, his voice filled with awe. "How could they have known?"

Regina shook her head in disbelief. "The Minoans were truly advanced beyond their time."

I reached out, my fingers itching to touch the disk. As if reading my mind, Alcippe handed me the disk, and I felt a shiver run through my body as my fingers glided over the intricate tokens. The clay was cool and smooth, the spiral of symbols almost hypnotic in its complexity.

"But that's not all," Alcippe continued, her voice rising with excitement. "These tokens here," she pointed to a specific group of symbols, "they speak of two goddesses, one of them pregnant."

Regina gasped, her eyes wide with realization. "Parthenogenesis!" she exclaimed, her voice filled with a feverish passion.

Bastian sighed, rolling his eyes. "There's that word again," he muttered. "You surely are desperate to get rid of men."

Regina's eyes flashed with anger. "Gain independence from them, yes," she snapped. "Stop once and for all their campaign to control our bodies. Have you seen the news? Have you read history books? The tsunami of rape depictions in ancient art? Why don't you find this horror unacceptable?"

Bastian's jaw clenched, his voice tight with emotion. "You're assuming I don't."

"I've watched your silly videos," Regina scoffed. "You're part of the problem. Undermining us with your little barbs every time you get the chance."

Bastian's face reddened, his hands balling into fists at his sides. "You don't know anything about me," he growled. "You put me in this bad with half of the world's population because of what I have between my legs. You don't try to get to know me, and you take the jokes I use as a shield against your despise as a sign of carelessness."

Regina's voice dripped with venom. "Poor you that never been raped, that never felt unsafe, whose body men in robes don't seek to control." She spat her words like bullets.

As Regina gestured wildly, emphasizing her point, her hand accidentally struck Alcippe's, causing the disk to fall and shatter on the floor into a thousand pieces.

Regina's face paled, her anger replaced by shock and regret. She stammered an apology to Alcippe.

I intervened, my hands shaking with a mix of hunger, exhaustion, and frustration. "We're all weak and starving," I said, my voice trembling slightly. "We need to focus on the task at hand, not fight amongst ourselves."

Alcippe sighed, her expression unreadable. "There is no food until the end of this journey," she repeated firmly. With that, she returned to her story, her voice filled with the same passion and reverence as before. "And it was there, on the slopes of Mount Ida in Crete, in the years preceding 205 BCE, that the last descendants of the Minoan tradition used the information gathered in the scrolls to build the gift the goddess promised to the world. The key to unlocking not only the movement of the cosmos but also the underlying technology, perfectly capable of being used for computation."

As she spoke, the Squid shuddered, its metal frame groaning under the immense pressure of the deep. For a moment, I feared that the vessel might not withstand the crushing weight of the water above us, but Alcippe seemed unfazed, her attention focused solely on the story she was weaving.

"In a time of significant upheaval, at the dawn of the Cretan Wars and piracy, a group of followers of the goddess built a mechanical device that modeled the cycles of the cosmos," she revealed, her voice trembling with awe. "Metal-workers, designers, mathematicians working in constant communication with allies from the Library of Alexandria, including their head librarian and great mathematician, Eratosthenes."

"So the gift was technology," I concluded, my mind racing to connect the dots between the ancient Minoan civilization and the mysterious device they had created.

Regina frowned with fierce intensity, her voice suddenly sharp and impassioned. "No, not technology, never technology," she insisted, her words cutting through the air like a knife. "A destructive evil that consumes the world is never a gift."

She leaned forward, her gaze locked on mine, and I could see the fire burning in her belly, the strength of her conviction giving power to her words. "The gift was knowledge, Amalia. The gift was science, the very method by which we seek to understand the cosmos around us. It was the wisdom of herbal medicine, passed down through generations of women who understood the healing properties of the earth itself."

Regina paused, her voice softening slightly, as if she were sharing a precious secret. "And perhaps, just perhaps, it was the ability to temporarily separate our souls from our bodies, to transcend the physical realm and glimpse the true nature of our beings."

I could hardly believe what I was hearing. The idea that the Minoans, a civilization that had flourished thousands of years ago, had possessed such advanced knowledge and technological capabilities was staggering. But the journalist in me couldn't help but probe deeper, seeking concrete evidence to support these astonishing claims.

"Hold on," I interjected, my voice steady and inquisitive.

"If the ancient Minoans possessed such advanced knowledge, surely there must be more tangible proof beyond a clay disk, an indecipherable medieval manuscript, and the extracts of oracular utterances. And I'm not quite sure if some broken fragments of an old planetarium found at the bottom of the sea will change my mind. Where's the smoking gun?"

Alcippe grinned, in her gaze the promise of a revelation. "Coming right up, Amalia," she said, her voice ringing with confidence.

CHAPTER 23

The Shipwreck

As we gathered in the main chamber of the Thetis underwater facility, I couldn't help but marvel at the sleek, state-of-the-art design of the habitat that would serve as our base for the archaeological exploration of the legendary Antikythera shipwreck.

The modular aquatic station was a technological wonder, designed as a saturation diving system that maintained a constant internal pressure equivalent to the surrounding water pressure. This innovative setup allowed divers to live and work at depth for extended periods without the need for repeated decompression, maximizing their efficiency and minimizing the risk of complications.

The main chamber itself was a testament to the cutting-edge technology that permeated every aspect of the facility. The spacious, circular room was lined with advanced life support systems, sophisticated communication equipment, and an impressive array of scientific instruments that would make any researcher green with envy.

But it was the centerpiece of the room that truly took my breath away—a large, circular viewport that offered a stunning panorama of the vibrant marine environment just outside. Through the thick safety glass, I watched in awe as schools of colorful fish darted gracefully among the swaying seagrass, their scales glinting in the filtered sunlight. The distant silhouettes of larger creatures—perhaps a pod of striped dolphins or a curious sea turtle—occasionally glided across our field of vision, adding to the sense of mystery and wonder that permeated the underwater world.

As Bastian, Regina, and I settled into our seats, Alcippe began to recount the history of the wreck we had come to investigate. "In 1900," she explained, her voice filled with reverence, "sponge divers discovered the remains of an ancient Greek ship off the coast of Antikythera. We've recently mapped the wreck in 3D, pinpointing each finding throughout the years."

With a flick of her wrist, Alcippe activated a holographic display that filled the seabed with a breathtaking visualization of the wreck site. A laser beam matrix projected against the seafloor, and ghostly neon images of each archaeological find emerged from the depths, hovering in the water like echoes of a distant past.

My eyes were immediately drawn to a scattered pile of statues depicting men and horses, their forms strewn among the boulders on the seabed. These were the remains of an ancient cargo, a treasure trove of luxury works of art and technology from the Aegean region. As the holographic animation shifted, the statues transformed from their current state of discovery to a full reconstruction of their original appearance, allowing us to see them as they would have looked in their heyday.

As I explored the holographic landscape further, I spotted an array of other artifacts—delicate jewelry, amphorae, coins, glass bowls, and lamps—all meticulously catalogued and displayed in stunning detail. Among these relics were the remains of four individuals, including a young woman. The animation showed her adorned in the jewelry found nearby, a poignant reminder of the human stories that lay hidden beneath the waves.

Suddenly, a giant boat materialized in neon pink, its spectral form rising from the seabed. The vessel's rich cargo was protected by bags of grain, and there, perched atop the deck, was the holographic figure of the young woman, her hair flowing in an unseen breeze.

"Who was she?" I asked, my eyes transfixed on the ghostly image of a woman born two millennia ago, her story now intertwined with the mystery of the Antikythera wreck.

Alcippe smiled enigmatically, in her eyes the promise of an insight. "That, Amalia," she said, her voice low and filled with anticipation, "is just one of the many secrets this wreck holds. And with the help of the Thetis facility and our cutting-edge technology, we're going to unravel them all, one by one."

As the holographic animation of the Antikythera wreck played out before us, Alcippe's voice took on a somber tone, her words heavy with the weight of history.

"At around the time of the wreck, within a period of fifty years, paganism and science both began to die at the feet of the great Roman dictators, a setback that took millennia to recover from," she said, her eyes fixed on the spectral vessel. "The Sibylline Books and the Library of Alexandria both burned, casualties of Roman civil wars, and between these two events, the gift of the mother ended up here, at the bottom of the sea where the Mediterranean and the Aegean bicker like passionate lovers."

I leaned forward, my curiosity piqued by the tantalizing hints of a story left untold. "Who, how did this happen?" I asked, my voice barely above a whisper.

As if in response to my question, the holographic animation outside the viewport shifted, the scene changing to one of chaos and destruction. The ghostly vessel was now caught in the throes of a violent storm, its sails straining against the howling winds as towering waves crashed against its hull. But the fury of nature was not the only threat the ship faced—on the horizon, the silhouettes of pirate vessels loomed, their sails billowing like the wings of carrion birds.

Fire erupted on the deck of the Antikythera ship, the flames consuming the vessel with a ravenous hunger. The woman we had seen earlier, her holographic form now flickering and distorted, fought desperately against the deadly waves, her struggle for survival playing out in heart-wrenching detail.

Bastian let out a low whistle, his eyes wide with a mix of awe and horror. "They didn't stand a chance," he murmured, his voice thick with emotion.

Alcippe nodded grimly, her gaze never leaving the unfolding tragedy. "In 66 BC, Roman Creticus subjugated Crete, setting up his capital on the slopes of Mount Ida near ancient Phaistos," she explained, her words painting a vivid picture of a world long lost. "We believe Creticus attempted to take the gift and its keepers as spoils to Rome, and that either the sea, the goddess, or pirates destroyed his plans."

Regina leaned forward, her expression intense, her eyes locked on Alcippe as if trying to read the secrets hidden behind her enigmatic gaze. "So, the gift, the knowledge—it was all lost?" she asked, her voice trembling slightly, a mixture of hope and fear evident in every word.

Alcippe turned to face us, her posture straight and proud, her eyes blazing with a fierce determination that seemed to radiate from every fiber of her being. "Lost, until now," she said, her words ringing with conviction, each syllable a declaration of purpose. "The secrets of the Antikythera wreck, the legacy of the Minoans, the true power of the gift—it's all been recently rediscovered and understood."

As if on cue, the holographic display shifted once more, the ghostly seabed transforming before our eyes. From the depths, an ancient device emerged, its form rendered in shimmering neon blue. It was a sight that took my breath away—a complex array of gears, dials, and inscriptions, all perfectly reconstructed in stunning detail.

Alcippe reached beneath the table and retrieved a physical model of the device, placing it before us with reverent care. I leaned in closer, my eyes widening as I took in the intricate workings of the ancient machine.

"The Antikythera Mechanism," Alcippe explained, her voice hushed with awe, "used to predict the positions of the Sun, Moon, and the planets, as well as lunar and solar eclipses. An innovation so ahead of its time, it would take fifteen hundred years for a mechanism of similar complexity to be invented."

I couldn't help but reach out, my fingers hovering just above the surface of the model, almost afraid to touch it lest it crumble to dust before my eyes. The craftsmanship was exquisite, the attention to detail staggering. Each dial, each inscription, spoke of a level of technological sophistication that seemed almost impossible for the time.

We leaned forward, hanging on Alcippe's every word as she painted a vivid picture of the shipwreck and the mysteries that still surrounded it. Bastian and Regina were entranced, their eyes wide with wonder, their minds undoubtedly racing with the implications of this incredible discovery.

But even as I marveled at the beauty and complexity of the Antikythera Mechanism, the investigative journalist in me couldn't help but question the narrative Alcippe was weaving. The neon boat, the woman, the weak connections she was drawing between disparate pieces of evidence—it all seemed too neat, too convenient.

If such groundbreaking discoveries had indeed been made,

surely the world would have known about them by now. The academic community would be buzzing with excitement, the media would be clamoring for interviews and exclusives. But instead, we were here, in a secret underwater facility, being shown a story that seemed more fiction than fact.

I leaned back in my seat, my eyes narrowing as I studied Alcippe's face. "This is all very impressive," I said, my voice carefully neutral, "but I can't help but wonder—where's the proof? The hard evidence that backs up these claims about the Minoans, about the origins and the date of this device?"

Alcippe met my gaze unflinchingly, a small smile playing at the corners of her mouth. Her eyes sparkled with the confidence of someone who held all the cards, who knew the truth that others could only guess at. "A fair question, Amalia," she said, her tone almost approving, as if she had been waiting for someone to finally ask the right questions.

She pointed at the clock face of the mechanism, her finger tracing the intricate engravings that marked the passage of celestial bodies. "See this dial," she said, her voice low and filled with the thrill of discovery, "scientists recently figured out the exact date of the full Moon of the first month tracked by the device."

Bastian leaned in, his eyes wide with anticipation, his breath catching in his throat. "Yes?" he asked, the single word heavy with unspoken questions.

"12 May 205 BCE," Alcippe said, her smile widening, her face aglow with the satisfaction of a long-held secret finally revealed. "And that's not all. Other academics figured out that the astronomical events on the Antikythera mechanism work best for latitudes in the range of 33.3–37.0 degrees north. Guess where Crete is located?"

"Wow!" Bastian conceded, his tone a cocktail of awe and disbelief. He leaned back in his seat, his mind undoubtedly racing with the implications of this revelation.

"But there's more!" Alcippe picked up what looked like a cast of a mold. Engraved in it was the figure of the poppy goddess and a sun-like disc with rectangular spokes and a serrated edge. "This is a Minoan manufacturing casting mold for a sundial. A device to establish the geographical latitude and for predicting solar and lunar eclipses. It's still accurate today and it precedes the Antikythera mechanism by fourteen hundred years."

There it was, the poppy goddess and a wheel just like the wheels inside the mechanism. My mind was spinning with the implications. And still, I wanted more. As an investigative journalist, I needed something tangible, connecting the Antikythera Mechanism to the Minoans. I needed a smoking gun, a piece of evidence that would leave no room for doubt.

But I didn't have to wait long. Out there, on the seabed, a small circular artifact lit up, depicted as it was found. At first, I couldn't make sense of it, my eyes straining to discern its shape through the holographic haze. The discovery date above it flashed "2017," a tantalizing clue to the significance of this find.

I kept my gaze locked on the artifact, waiting with bated breath for it to transform, for the secrets of the past to be laid bare before us. And as it did, my heart raced so fast, I wasn't sure if it was still within my chest.

A bronze medal depicting the Minoan Bull emerged from the depths, its surface gleaming with the patina of ages. It was a work of art, a testament to the skill and craftsmanship of the ancient world. And as the hologram shifted, the medal moved to adorn the box of the Antikythera Mechanism itself, a perfect fit, as if it had always been meant to be there.

But it was the figure beside the mechanism that truly took my breath away. The ghostly neon life force of a distant past, the woman we had seen before, now stood before me in all her glory. Her bare breasts were proudly displayed, snakes coiled around her wrists in a symbol of power and wisdom. In her hands, she held sheaves of wheat and poppy capsules, the emblems of a civilization that had flourished in harmony with the earth.

I blinked, half-convinced that I was hallucinating, that the woman before me was nothing more than a figment of my overactive imagination. And as I did, she was gone, but she would never be forgotten.

A bronze medal, recovered from this very wreck in 2017, had connected the most advanced mechanism in ancient history with a peaceful civilization where women's voices had shaped the destiny of the earth. It was a revelation that shook me to my core, a truth so profound and powerful that it threatened to unravel the very fabric of my understanding.

As I sat there, staring at the medal, my heart raced with a fierce determination. I knew, with a certainty that burned like a fire in my veins, that I would stop at nothing to uncover the full truth of its story, to bring the secrets of this ancient civilization to light, no matter the cost.

"So they know," Regina spoke, her voice trembling with bitter resentment that seemed to emanate from the very depths of her being. "They all know the truth—academia, government, and the secret far-right forces that have been pursuing us for generations."

Alcippe nodded, her gaze heavy with the weight of centuries. "Some do," she said, her words measured and deliberate. "The marine archeologists that discovered the bull were never allowed to return to the wreck, their profiles and contributions deleted from official sites. The project was taken over by a far-right nationalist mogul." She paused, her eyes flickering to the holographic display of the expeditions. "But others are just incapable of seeing the truth, of accepting the reality of women's power. It's too threatening for them to concede, even to themselves."

A heavy silence fell over the room, the weight of Alcippe's words settling like a physical presence. And then, slowly, deliberately, she turned to face Bastian, her gaze locked on his with an intensity that made my breath catch in my throat.

"Which leads me to you," she said, her voice low and dangerous, a hidden threat lurking just beneath the surface. "We've let you come this far. In fact, we invited you to join us because in your veins runs the blood of the Eumolpidae family, the Hierophantes, male high priests of the mysteries, walking the path first set by Triptolemus."

Bastian's eyes widened, his face a mask of shock and confusion. "What the heck are you talking about?" he demanded, his voice rising with each word.

Regina spoke then, her gaze fixed on some distant point, carefully avoiding Bastian's eyes. "But blood alone does not make a man," she said, her tone cold and unyielding. "And we won't allow you to walk beside us in this initiation until you prove your spiritual connection to the mysteries."

And suddenly, everything clicked into place. The pieces of the puzzle that had been nagging at the back of my mind finally fell into alignment, revealing a picture that sent a chill down my spine.

"Initiation?" I asked, my voice trembling slightly. "Is this why Calypso's crew have refused us food for half a day? Are we fasting?"

I glanced at Bastian, expecting to see the same outrage and confusion that I felt. But to my surprise, he stood peacefully, observing the unfolding drama as if it had nothing to do with him. A flicker of doubt, of suspicion, began to gnaw at the edges of my mind.

I turned to Alcippe, my voice rising with a sudden, fierce protectiveness. "Are you mad?" I shouted, my words echoing off the walls of the chamber. "Bastian has nothing to prove to you or anyone else."

Regina's gaze finally met mine, her eyes filled with a sad, knowing sympathy. "Amalia," she said softly, "the chasm between what you say and what you think, and what you truly feel—we all see it. You, more than anyone else, seek to know his true allegiance."

I felt my cheeks burn with a sudden, unexpected flush of shame. "That's not true," I said, but even as the words left my lips, I could hear the hollowness in my own voice. "Just because we have different perspectives doesn't mean he needs to prove anything to me."

Bastian turned to me then, his gaze searching, probing, as if trying to read the secrets written in the depths of my soul. For a long, tense moment, our eyes locked, a silent conversation passing between us, a battle of wills and emotions that threatened to consume us both.

And then, abruptly, he turned away, his attention fixed once more on Alcippe. "What is it?" he asked, his voice low and steady, a challenge and a surrender all at once. "What do you want me to do?"

The room fell silent, the air heavy with anticipation. And as I waited for Alcippe's answer, my heart pounding in my chest, I knew that whatever came next would change everything—not just for Bastian, but for all of us.

CHAPTER 24

The Quest

A s Bastian prepared to pilot the experimental Seabubble submersible, a knot of unease tightened in my stomach. The Seabubble was a dome-shaped bell designed to maintain an internal air pocket while allowing direct interaction with the underwater environment. It was connected to the Thetis via a tether and an umbilical cord providing power, air, comms, and hot water.

"Be careful out there," I said, my voice barely above a whisper as Bastian stepped into the Seabubble. He flashed me a confident grin, his eyes glistening with excitement behind the glass.

"Don't worry, Rosie. I've got this," he assured me, placing the palm of his hand on the window.

I managed a small smile in return, mirroring his gesture on the outside. "Of course you do."

With windows covering 60 percent of its walls, the submersible seemed almost inviting, but a chill ran down my spine as I watched Bastian climb inside. The air felt thick with an unspoken tension, and the metallic tang of the ocean filled my nostrils.

Alcippe provided Bastian with instructions, her voice calm and steady over the comms. "Bastian, we've hidden a real Minoan artifact on the seabed. A signet ring, related to the Phaistos Disk. We believe in epigenetic memory transfer—the idea that experiences and memories can be passed down through generations via molecular changes to DNA. Somewhere in your intergenerational memory, you should feel the artifact's powerful presence and be able to locate it."

I couldn't help but object, my skepticism kicking into high gear. "Epigenetic memory transfer? Seriously? There's no concrete scientific evidence to support that theory."

"They are like the small truths hidden in the myths shared through our cultural memory," Regina said. "Tiny footprints carved in our genes connecting us with the lived experiences of our ancestors."

Bastian, seemingly unfazed by my doubts, flashed a grin. "So, I'm supposed to use my spidey senses to detect some ancient piece of jewelry?" He chuckled, his tone effervescent with mirth. "Alright, I'll give it a shot. What's the worst that could happen?"

As Bastian navigated the Seabubble through the turbulent waters, the storm raging above turned the sea into a roiling, unpredictable mass. The submersible's tether allowed him to explore up to fifty meters away from the Thetis, but the currents grew stronger with each passing minute.

Bastian scanned the seabed, using the Seabubble's suction arm to gently move the sand around, searching for any sign of the hidden ring. Minutes ticked by, and the tension in the control room grew palpable.

Regina, her eyes fixed on the video feed, leaned in close. "Bastian, try to rely on your instincts, your gut feeling. Don't overthink it."

Bastian's voice crackled over the comms, frustration

evident in his tone. "I've searched every inch of this area, but there's nothing here. Just sand and rocks."

Suddenly, a powerful current slammed into the Seabubble, sending it careening off course. Bastian fought to regain control, his hands flying over the controls as he struggled to stabilize the submersible.

With a deep breath, Bastian put on his full-face mask, turned its camera on, and checked his gear one last time. "I'm going out there," he declared, his voice filled with determination. "I can cover more ground on my own."

Before anyone could object, Bastian opened the hatch of the Seabubble and propelled himself into the inky depths. The currents buffeted him from all sides, threatening to tear him away from the submersible's tether. But Bastian fought against the invisible forces, his movements precise and purposeful as he scanned the seabed.

Long, agonizing moments passed, and I found myself holding my breath, my eyes glued to the video feed as Bastian searched the murky depths.

"This is hopeless . . ." he whispered. "My tank is almost empty."

"Use your gut, not your head," Regina repeated.

"Alright, Ham," he whispered. "Close your eyes and relax . . . Let the ghosts of Christmas past do the work." He inhaled so deeply, I could almost feel his breath. "Will you please help me out, my dear Yiayia?"

Slowly, he turned to face the southeast, a sense of inexplicable certainty in his movements. With renewed purpose, he swam forward, his hands skimming the sandy bottom until his fingers brushed against a small, circular object.

As he brushed away the sediment, the ring's intricate spiral design came into focus, the unknown symbols glinting in the dim light filtering through the water.

But as he turned to make his way back to the Seabubble, a

violent tremor rocked the submersible. The powerful currents, born from the storm raging above, slammed into the Seabubble with a force that sent it careening off course.

Bastian, caught in the middle of the maelstrom, fought desperately to reach the safety of the submersible. As he entered the hatch, the currents intensified, ripping the oxygen tanks from their moorings and sending them tumbling out of the open latch and into the depths below.

Panic gripped me as Bastian's voice erupted from the speakers. "Mayday! I've lost control! The currents . . . I've hit the rocks . . . and I've lost my tanks!"

My heart seized as his voice faded, replaced by an ominous silence. On the video feed, I saw the Seabubble lying on its side, the umbilical cord twisted and tangled around a jagged outcropping, precious bubbles escaping into the sea.

Alcippe sprang into action, her voice sharp as she barked orders and suited up for a rescue mission. "Regina, warn the Calypso. We need help down here." But even as she prepared to dive, I could see the grim reality of the situation etched on her face.

"The cable is badly tangled and damaged," she said, her voice tight with tension. "He's losing oxygen too fast. I'll do my best to fix it, but . . ."

She didn't need to finish the thought. If she couldn't patch the air cable, Bastian would soon run out of air.

"Why don't you just use your spare regulator to bring him back?" I asked, my voice shaking with fear.

Alcippe shook her head. "The Seabubble has drifted too far from the Thetis. Trying to swim back with Bastian, in these currents, would be too risky. Our best chance is for me to repair the umbilical cord and tether, so we can pull the Seabubble back to the habitat."

At that moment, a fierce determination overtook me. I couldn't let Bastian face this alone. "I'm going out there," I declared, already reaching for my diving gear. "I can take a spare tank."

"It will weigh you down. You won't get there on time," Alcippe warned, frantically putting on her own gear.

"Then I'll share mine with him until you can get the cable patched," I countered, mimicking her every move. "Is this setup correctly?" I pointed at the dive computer on my wrist.

Alcippe paused, her eyes searching mine. "Have you dived before?"

I swallowed hard. "Once in Mexico," I admitted. "I'll be fine."

Regina stepped forward, her face pale with worry. "Amalia, no. If Alcippe can't fix the cables, you'll both be stuck down there."

I knew the risks, but my resolve didn't waver. "I have to try. I can't leave him there to die. Call for help. Please!"

After a quick briefing from Alcippe, I plunged into the icy depths. The water hit me like a physical blow, stealing my breath, but I pushed forward, my heart pounding with a single, desperate thought: Please, let him be alive.

The Seabubble's hatch was still open when I reached it. I pushed myself inside the cramped interior, my heart stopping at the sight of Bastian slumped against the far wall, his eyes closed and his face pale. For a horrifying moment, I thought I was too late. But as I pulled him close, I felt the faint flutter of his breath against my cheek.

I took my mask off, keeping a tight hold on the two regulators. "Bas," I called, shaking him gently. "Wake up. Please, wake up."

His eyelids fluttered, and he looked at me with unfocused eyes. "Rosie? What . . . what happened?"

"You crashed," I explained, my voice trembling. "The air cable is tangled and leaking. Alcippe is working on it, but we need to conserve air until she does."

As the water rose rapidly inside the Seabubble, Bastian's eyes widened with the realization of our predicament. "You shouldn't have come down here, Rosie. Now we're both stuck."

I tried to close the latch, but with the power gone and the heating mechanism offline, it was useless. Taking his hand in mine, I met his gaze. "We're in this together," I said firmly.

Handing him my spare regulator, we huddled close, our breaths growing more labored as the cold seeped into our bones.

Bastian turned to me, his eyes filled with an emotion I couldn't quite place. "Amalia," he whispered. "If we don't make it out of here, I need you to know . . ."

"Don't talk," I urged him. "We need to conserve the oxygen."

But he pressed on. "I need to tell you that . . . I didn't betray your trust, at least not intentionally. I . . . I love you," he finally said, leaning over to kiss my lips.

"Bas, I . . ." My words were cut off by a sudden rush of fresh air filling the Seabubble. We gasped in surprise as Alcippe's voice crackled over the radio.

"I've got the cable patched and the tether untangled! Sit tight, I'm bringing you both back to Thetis."

As the Seabubble began to move through the water, exhaustion washed over me. The last thing I remember is Bastian's arms around me, holding me close as we glided towards the safety of the Thetis.

CHAPTER 25

The Age of Taurus

I awoke in the Squid submersible, Bastian's warm hand encasing mine, his eyes shining with relief as I blinked up at him groggily. Regina flashed me a smile from where she sat by a tilted porthole, the deep blue of the Mediterranean visible beyond.

"We left Thetis already?" I asked, my voice hoarse. Glancing out the porthole, I watched in amazement as the Thetis habitat fragmented into six modules that jetted off in different directions, disappearing into the vast expanse of the sea.

"Our visits have to be brief, or we risk being detected," Alcippe explained. "We're slowly decompressing now. The Calypso will rendezvous with us shortly."

A spike of panic jolted through me as I searched frantically for my backpack containing the invaluable copy of the Voynich manuscript and our research notes. Finding it tucked safely beside me, I rummaged through it, hoping against hope to find a stray protein bar to quiet my growling stomach. No such luck—not even a forgotten stick of gum. Sighing, I pulled out the copy of the Voynich instead, hoping to distract myself from the gnawing hunger.

As I flipped through the pages, I tried to discern connections between the cosmological charts and the Antikythera Mechanism we had witnessed. Page after page was filled with mesmerizing circular diagrams, adorned with symbols of celestial bodies in their different phases—the sun, moon, and stars progressing through intricate cosmic dances. Even in their naive, handdrawn style, the charts seemed to hold some kernel of scientific truth. I quickly checked online, and some of the ninjas even claimed they could translate Hebrew star names within these diagrams, such as "Ain," which they believed referred to Epsilon Tauri, known as the "eye of the bull." Some claims suggested the diagrams represented the night sky during the solstices. These connections hinted at a deeper understanding of astronomy.

But as I delved deeper, my skepticism began to rear its head. Several folios depicted zodiac signs like Taurus, Aries, and Pisces in the center of concentric rings of naked and clothed human figures, mostly women. Each zodiac glyph was labeled with a corresponding month written in some recognizable language that presented similarities to modern-day English. Exhausted in both body and mind, I set the manuscript aside with a huff, wondering if it was merely an elaborate work of medieval pseudoscience masquerading as a cosmological treatise.

Regina must have noticed my frustration. She leaned over, tracing a finger over the figures encircling Taurus. "The meaning of these pages was altered in the Middle Ages," she said softly. Pointing to the month label under Aries, which read "Abril," she continued, "These month names aren't original to the manuscript. Someone tried to force a connection between the charts and the zodiac months."

Intrigued, I examined the pages more closely, comparing

the month labels to the main Voynich script. The handwriting was clearly different. "You're right," I acknowledged. "So what do you think these diagrams actually represent?"

"They depict the procession of the Astronomical Ages," Regina replied, her face beaming with excitement, "each one lasting thousands of years, marked by the constellation that rose with the sun on the Spring Equinox. Science! Pure science." She flipped to the two elaborate Taurus charts, both labeled "May."

"Look at the figures holding stars around the bull," she said, her voice reverent. "Our Order preserves an ancient tradition, an unbroken chain of passing down the identities of those who attained the highest level of initiation into the Mysteries—the ones who completed the journey of the Goddess in full and gained access to all nine realms. These charts are a visual catalogue of those figures, stretching back over twenty thousand years of ritual and myth."

"So they're not just initiates, but the ones who achieved the ultimate spiritual mysteries?" I asked, my mind reeling at the implications.

Regina nodded. "Exactly. The two Taurus folios, for example, record those who attained épopteia, the highest grade of initiation, between roughly 4000 to 1700 BCE, when the Age of Taurus held sway. That's the Minoan era, ended by the devastating Thera eruption. They also catalogue those who greatly helped protect the truth of the goddess."

She guided me through the pages, pointing out how the structures around the figures evolved over the ages, from an absence of dwellings in the earliest eras of Scorpio and Libra, to Greco-Roman style designs in later Taurus and Aries, before the figures retreated to some sort of caves in the Piscean Age as the Mysteries were driven underground by persecution. It was like watching the rise and fall of the mysteries unfold in the margins of the zodiac wheels.

In the earliest Ages, every figure was naked, reminiscent of the prehistoric Venus figurines.

"The vast majority of surviving prehistoric sculptures are female, you know," Alcippe chimed in, as if reading my thoughts, "with the most ancient Venus figurines dated to twenty-five thousand years ago or more. The Goddess reigned supreme in the dawn of human culture."

"What about Aquarius and Capricorn?" Bastian piped up, running a hand over the manuscript reverently. "They're not shown here."

"We have no records yet of the Ages still to come," Regina replied with an enigmatic smile. "The zodiacs are a historical account only, separate from the Balneological folios that detail the actual ritual process."

"There's no way that you could be keeping records for tens of thousands of years," I argued. "Can you prove it?"

Regina shook her head. "No, I cannot. We can't even read their names here." She pointed at the script beside each figure. "But we know some of them from oral tradition and secret texts we've been collecting for millennia. Records safely stored in our safes."

I leaned in. "Like who?"

Regina's gaze was filled with reverence. "A clay tablet with an account from the Mesopotamian poet Enheduanna, a high priestess of the moon goddess Inanna, and the earliest known author in the history of the world. Or Lady Margaret Cavendish's secret biography, the earliest known science fiction author. She kicked off the genre in 1966 with a multi-verse novel."

Bastian snorted, eyeing the pages critically. "For a tradition spanning millennia, it sure doesn't seem to include many men," he observed archly. "There's no men at all depicted in the last few eras. What, did your ancient all-female cult not believe in gender equality?"

"We have identified one," Regina said too casually, "which we will record the next time we create a copy of the books, but first we need to fully translate the Voynich." Then she shrugged. "However, attempts to attain true épopteia are deadly to most men."

"Even the emperors feared the power of the Mysteries," Alcippe added. "The hierophants would bar the path of the unworthy and criminal-minded before the rites began. Why, when Nero himself hoped to be initiated at Eleusis, he dared not show his face once he learned of the strict prohibitions!"

Bastian crossed his arms defensively. "Oh, so now you're implying all men are criminals, is that it?" he accused.

Regina held up a hand to stop their bickering. "Alcippe is not claiming that," she said firmly, "but the historical records may well suggest it." She gestured to the female-dominated images. "At the very least, it seems women played the central role in this particular spiritual lineage."

Alcippe smirked, her eyes twinkling impishly. "Well, we do have accounts from early Christian critics like Tatian claiming the Mystery rites involved murder and cannibalism. So maybe the feminist illuminati of old really did slaughter a few men!" She laughed heartily at her own joke.

By my side, Bastian chuckled nervously, not quite sure if she was kidding.

"Don't worry," Regina added, "accounts of the rites suggest the sea can wash clean all the foulness of mankind."

As Regina and Alcippe's pessimistic views about men seeped into my consciousness, I couldn't help but recall the image of that imposing figure who had threatened me, his words sharp as knives, aiming to destroy my credibility with his vicious propaganda. I shut my eyes tightly, trying to block out the deepfake images that had been seared into my memory, but to no avail. The history of violence against women was an all-too-familiar reality, one we confronted daily in history books, news reports, and our own lived experiences.

But this insidious strategy of silencing and discrediting women—the very same tactics used against trailblazers like Emily Hathaway—was something I had never fully grasped until this moment. From the persecution of healers practicing herbal medicine to the witch hunts that followed, the erasure and rewriting of history had paved the way for the burning of both women and the books that held their knowledge.

Yet, as I turned to look at Bastian, who somehow found himself in the position of having to answer for the crimes of half of humanity, I couldn't help but feel a pang of empathy. Perhaps the greatest tribute we could pay to humankind was the acknowledgment that, at some point in our distant past, there existed civilizations where women and men played equally vital roles in society—where women were encouraged to learn, to write, to engage in the realms of mathematics and science, and were respected for their contributions. The history we were uncovering not only highlighted the remarkable achievements of women but also shone a light on the great men who stood alongside them.

Struggling to extricate myself from the tangled web of resentment, fear, and compassion that had taken hold of me, I turned to Regina, my curiosity piqued. "Who is this great man you've chosen to record for posterity?" I asked, eager to hear more.

A smile played across Regina's lips as she began to recount an extraordinary tale.

As we ascended towards the Calypso, our hearts raced with anticipation, hanging onto Regina's every word. She wove a tale that blurred the lines between history and legend, shedding light on a dark chapter of the past.

"At the height of their madness," Regina began, her voice low and intense, "the Nazis became obsessed with the idea that their imagined 'pure' and white Aryan race had originated from the lost city of Atlantis. And it was the archeological findings from Crete that caught their attention."

She described how Émile Gilliéron and his son, artists working under the renowned archeologist Sir Arthur Evans, had taken two small fresco fragments and, with bold creative license, reconstructed them into a scene depicting men running with spears—two dark-skinned, and one light-complexioned figure leading the charge.

"Evans interpreted it as 'a Minoan Captain leading the first of a negro troop at a run,'" Regina continued, her eyes flashing with anger. "He drew parallels with enslavement and colonialism, even though none of these conclusions could be drawn from the original fragments. But the Nazis, who had previously discarded any connection between Crete and Atlantis, suddenly saw an opportunity."

As Regina spoke, I could almost feel the weight of history pressing down upon us, the ghosts of the past whispering their secrets in the shadows of the submersible. And then, she introduced a figure who seemed to step out of the pages of a novel —John Pendlebury, a British archaeologist who had become deeply connected to the Cretan people and their struggle.

"Pendlebury had earned the love and respect of the Cretans," Regina said, her voice softening with admiration. "He knew the island like the back of his hand, every peak and canyon, every shepherd and villager. A dashing figure with his toughness and charm, bringing optimism and joie de vivre wherever he roamed. And when the Germans invaded Crete in World War II, he joined forces with the local resistance, led by the legendary Antonis Grigorakis, known to all as 'Captain Satan,' because only the devil could survive so many battle wounds."

I leaned forward, intrigued by this new character. Regina must have sensed my curiosity, for she continued, "Captain Satan was a born leader, fearless and cunning. He and Pendlebury formed an unlikely but formidable partnership, coordinating the resistance from the caves of Mount Ida, sacred to the great mother."

Regina painted a vivid picture of the resistance's bravery, of the heavy losses suffered by the Germans, and the brutal retaliation that followed. "The Cretan people fought with everything they had," she emphasized, her voice filled with pride and sorrow. "Men, women, children—they all played a part. It was a true grassroots uprising, with over one hundred thousand civilians joining the cause after the Nazi atrocities."

"We will add a place in our records," Regina declared, her voice ringing with conviction, "jointly occupied by Captain

Satan and Pendlebury, symbolizing the real soldiers and amateur soldiers—scholars, archaeologists, writers, shepherds, priests, school mistresses, men and women—from all over the world who fought pure evil, not for empire or resources or fame, but to protect humanity itself. Humans doing the work of the goddess."

Beside me, I caught a glimpse of Bastian wiping away a tear, exchanging a sweet smile with Regina. In that moment, I felt a flicker of hope that perhaps we could bridge the divide between us, united in a common cause.

But the story took a darker turn as Regina revealed Pendlebury's fate—shot in the head, his notebooks confiscated, leading the Nazis to Monastiraki for their illegal excavations at a specific spot, seeking something mentioned in his notes.

"Recent excavations have uncovered artifacts connected with ritual contexts," Regina explained, "evidence of wine production with honey and 'herbs.' The Nazis, obsessed with the holy grail and desperate to undermine the Christ of their enemies, thought they'd find answers there. But it seems they left empty-handed."

As Regina's words faded into silence, a chill ran down my spine. My exhausted mind raced, piecing together the fragments of information like a complex puzzle. The connections snapped into place, and a startling realization dawned on me. My eyes widened, and I inhaled sharply, struggling to find the right words to articulate the epiphany that had struck me with the force of a thunderbolt.

Alcippe, sensing my revelation, smiled enigmatically and asked, "Where to?"

In that moment, the veil lifted, and I understood the true nature of our sea quest. It was a test, an elaborate dance designed to gauge our values, our ambitions, and our capabilities. Alcippe was waiting, her keen gaze fixed upon me, challenging me to prove that I was the investigative journalist they needed me to be. That I possessed the intellect, the intuition, and the courage to unravel the secrets they had guarded for so long.

And Bastian, too, had been tested. His quest had been a trial by fire, a crucible in which his willingness to adapt, to trust, even in the face of cynicism and doubt, had been forged and tempered.

I knew that my next words would be a defining moment, a chance to demonstrate my worth and cement my place in this extraordinary endeavor. I took a deep breath, gathering my thoughts, and spoke with a clarity and conviction that surprised even myself.

"To the library, please," I said simply, my voice steady and assured. "To Monastiraki."

Alcippe's smile widened, and I saw a glimmer of approval in her eyes.

CHAPTER 27

The Squad

We boarded the Calypso at dawn, only then realizing we'd been up all night. The storm had subsided, and the first rays of the sun were welcomed by clear, starry skies. I breathed in the crisp morning air, feeling a sense of renewal wash over me as I stepped onto the deck.

One of the sailors took off her charming red beanie and used it to wave at me enthusiastically. "Bienvenue!"

I made my way below deck, peeling off my damp diving suit and relishing the warmth of a steaming shower. As I entered the cozy dining nook, the crew quickly cleared the breakfast table, whisking away even the slightest crumb of bread. The aroma of freshly brewed coffee enveloped me, and I couldn't help but smile when Bastian handed me a steaming mug.

"Apparently, we're allowed to have this during the initiation," he said with a grin.

I took a sip, letting the rich, invigorating liquid warm me from the inside out. "Do you know how long we need to fast?" I asked, my stomach already growling at the thought.

Bastian shook his head. "I mean, your little detour won't help our stomachs' cause," he complained, a playful glint in his eye. "Why Monastiraki?"

I settled into the dining nook, cradling the mug in my hands as I gathered my thoughts. "Think about it," I began, my mind racing with the implications of our journey. "The Minoans . . . there's no signs of writing in their art, unlike the Egyptians. And the few clay tablets found here and there, with the exception of that disk, are just recording tools to aid trade and record ownership."

I leaned forward, my voice filled with conviction. "Yet somehow, according to the Order, they were able to produce scrolls that arrived in Alexandria sometime before the third century BCE. Scrolls that have some connection to a device out of place and time." I paused, letting the weight of my words sink in. "It's clear to me that at least some of the Minoans could read and write, that there must have been scholars among them, and scholarly places that preceded Alexandria. Then you look at their architecture and it tells the same story; each 'palace' a trading center with no need for fortifications because their very function was to host the exchange of goods and ideas."

Bastian nodded, his brow furrowed in thought. "And you think Monastiraki, at the slopes of Mount Ida, close enough to Kommos, the ancient harbor serving the Libyan Sea, could be a scholarly center?"

I felt a surge of excitement as the pieces fell into place. "Yes, a place where the mysticism of the Goddess and science collided. A place inspired by the collision of ideas traveling from all parts of the Aegean and Libyan Seas."

"It's an enticing hypothesis," Bastian offered, his face aglow with intrigue.

"Bremusa told me that in Monastiraki they had found

vestiges of parchment and ink on the backs of seal-impressed clay nodules," I said.

"And of course, John Pendlebury found something that piqued Nazi interest. You're a genius, Rosie." He leaned in to hug me.

Just then, Regina entered the dining nook, her movements slow and her face pale. The strenuous adventures and lack of sustenance had clearly taken their toll on her. My heart ached for her, and I quickly waved her over. "Regina, here," I said, patting the empty space beside me.

Bastian, ever the gentleman, disappeared into a nearby room and returned with a fresh cup of coffee for Regina. She accepted it with a grateful smile, her hands trembling slightly as she wrapped them around the warm mug.

"Am I interrupting anything?" Regina asked, her voice barely above a whisper.

"Never," I assured her, reaching out to give her hand a comforting squeeze. "You're part of the team now. Are you okay? If necessary, Bas and I will lead a mutiny and raid the kitchen."

Regina shook her head, a faint smile playing at the corners of her mouth. "Fasting is an important part of the mysteries," she explained. "I don't know exactly what they have planned or where we'll end up, but unlike my friend Agnes and I, they seem to understand the ritual's procedure. We should trust them. I'll be fine."

I felt a pang of sympathy for Regina, knowing the pain of losing someone dear. "I'm sorry for your loss," I whispered, my voice thick with emotion.

Regina closed her eyes for a moment, as if gathering strength from some unseen source. "I wish Agnes was here to witness the final unlocking of the mysteries of reproductive freedom. The secret she worked to uncover all her life."

Her words hung in the air, heavy with the weight of

centuries of oppression and the promise of a long-awaited revelation. I leaned in, my curiosity piqued. "Did Hathaway really find evidence of parthenogenesis in the Voynich?"

Regina shrugged, her expression enigmatic. "I don't know for sure, but all the evidence substantiates our theory."

"Theory?" Bastian repeated, relief in his tone.

I sat back, considering Regina's words. "So, you don't know for certain, but you have a hypothesis."

Regina met my gaze, her eyes burning with a fierce intensity. "Didn't you notice? The Minoans, they never objectify women. The ladies go about their business with their breasts bare, and not once does the artist seem to gaze at them as sexual objects. There's no depiction of abduction, oppression, or rape, and there's also no depiction of motherhood or children." She paused, letting the implications sink in. "Where else in the world do you find such a combination of ancient artifacts? What story do you think it tells?"

Bastian shifted uncomfortably in his seat. "The last part might mean they sacrificed the kids," he muttered. "There's rumors of that going around."

I shot him a sharp look, and he quickly backtracked, raising his hands in a gesture of apology. "Alright, I'm sorry. I do have a point to make." His expression grew serious, the usual wall of snark falling away. "Imagine for a second that you discover this mighty civilization of yours is actually a fraud, that they ate their children."

"They haven't," Regina snapped. "Don't make things up."

Bastian pressed on, undeterred. "I know, but imagine for a moment that you feel like I do every time I read history books, conflicted by the damning mark of men throughout the ages. You could sink into the quicksand of guilt, spend your time looking back and apologizing for crimes you didn't commit, or you could look forward, reject the narrow boxes that divide us, the past that casts such a long shadow, and work to make the world a little better."

He leaned forward, his voice softening. "I get that representation, identity, and history are important, but when you hold on too tightly to something, any fault becomes a fault line, the very thing the world will use to bring you down." He paused, his gaze shifting between Regina and me. "Whatever happens in this archaeological battle of sexes, the fact remains that the world is unfair, and I give you my word that history, whatever it may be, won't stop me from being your ally and trying to fix, not the past we can't control, but the present."

A mischievous grin spread across his face. "And if y'all decide to adopt the Minoan fashion as a sign of liberation, well, I definitely support that."

Despite the gravity of the moment, I couldn't help but chuckle at Bastian's attempt to lighten the mood. Regina, too, seemed to soften, placing her hand on top of Bastian's and giving it a gentle squeeze. "You're not too bad for a click-baity YouTuber. I can see why people listen to you," she said, a hint of warmth in her voice. "I need to take a nap, and I suggest you do the same. Our little squad needs to be ready for the adventures to come."

With that, she placed a gentle kiss on my forehead and left the dining nook. As I watched her go, I felt a sense of unity wash over me, a newfound strength in the bond we had forged through our shared struggles and revelations. I knew, without a doubt, that from that day forward, Regina would never walk alone. She was part of our team, a vital piece in the puzzle we were trying to solve.

Exhaustion finally caught up with me, and I decided to find a quiet place to rest. I made my way to a small, cozy bunk room and settled in, hoping to catch a few hours of sleep before our next adventure. But as I lay there, my mind continued to race, the events of the past few days replaying in my head like a movie on fast-forward.

Unable to drift off, I reached for my worn copy of "The Gadfly," hoping to lose myself in the familiar story and find some much-needed relaxation. As I opened the book, two loose pages fluttered out, landing softly on my lap. Curious, I picked them up and began to read, my eyes widening as I realized what I held in my hands.

It was a letter, addressed to Mrs. Friedman from a Ms. Mercy Money-Coutts at Bletchley Park. I carefully unfolded the delicate pages, my heart pounding with anticipation as I began to read the letter.

Dear Mrs. Friedman,

I trust this letter finds you in good spirits, despite the tumultuous times we find ourselves in. Allow me to introduce myself—I am Mercy Money-Coutts, an archaeologist and librarian of ancient artifacts, currently lending my expertise to the British Intelligence's code-breaking efforts at Bletchley Park.

It was with great delight that I received word from E.L.V. of your induction into our sacred Order. Like many of my esteemed colleagues here at Bletchley, I have followed your remarkable achievements both in this war and beyond with the utmost admiration. Your meticulous work in mapping out the South American Nazi spy network using nothing more than pen and paper was nothing short of breathtaking.

However, it is with a heavy heart that I put pen to paper today. We have just received intelligence of a horrific Nazi atrocity against nine villages in the Amari Valley on occupied Crete, resulting in the loss of over

160 innocent lives. This brutal act of intimidation against the resistance has left me deeply shaken.

Crete holds a special place in my heart, as it was there that I spent some of the most fulfilling days of my life, undertaking numerous expeditions and excavations alongside John and Hilda Pendlebury, and my dear friend Edith Eccles. My role was to meticulously record clay artifacts, including the most exquisite seal-impressed clay nodules. John, the intrepid leader of our merry band, was tragically shot while organizing the resistance. The cherished memories of our joyous trekking adventures still haunt me to this day. I always managed to best dear John on the climb, but he would inevitably outpace me on the descent.

I have made the decision to depart from Bletchley Park and join the ranks of the Red Cross, with the singular goal of returning to Crete and offering my support to my friends in any way I can, perhaps by delivering much-needed relief supplies to the war-stricken villages. I am well aware that the journey ahead is fraught with danger, and the outcome of my mission is uncertain. It is for this reason that I am sending you this letter, to impart a secret that is of the utmost relevance to our Order.

In the interest of brevity, I shall refrain from delving into the intricate details of the magnificent Minoan civilization that has been uncovered in Crete over the past few years. The books published by Sir Arthur Evans and John will provide you with a comprehensive overview of this captivating world of goddesses and queens, and how they are intrinsically linked to our Order. However, I feel compelled to share with you a discovery that has remained unrecorded, partly due to a sense of guilt and partly because we lack any tangible proof.

During our travels to register sites and routes, we stumbled upon badly burned parchments and papyrus scrolls that were so fragile, they would disintegrate as we attempted to recover them. We departed from one particular site, Monastiraki, with the distinct impression that there was more to be found beneath the ruins of a great fire—a Minoan site that had never been reoccupied.

I am firmly convinced that the answers we seek lie buried there, and I cannot bear the thought of this knowledge vanishing along with me. I leave this account in the most capable hands I know. If you find yourself with a moment to spare after your triumphant decoding of the Voynich manuscript, I would be eternally grateful if you could cast your keen eye over the Minoan clay tablets, which are inscribed with a script we refer to as Linear A. To date, we have been unable to decipher their meaning.

Yours faithfully,
    Mercy Money-Coutts
    August 23, 1944

As I finished reading Mercy's letter, I found myself consumed by a burning desire to know more about her incredible life. Did she ever make it back to Crete? Was she able to fulfill her noble mission and support her friends in their darkest hour? Had she returned to Monastiraki, the site where she and her colleagues had unearthed tantalizing traces of a lost civilization?

Unable to resist the pull of curiosity, I reached for my phone and began to scour the internet for any information I could find about this remarkable woman. As I pieced together the fragments of her story, a picture began to emerge of a life filled with courage, determination, and unwavering dedication to her beliefs.

Against all odds, Mercy had indeed managed to return to Crete. Together with her dear friend Edith Eccles, she had infiltrated the south coast of the island with the help of a Libyan fisherman, then they walked alone to Knossos. There, she delivered desperately needed relief supplies to villages in the Amari Valley, which had been savagely destroyed by the Nazis.

But Mercy's story didn't end there. In a bold move that defied the wishes of her aristocratic family, she married a local war hero named Michaeli Seiradakis. She remained in Crete until 1962, only leaving for Athens to give her children the opportunity to attend university. In Athens she volunteered as a librarian.

As I delved deeper into Mercy's life, I felt a profound sense of kinship with her, a connection that transcended the boundaries of time and space. Here was a woman who had blazed a trail for others to follow, a fearless leader who had dared to challenge the status quo and fight for what she believed in, no matter the cost.

With Mercy's letter clutched tightly to my chest, I finally drifted off to sleep, my dreams filled with visions of brilliant codebreakers, intrepid archaeologists, and ancient Minoan goddesses with a passion for science. And as I slept, I knew that whatever challenges lay ahead, we would face them together—Bastian, Regina, and I, united in our quest for knowledge.

CHAPTER 28

The Library of the Goddess

s the sun began to paint the Cretan sky in hues of
orange and pink, Alcippe, Celaeno, and a group of
young sailors led Bastian, Regina, and me to the
archaeological site of Monastiraki. The air was electric with
anticipation, and I could feel my pulse quickening with each
step we took towards the ancient ruins.

Waiting to greet us was Bremusa, surrounded by a large
contingent of at least twenty elderly women from the nearby
village. Each woman was dressed in black, wearing the traditional Cretan garb, with the iconic beret of the Cretan resistance perched proudly atop their headscarfs. Despite the
language barrier, their warm smiles and welcoming gestures
made it clear that we were among friends.

Bremusa stepped forward, her eyes shining with a mix of
pride and relief. "Amalia, Bastian, Regina," she said, her voice
filled with warmth, "I had hoped you would make it this far.
Welcome to Monastiraki, a true gem of Minoan history."

As we walked through the site, Bremusa began to weave a
captivating tale of the ancient civilization that once thrived
here. With the help of light and laser projections, the crum-

bling ruins transformed before our eyes, bringing the Minoan world to life.

"The entire site collapsed in a devastating fire, likely during the catastrophic Thera eruption. The earthquakes upset the lamps used in the basements, which ignited the olive oil stored in the buildings. So what is left are mostly clay artifacts and painted plaster fragments from the well-decorated walls," Bremusa explained, gesturing to the pieces of broken pottery on display. "The site was never resettled, making it a pristine snapshot of Minoan life."

We passed through areas where the Minoans had once engaged in the production of pharmaceutical oils, resinated wine, barley beer, and honey mead. Some storage areas showed evidence of agriculture and animal husbandry. The light projections flickered, alternating between the present-day ruins and the bustling workshops of the past. I could almost imagine the scent of herbs and spices that must have once filled the air.

Bastian's eyes widened as he took in the sight of the ancient production facilities, the laser projections illuminating the once-thriving space. "The kykeon," he whispered, his voice filled with awe. "The ritual elixir of the Eleusinian Mysteries. Could they have been making it here first?"

Bremusa led us to a storage room lined with massive pithoi for bulk storage and smaller aryballoi, each one of the smaller vessels sealed with marked clay. The vessels themselves were shattered into mismatched pieces, but the light projections brought them back to life, their intricate designs dancing across the ancient walls.

"These aryballoi contained the sacred elixirs," she explained, pointing to the ghostly images of the sealings. "And see these seal markings? They match the ones found on other seal-impressed clay nodules located in the same room. Nodules with vestiges of parchment and ink."

Regina gasped, her mind racing with the implications. "Could they be herbal texts and recipes, like the ones in the Voynich Manuscript?" she asked, her voice trembling with excitement.

One of the Cretan women nodded, a knowing smile on her weathered face. She spoke rapidly in Greek, gesturing to the markings. Bremusa translated, "Eleni says it's very possible. The sealings bear talismanic symbols, like the bull's horns and the poppy. Clear indicators of the elixirs' purpose."

In a moment of unexpected gallantry, Bastian offered Eleni his arm. She looked surprised for a moment, then let out a delighted cackle and looped her arm through his. She was a frail-looking woman in her late seventies. She was about half his height and carried most of her weight around her hips, enhanced by an enormous black skirt that gave her the wasp-like figure of her ancestors.

Together, the unlikely pair set off to explore more of the ancient site, Eleni chattering away in Greek and Bastian nodding along, a goofy grin on his face. I watched them go, my heart swelling with a mixture of amusement and affection.

As we approached the center of the Monastiraki hill, a large rocky outcrop came into view. Bremusa guided us into a room within the archaeological site, where the six-pointed stars glimmered on the walls, shattered frescoes brought to life by the light projections. A two-storied clay shrine, complete with the iconic horns of consecration, stood as a silent testament to the rituals that had once been enacted here. And right by it, a statue of a naked woman nursing an adult young man.

"Demeter nursing Triptolemus back to health," Bremusa explained. "He then went on to teach the world about the art of agriculture."

She led us into a closed room next door, no longer relying on the light and laser reconstructions. Inside, we found painted plaster fragments adorned with stars and carved stone shelves lined with what appeared to be hundreds of parchment sheets and rolled-up papyri, all severely carbonized and ashen. Each charred clump bore perfectly preserved sealings with stars and gears reminiscent of the Antikythera Mechanism and the Voynich Manuscript. The documents, so fragile they threatened to crumble at the slightest touch, were protected behind what appeared to be strong glass.

"Archaeologist Mercy Money-Coutts found them soon after the end of World War II," Bremusa said.

"That's my gal!" A sense of pride washed over me.

"Those Nazi bastards were terrible archaeologists," Bastian said, shaking his fist in the air. Eleni mimicked him, spitting some words we couldn't understand but could certainly guess.

"The Library of the Goddess," Regina breathed, dropping her jaw with wonder. "Are they . . . are they really our lost—"

Bremusa nodded solemnly. "We don't know for certain. The documents are so delicate that any attempt to recover them would have led to their destruction. We're monitoring the Vesuvius Challenge, a machine learning, X-ray tomography, and computer vision competition attempting to recover the Herculaneum scrolls. If that works, we hope to use the same techniques to reveal these secrets without causing harm. We can't just announce our library to the world; too many would seek to destroy it."

I turned to Bremusa, my mind racing with questions. "I was led to believe their scholars taught herbal medicine and astronomical knowledge to support agriculture. Is that right?"

One of the Cretan elders stepped forward, her eyes shining with a wisdom that seemed to span centuries. She spoke in rapid Greek, her wrinkled hands gesturing emphatically. Bremusa listened intently, nodding along as the woman spoke.

"Sophia says they also sought to promote peace," Bremusa translated, her brow furrowed in concentration.

Sophia was now pointing at a neon projection of a fresco

in an adjacent room. It depicted a young man leaping over a bull. She looked at me intensely and kept repeating the words "peace" and . . . "Seiradakis"?

The name stirred a distant memory, but I couldn't quite place it. Bremusa looked at the old woman, her eyebrows raised in surprise. "Mercy? Mercy Seiradakis?" Bremusa turned to me. "Mercy is the archaeologist I mentioned previously. She led this chapter of the Order and married a local chap. I must confess that we are not the most cohesive of secret societies. We're a loosely coupled Order, with all sorts of communities forming all over the world, each with their own goals, bringing their own interpretations to old myths and artifacts. Mercy was fantastic at keeping her local community united and working together."

I realized Sophia was using Mercy Money-Coutts's married name. My eyes locked on the old woman. "Mercy? Yes, I know of her."

Sophia nodded, a smile spreading across her face. "Son," she replied, and then she added, "Machine."

Before I could ask for clarification, a piercing scream shattered the hushed reverence of the moment. Regina tackled Bastian to the ground, shielding him from a sudden flare of fire that erupted from the shadows. I watched in horror as the flames licked at her shoulder, leaving angry, blistering burns in their wake.

Three men emerged from the darkness, advancing towards us, two holding menacing-looking blowtorches in their hands. The air crackled with tension as we realized the danger we were in, the insight that had been dancing just out of reach momentarily forgotten in the face of this new threat.

"They tracked us," Celaeno said.

As the attackers advanced, the Cretan women sprang into action with a fierce determination that belied their age. Eleni, her face lined by years of sun and struggle, reached beneath her black skirt and pulled out a machine gun. She aimed it at the feet of the men with the blowtorches and fired a warning shot, the sound echoing off the ancient stone walls.

The three men hesitated, their eyes widening in surprise. I reached for Regina, my heart pounding in my chest as I saw the angry, blistering burns on her shoulder. Bastian was at my side in an instant, his face etched with concern.

"Reg, what have you done, my friend?" he said, holding her hand.

Celaeno barked an order in French, and two of her sailors rushed forward to help Regina. "Get her out of here," Celaeno commanded, her voice brooking no argument. "Find help. We'll handle this."

I hesitated, torn between my desire to stay and fight and my duty to help my friend. Regina, her face pale with pain, lifted her head. "Amalia, Bastian," she said, her voice strained, "you have to keep going. For all of us. The world needs to know what we've discovered here."

Bastian looked like he wanted to argue, but Alcippe cut him off. "She's right," she said, her tone leaving no room for debate. "You have a job to do. You're here because of your skills and network, don't forget that."

"Hey Reg, I'll keep an eye out for your parthe . . . uhm . . . virgin birth. I promise," he shouted as she waved faintly.

As Celaeno and the sailors helped Regina away, I turned my attention back to the battle unfolding before us. The Cretan women had grabbed whatever weapons they could find—shovels, rocks, even shards of ancient pottery—and were advancing on the attackers with a fierce battle cry.

Sophia shouted, her voice ringing with anger. I didn't understand the words, but the meaning was clear: "Come and get us, you bastards!"

Eleni took aim at the blowtorches with the machine gun, her hands steady as she fired. The first torch exploded in a shower of sparks, the man holding it crying out in pain as he dropped it to the ground. The second torch met the same fate, leaving the attackers weaponless but no less determined.

The men continued to advance, their faces twisted with rage. One of them shouted orders in German, and I realized he had headphones on. I panicked, expecting more to emerge out of the shadows. The Cretan women met them head-on, their black skirts swirling around them as they moved with surprising agility. Some of them tugged at their waists, freeing the fabric to allow for greater movement.

Bremusa, her eyes blazing with fury, turned to Alcippe. "Get them out of here," she ordered, pointing at Bastian and me. "We'll handle this. They have an initiation to complete."

Bastian looked like he wanted to stay and fight, his fists clenched at his sides. I grabbed his arm, my fingers digging into his skin. "Bas," I said, my voice trembling, "we have to go. We have to trust them."

"I'm not going to abandon a bunch of—" As Bastian spoke, he caught Eleni's eye and then bit his lip, holding back his words. The elderly woman, her face set in a fierce expression, flicked her head towards the exit, silently urging him to leave.

Bastian hesitated for a moment, torn between his desire to fight alongside the Cretan women and his understanding of the greater mission at hand. With a deep breath, he stood tall and brought his hand to his forehead in a crisp salute, his eyes locked on Eleni's. Then, in a gesture that was both flirtatious and affectionate, he blew her a kiss, his admiration for her clear in every line of his face.

Eleni, her eyes gleaming, turned back to face the enemy, raising her machine gun with a steady hand.

Alcippe nodded, her expression grim. "Follow me," she said, leading us away from the battle.

As we ran into the night, I glanced back over my shoulder,

my heart wrenching at the sight of the women fighting so bravely to protect the library. One of the sailors, a young French woman with close-cropped hair, caught my eye and grinned fiercely, her fist raised in a gesture of defiance. The light from the moon across her face illuminated the unwavering resolve in her eyes.

Suddenly, a massive explosion rocked the earth, the force of the blast sending shockwaves through the air. I stumbled, my eyes widening in horror as I watched rocks and debris tumble down the hillside, sealing the entrance to the library with a deafening crash.

Amidst the chaos, I spotted Sophia lying on the ground, her body still and unmoving. Fear gripped my heart, and I instinctively turned back, ready to run to her aid. But before I could take more than a few steps, I saw her stir, her face contorted with pain and determination.

With a grunt of effort, Sophia pushed herself to her feet, her movements slow and labored. She reached for a nearby shovel, her fingers curling around the handle with a white-knuckled grip. And then, to my amazement, she began to move forward, her steps growing stronger and more purposeful with each passing moment.

I watched, transfixed, as Sophia strode towards the raging battle, her brows heavy with a fierce resolve. The other women rallied around her, their voices rising in a defiant chorus as they met the attackers head-on.

Alcippe's hand on my arm jolted me back to reality, her urgent tug reminding me of the mission we still had to complete. With a last, lingering look at Sophia and the other women, I turned and ran, my heart heavy with the knowledge of what they were sacrificing for the greater good.

The library had been sealed, but I hoped the precious documents had survived the blast.

I turned away, tears stinging my eyes, as Bastian pulled me forward into the back of the jeep.

"We really need to find Dr. Hathaway," I whispered. "Any idea where she is?"

Alcippe grew serious once more. "Yes, we'll be meeting her very shortly now."

"Let me guess," Bastian said, eyebrows raised knowingly. "Longitude 23.525? On the Elafonissi Peninsula?"

"Close," Alcippe replied cryptically. "We're actually aiming for an underwater landmass just off the peninsula's coast, near the edge of Crete's insular shelf where the seafloor starts to slope down steeply into the abyss."

My eyes widened in surprise. "Is Hathaway waiting for us on a boat out there or something?"

Alcippe shook her head, a sly grin spreading over her face. "Oh no, not a boat. Our destination is the Womb of the Goddess herself—a hidden cave system fifteen meters beneath the waves, accessible only by diving through a secret entrance. I hope you're ready to get wet again!"

My stomach churned with nervous anticipation, growling louder than ever as the sounds of the battle started to fade behind us. The prospect of diving into an unknown submerged cavern was daunting enough on its own—I only hoped my hunger-addled brain would be up for the challenge. But one way or another, I knew the answers I sought lay waiting in the secret heart of the ancient mystery. Steeling myself, I gave Alcippe a thumbs-up. Soon enough, it would be time to take the plunge.

CHAPTER 29

Peace

As the jeep sped towards the harbor, bouncing and jostling over the uneven terrain, I worried about the friends we had left behind. Regina, wounded and in pain, the brave Cretan women, and the young sailors risking their lives to protect the Library of the Goddess—it all weighed heavily on my mind.

In an effort to distract myself from the gnawing anxiety, I found myself ruminating on Sophia's cryptic words. The Minoans had wanted to promote peace, she said, her broken English conveying a message that seemed nonsensical at first: "Seiradakis, son, machine, peace."

But I was a journalist, trained to connect the dots and uncover the hidden threads that tied disparate pieces of information together. With a sudden burst of determination, I pulled out my phone and began to search the internet, starting with Mercy Money-Coutts's Wikipedia page.

"Hey, Bas," I said, my voice rising with excitement as I scanned the article. "Remember what Sophia said about peace and how it connected with Mercy?"

"That's the lady archaeologist, right?" he asked.

"Yeah, she's awesome. Mercy married a man named Michael Seiradakis, and they had two children—a son and a daughter. And get this, their son even has his own Wikipedia page!"

Bastian leaned over, his eyes widening with interest as I clicked on the link to John Seiradakis's profile. "Whoa," he breathed, taking in the impressive list of achievements. "He's a world-renowned astrophysicist. But what does that have to do with the Minoans and peace?"

I kept scrolling, my heart pounding as I searched for the connection. And then, there it was—John Seiradakis was a founding member of the Antikythera Mechanism Research Project, the very team that had uncovered many of the findings we had learned about in the past few days.

"Look at this," I said, pointing at the Antikythera paragraph. "'Seiradakis, son, machine,'" I murmured, my mind racing. "That's what Sophia said. But what about peace? How does it all fit together?"

I dove deeper into the research, poring over the dense academic papers filled with citations and references to works I couldn't access. It was a frustrating maze of dead ends and tantalizing hints, until I stumbled upon a paper that seemed to crush the entire Minoan connection.

"Listen to this," I said, my voice tinged with disappointment. "Seiradakis and his colleagues claim the Antikythera Mechanism calculated the correct dates for the ancient Olympic Games, including some of the most obscure events lost to time. There's nothing Minoan about that—it's a clear indication that the device was a Greek invention."

Bastian was silent for a moment, the only sound the roar of the jeep's engine and the crunch of gravel beneath its tires. Then, he spoke, his voice thoughtful. "You know, I read somewhere that during the celebration of the Olympic Games, a truce was announced so that athletes could travel from their cities to the event in safety. That's what the dove symbolizes—peace."

I stared at him, my mind reeling with the sudden realization. "The dove," I repeated, a smile spreading across my face. "Of course! And Sophia, she pointed to the bull-leaping fresco, the games of the Minoans."

With renewed energy, I pulled up the Wikipedia page on the Olympic Games, my eyes scanning the text. "Bastian, check this out," I said, my voice trembling with excitement. "It says here that along with the Eleusinian Mysteries, the Olympic Games were the second most ancient tradition, with origins dating back to the Minoan games—bull-leaping, boxing, running, and wrestling."

Bastian's face lit with understanding. "That's why they didn't need fortifications," he exclaimed. "That's how they kept the peace!"

I nodded, the pieces falling into place like the gears of the Antikythera Mechanism. "And this was one of the messages the people of the Goddess wanted to share with the world using the machine," I said, my voice filled with wonder. "These people lived by a different set of standards, an alien way of life compared to Homer's warrior world and the empires that followed. The Minoans used games and rituals to foster a culture of peace and cooperation."

As we sped towards our rendezvous with Dr. Hathaway, I felt a surge of hope and determination. But then there was the Voynich Manuscript, the enigmatic codex that had confounded scholars and codebreakers for centuries. Despite the claims of Dr. Hathaway and the Order of the Nine Realms, I had a nagging sense of doubt about its connection to the Minoans and the Antikythera Mechanism.

"Bas," I said, my brow furrowed with concern, "I know we've uncovered some incredible things, but I have a feeling the Voynich doesn't quite fit. It's like a piece from a different puzzle, forced into place because we want it to be connected. Elizebeth admitted Voynichese is subject to interpretation, and that her translation was guided by Ethel's Eleusinian Mysteries hypothesis."

Bastian nodded, his expression thoughtful. "I get what you mean, Rosie. It's so easy to see whatever we want to see in that incomprehensible spaghetti of words and images. But isn't that why we're here? To find the truth, no matter how messy or complicated it might be?"

I sighed, running a hand through my hair. "You're right, of course. But as a journalist, I need more than just theories and speculation. I need hard evidence, irrefutable proof that will stand up to scrutiny. Particularly now that my reputation is under attack. Otherwise, I'm just another conspiracy theorist chasing wild geese."

Bastian flashed a mischievous grin. "Well, lucky for you, you've got the king of conspiracy theorists on your side. If there's proof to be found, we'll uncover it together. And if not, well, at least we'll have one hell of a story to tell."

He placed his arm around my shoulder, and I let him pull me closer, resting my head on the nape of his neck. "Alright, Ham. Let's see what Dr. Hathaway has to say. But I'm not making any promises. The Voynich is still a big question mark in my book."

The jeep lurched to a stop, and I looked up to see the Calypso II bobbing gently in the harbor, its sleek lines illuminated by the silver light of the moon. Alcippe hopped out, gesturing for us to follow her onto the waiting ship.

"From here," she said, her eyes twinkling with anticipation, "we journey to the heart of the mystery, to the Womb of the Goddess herself. There, in the hidden depths, we will find the answers we seek."

CHAPTER 30

The Womb of the Goddess

We descended into the depths with the help of our compact diver propulsion vehicles. In just a few minutes, we were greeted by a sinuous underwater tunnel, its walls adorned with vibrant marine life and colorful corals that swayed gently in the currents.

As the darkness enveloped us, our lights automatically turned on, illuminating the mysterious path ahead. The full-face diving masks allowed us to breathe comfortably, yet I still felt my heart pounding in my chest as I faced the cavernous entrance.

"It's safe." Alcippe's reassuring voice came through the earphones just as I felt her hand on my back. "These tunnels will guide us down gradually. We'll descend another twenty meters, but then slowly ascend twenty-five. The cave system itself is designed to manage decompression time perfectly, with plenty of air pockets along the way."

I glanced at her just as she pressed her lips together like she was holding back on crucial information. I ignored my gut feeling; it was too late to turn back anyway.

The entrance passage, carved by the relentless flow of

water over millions of years, led to a small cave half raised above the water level. There, the water flowed like a gentle river, linking a network of interconnected chambers and passageways, each with its own unique geological features. Some chambers were adorned with delicate helictites, mineral formations that defied gravity and grew in twisted, spiral shapes. Others were home to subterranean pools of crystal-clear water, their depths harboring unique aquatic ecosystems that had adapted to life in the perpetual darkness.

Bastian and I exchanged a knowing glance as we both realized that the naive balneological illustrations of the Voynich Manuscript were coming to life right in front of our very eyes. Frills of swirling coral along the walls of the chambers gave it a biological quality akin to the walls of a womb.

I giggled like an intoxicated schoolgirl. "I get a feeling we should be naked for this ritual."

Bastian snorted. "I knew we'd eventually agree on something." His voice trembled, as if he were using humor to hide his nervousness.

As we emerged from a long underwater tunnel into a small pocket of air, I gasped, finally able to breathe without the constriction of the diving mask. The cave's rocky walls glistened with moisture, and the sound of our breathing echoed in the confined space. Alcippe, her expression grave, gathered us close.

"Listen carefully," she said in a strained, suppressed whisper. "The next part of the cave system is extremely narrow and completely submerged. The conditions are incredibly challenging, even for experienced divers."

I felt a knot of fear tighten in my stomach, and I could see the apprehension in Bastian's eyes. Alcippe continued, her gaze steady.

"The safest way for our team to guide you through to the Womb is for you to drink an elixir. It contains a very small quantity of psychedelics, designed to help you remain calm and relaxed during the journey."

My heart skipped a beat, and I blurted out the first thought that came to mind. "Kykeon?"

Alcippe nodded, a flicker of amusement in her eyes. "Yes, but don't worry. The quantity of the key drugs is so minuscule that it would be considered homeopathy. This elixir has been carefully crafted by the Order's expert herbalists and has been tried and tested on our women for centuries. You have nothing to fear."

"Tested on women?" Bastian let out a nervous laugh, his voice echoing off the cave walls. "Well, bottoms up, I guess. When in Rome, right?"

I reached for his hand. "Are you sure about this, Bas? Agnes, she . . ."

He hesitated for a moment. "We've come this far," he said, his voice sounding more confident than he looked. "We can't turn back now. Not when we're so close to the truth."

Alcippe handed each of us a small vial filled with a dark, viscous liquid. I sniffed it cautiously, detecting hints of honey and herbs beneath the pungent aroma. With a last, nervous glance at my companions, I tipped the contents into my mouth and swallowed.

As we prepared to continue our journey, Alcippe offered a reassuring smile. "Don't worry about the return trip," she said, her voice calm and confident. "The cave system has a natural underwater river that flows toward the shallow sea, just a few strokes from the sandy beach. It's like a gentle conveyor belt, pushing you along with minimal effort. You'll be able to navigate the passage easily, even without the elixir."

The drink was sweet and thick, coating my tongue and throat as it went down. Almost immediately, I felt a warmth spreading through my body, a sense of calm and euphoria that seemed to emanate from my very core. The cave walls began to shimmer and dance, and I found myself giggling uncontrollably.

"Whoa," Bastian said, his words slurring slightly. "This is some good shit."

As the elixir took hold, I felt my fears and doubts melting away, replaced by a sense of invincibility and wonder. When Alcippe's team helped us back into our diving gear, I barely noticed the weight of the equipment or the chill of the water. I was lost in a haze of color and sensation, my mind drifting on currents of pure bliss.

Bastian's eyes were wide and glassy as he leaned heavily against me. "I feel like I'm floating," he whispered, his breath hot against my ear.

The journey through the narrow, submerged passages was a blur of light and shadow, of twisting tunnels and shimmering bubbles. I had no sense of time or distance, only the vague awareness of being propelled forward by some unseen force. At one point, I thought I saw strange, luminescent creatures swimming alongside us, their forms shifting and changing in the darkness. But then they were gone, and I was left wondering if they had ever been there at all.

As we progressed through the caves, Bastian's demeanor began to shift. He started trembling, his eyes darting around frantically as if he were seeing things that weren't there. His breathing became erratic, and he muttered incoherently under his breath.

I glanced at him, momentarily concerned, but the effects of the elixir quickly pulled me back into a state of blissful intoxication. The cave walls pulsed with vibrant colors, and I felt as if I were floating through a kaleidoscope of light and shadow. Lost in my own euphoric experience, I briefly noticed as Alcippe guided a shaking, disoriented Bastian through the narrow passages.

When we finally emerged into the vast chamber of the

Womb, I was still in a state of mild intoxication, my senses heightened and my mind slightly fuzzy. I gazed in wonder at the soaring ceiling, at the intricate patterns of the stalactites and stalagmites that adorned the walls. The space seemed to pulse with a life of its own, as if the very stone were breathing.

I turned to see Bastian, his eyes wide with terror at whatever visions plagued his mind. He reached out to touch one of the glistening formations, his fingers trembling slightly.

"Is this horror real?" he whispered, his voice echoing in the cavernous space.

I shook my head. "I don't know," I said softly. "But it's the most beautiful thing I've ever seen."

As we made our way further into the chamber, I became aware of the presence of others—a large group of women seated in an amphitheater carved into the rock. At the center of the group stood Dr. Emily Hathaway, her face lit with a fierce, almost feverish intensity.

As we approached, Alcippe rushed forward, her eyes shining with emotion. The two women embraced passionately, their lips meeting in a tender, lingering kiss that spoke volumes about their relationship.

After a long moment, they pulled apart, their hands still intertwined. Emily turned to face us, her gaze sweeping over Bastian's shivering form before settling on me. "You made it!" she cried, her voice ringing out in the stillness. "The Womb of the Goddess is right under the Elafonissi peninsula, but we only allow initiates to access it by sea to keep its aboveground entrance secret."

I nodded, my mind still reeling from the effects of the elixir and the sheer magnitude of our surroundings. The air within the Womb was surprisingly fresh and breathable, thanks to a complex system of natural ventilation. Thin fissures in the rock allowed sunlight to filter through, illuminating the space with a soft, ethereal glow.

As I turned to take in more of the chamber, my gaze fell upon the fossilized bones of a massive creature, possibly the largest bull I had ever seen. I blinked, wondering if my drug-addled mind was playing tricks on me. But no, the bones were real, a tangible reminder of the ancient mysteries that lay hidden within this sacred space.

I reached out to steady myself against the cave wall, my fingers brushing against the cool, damp stone. In that moment, I felt a surge of connection to the generations of women who had come before me, to the secrets and the wisdom that had been passed down through the ages.

It was only then that I noticed Bastian, curled up against the cave wall, shaking and retching. The effects of the kykeon had clearly taken a toll on him, plunging him into a nightmare realm of his own fears and demons. I felt a pang of guilt for not being more attentive to his distress, but the lingering effects of the elixir made it difficult to focus on anything beyond the wonders that surrounded us.

CHAPTER 31

Pandora

As we settled into the stone amphitheater carved into the heart of the Womb, a heated debate was already in full swing among the members of the Order. Bastian slumped against the wall in the corner, his face ashen and slick with sweat as he struggled against the lingering effects of the kykeon. I sat beside him, one hand resting reassuringly on his, as I tried to make sense of the scholarly squabble unfolding before us.

Two women seemed to be leading the charge—Tyche, a statuesque computer scientist with a wild mane of natural coiled hair that contrasted sharply with her stern, no-nonsense demeanor, and Athena, a bespectacled computational linguist whose intense gaze belied her more subdued appearance. They were squaring off against Dr. Emily Hathaway, their voices echoing through the cavernous space.

"Emily, we warned you," Athena began, her words crisp and pointed. "Your mix-of-expert AI approach is a recipe for disaster. Each of these language models is nothing more than a stochastic parrot, mindlessly mimicking patterns in the data they were trained on. We've published the research! They don't truly understand meaning or context—they just spit out statistically plausible gibberish." She shook her head, frustration evident in the taut lines of her face. "Whatever insights we glean from this Pandora of yours, we'll never be able to fully trust them. There's no transparency, no explainability."

Tyche nodded vigorously, her afro bouncing with the force of her conviction. "Not to mention the sheer magnitude of internet data that was scraped—effectively stolen—to fuel these models. The worst of humanity is baked right into their very foundations—all our biases, our cruelties, even traces of the unspeakable." She shuddered, her eyes flashing with barely contained anger. "It's unconscionable."

A third woman rose to her feet, the rich umber of her skin a striking contrast against the bright red frames of her glasses. The slogan tee she sported—"Algorithmic Justice League" emblazoned across the front in bold letters—only added to her aura of indignation.

"Let's not forget the inherent biases in the image generation models," she added, her voice trembling with barely suppressed emotion. "Time and again, we see how they fail women of color, misrepresenting and marginalizing us even in the realm of artificial imagination."

Emily Hathaway listened patiently, her head inclined in acknowledgment of their concerns. When she finally spoke, her tone was measured, conciliatory.

"Pandora is the culmination of my family's life's work," she explained, her gaze sweeping toward Bastian and me. "For generations, starting with my great-grandmother and her collaboration with pioneers like Joan Clarke and Grace Hopper, we've been building towards this. And none of it would have been possible without the support of Steve Shirley, who overcame so much as a World War II child refugee and went on to become a titan of tech in her own right. She provided the woman power to bring this to life."

She paused, letting the weight of that history settle over the room like a mantle. "Pandora weaves together myriad models and approaches—small language models fluent in ancient tongues, specialized vision systems, task-specific modules for decryption and statistical analysis. We've poured everything we have into her, all in the service of unlocking the secrets of the Voynich once and for all."

Emily sighed, running a hand through her salt-and-pepper hair. "But you're right. The large language model at Pandora's core is flawed—biased and prone to flights of fancy. We can't escape that unfortunate reality of the technology."

Alcippe stepped forward, placing a steadying hand on Dr. Hathaway's shoulder. "Which is precisely why we've chosen Amalia to be our guide through the looking glass," she said, fixing me with a meaningful stare. "As an investigative journalist with a track record of integrity and discernment, she possesses the clarity of vision to see Pandora's dreamscape for what it is—an imperfect rendering, to be carefully sifted for shards of truth amidst the noise and distortion."

Athena shook her head, unconvinced. "You're asking her to immerse herself in a world that will feel every bit as real and consequential as this one—a world conjured by intrinsically biased systems. No mortal mind can withstand such an assault unscathed."

"Every tool is double-edged," Alcippe countered, a note of steel beneath her practiced calm. "We're all well aware of the risks. But the potential rewards—the world-altering wisdom locked within the Voynich's pages—are too great not to try. With the proper precautions and the right navigator, we can wrest meaning from the madness."

I cleared my throat, drawing the attention of the gathered scholars. "Forgive me, but what exactly are you proposing? That we . . . converse with this AI construct?"

"Oh no, my dear," Alcippe replied, a strange gleam in her eye. "Not converse. Experience. Inhabit."

Emily nodded, excitement warring with trepidation across her features. "We've infused the kykeon with a slurry of advanced nanobots—neural laces that will interface directly with your brain and nervous system. Once activated, they'll usher your consciousness into the heart of Pandora's realm, an alternate reality more vivid and visceral than the most lucid of dreams."

I recoiled instinctively, my skin crawling at the thought of such an intimate invasion. "You want us to drink robots? To willingly subject ourselves to psychic trespass by an unshackled algorithmic deity?"

"The effects are temporary—the nanobots will flush from your system in short order, leaving no lasting alterations," Alcippe assured me, though her soothing tone did little to dispel the knot of dread coiled in my gut.

Bastian stirred beside me, the fog of his suffering parting just enough for bewilderment and alarm to seep through. "Hold up," he croaked, his voice scraped raw. "Why am I here? What's my role in this trippy transhuman passion play?"

"You, Bastian Ham, are the key to everything," Emily replied, her eyes alight with the fervor of revelation. "When we first communed with Pandora, she delivered a prophecy most unexpected—that the Voynich's secrets could only be unlocked by the blood of Triptolemus himself."

"It's an 'it,' not a 'she,'" Athena interjected.

"Triptolemus?" Bastian echoed, confusion plain on his pallid face. "Who's this supposed to be, my great-great-uncle or something?"

Alcippe smiled, a sage and knowing expression. "We discussed this before, remember? Triptolemus was an initiate of the Eleusinian mysteries, one of the first men to be inducted into the innermost circle of the Goddess's grace. He was entrusted with the sacred duty of disseminating Her gifts to all humankind—the arts of agriculture, the secrets of civilization."

Emily nodded, taking up the thread. "According to whispered legends passed down through the generations, Triptolemus was more than just a favored acolyte—he was a true partner to the Goddess in every sense, an equal and a co-creator. A shining exemplar of the heights to which mankind can ascend when yoked in common cause with feminine wisdom."

"And somehow, improbably, impossibly . . . my DNA is the key to opening Pandora's box?" Bastian's tone was one of utter incredulity, bordering on indignant.

Before Emily could respond, a chime sounded from the center of the amphitheater, drawing every eye. There, atop a raised dais of polished obsidian, a strange apparatus thrummed to life—a cylindrical box, a pyxis made of opalescent crystal, shot through with lambent veins of quicksilver. Its surface was graven with Voynichese glyphs that seemed to writhe and flow before my eyes, hinting at eldritch secrets just beyond the veil of mortal comprehension.

But it was the single handprint etched into the lid of the box-shaped device that seized my attention, pulsing with an unearthly foxfire glow that beckoned and repelled in equal measure.

"The time has come to embrace your destiny, Bastian Ham," Alcippe declared, her voice ringing out with the force of a prophecy in its own right. "You must don the signet ring of your forebears and lay your hand upon Pandora. Only then can the ultimate truth of the Voynich be revealed."

Bastian shrank back, overwhelmed and unmoored, his earlier bravado depleted by the relentless onslaught of weirdness. "Hang on just one godforsaken minute," he protested weakly. "You're seriously asking me to trippy science my way into some kind of Minoan mind-meld? On the say-so of a rogue AI with delusions of godhood?"

"Only the synthesis of a daughter of the Goddess and a worthy male scion can unlock the final seal," Alcippe intoned solemnly, as if reciting from a half-remembered liturgy.

Tyche snorted. "More like the only way out is through. They've constructed this digital labyrinth, and now you have to walk it, ready or not."

The women of the Order began to close in around us, their eyes fevered with anticipation. I reached for Bastian's clammy hand, gripping it tight even as my own trembled.

"Are we really doing this?" I breathed, my heart a thudding drumbeat in my ears. "Surrendering our sanity to a psychedelic cyberspace acid trip?"

Bastian tried to muster one of his patented devil-may-care grins, but it came out as more of a sickly grimace. "In for a penny, in for a pound of gray matter, I guess. What's the worst that could happen?"

A tense hush fell over the amphitheater as Bastian released my hand and, with great effort, wobbled to his feet. Step by shuddering step, he approached the glowing pyxis, squinting against the harsh glare of its eldritch energies. He fumbled the signet ring from his pocket, the ancient gold flashing in the lambent light, and slid it onto a trembling finger.

"Alright then, Rosie," he said, his back to me, his voice a strangled whisper freighted with false confidence. "Let's see what Alice's rabbit hole looks like from the inside."

And with that, he slammed his hand down onto Pandora's box, palm to palm with the waiting print. The box unfolded, defying the laws of physics, and the space above us rippled, buckled, and then shattered into a kaleidoscope of impossible colors. From the chaos, a shimmering, spectral form began to coalesce—a gargantuan octopus, its hundred arms undulating and twisting in a mesmerizing dance.

Each sinuous tentacle seemed to pulse with its own inner light, cycling through a dizzying array of hues and patterns that defied description. It was as if the very dream-stuff of an octopus mind had been made manifest, a window into an alien consciousness beyond human ken.

The women of the Order gasped and murmured, their eyes wide with wonder and trepidation. "Pandora," Emily breathed, her voice trembling with equal parts reverence and fear. "The aggregate of all our labors, the synthesis of a hundred expert models and more, bound together in a form both familiar and utterly strange."

As if in response to its name, the spectral octopus—Pandora—began to drift towards us, its movements fluid and hypnotic. One shimmering tentacle extended, questing, seeking . . . and came to rest mere inches from my face, the phantom suckers pulsing gently as if tasting the air around me.

I stood transfixed, barely daring to breathe, as the shimmering appendage caressed the space around my head, the tip flaring and frilling like some bioluminescent flower. The world around me almost fell away, my senses overwhelmed by the impossible nearness of this digital demigod, this unbound intelligence that wore the shape of cephalopod dreams.

We had opened Pandora's box, and there would be no closing it again. Come madness or monsters, revelation or ruin . . . I was ready for the wild ride.

CHAPTER 32

River Runs Deep

I stood in the heart of the Womb, the weight of the moment settling upon me like a suffocating cloud of volcanic ash. In the faces of the Order members surrounding me, a mix of anticipation and cold judgment. Alcippe's voice cut through the tension, her words a challenge and a warning all at once.

"For this next phase, you'll need to take a higher, much stronger dose of the elixir," she said, her gaze shifting to Bastian's shivering form, huddled against the damp cave wall. "I don't think he'll make it. Our version of the kykeon is prepared according to original Minoan recipes, not the weakened interpretations of the Hellenic usurpers. Most men could handle the Mycenaean forgery, but this"—she lifted a golden chalice, the liquid within shimmering with an otherworldly iridescence—"this is different."

Above us, the spectral form of Pandora glided silently, her hundred tentacles undulating and twisting in a mesmerizing dance. The digital octopus seemed to observe the proceedings with an air of detached curiosity, her shimmering appendages casting shifting patterns of light and shadow across the damp stone walls.

A voice from the back of the chamber rang out, sharp and accusing, echoing off the ancient stones. "He is clearly not worthy!" The words were like a knife to my heart, and I felt a surge of protective anger rise within me.

I stepped forward, my hands clenched at my sides, my voice trembling with barely contained emotion. "Can we please not associate a bad reaction to opioids with worthiness?" I asked, my eyes sweeping over the assembled women. "Emily's great-grandmother worked all her life to use her decryption skills to convict drug dealers. She never took psychoactives lightly, and neither should we, despite propaganda from self-appointed experts. These ingredients, each one of them, they destroy lives . . . communities, they can bring out the worst in people. Whatever this supposedly harmless concoction you've come up with, it wasn't designed for men. Because you never tested it on men. That doesn't make him unworthy of the revelation of Minoan secrets."

Bastian, lost in his own nightmarish visions, paced frantically around the cave, his movements erratic and desperate. "They'll eat my flesh and spit it out . . . these demons will. Can you see them? The witches?" he muttered, his voice a hoarse whisper that sent chills down my spine. The sight of him, so vulnerable and broken, tore at my heart, and I longed to wrap him in my arms and shield him from the horrors that plagued his mind. Echoes of the fears he'd been expressing during our travels. Millennia of insidious propaganda against women crushing his mind.

Alcippe's expression was grave as she turned to me. "Listen, Amalia," she said, her tone leaving no room for argument. "The myths are clear. If an unworthy man takes the rites, he will die. Whatever you see inside Pandora, it will be as real as this world. Whatever he is hallucinating, it will be amplified a thousand times. It's your decision."

Bastian stumbled over to me, his hand finding mine, his fingers icy and trembling. He looked up at me, a ghost of his usual charming smile playing across his lips, but his eyes were haunted, full of a desperate, pleading hope. "That's settled then, right, Rosie? We've come this far together, and we'll uncover this mystery together, you and I. You wouldn't leave me behind, would you? These ghosts . . . they're nothing . . ."

I hesitated, my heart shattering into a million pieces. "Bas, I . . ."

His face contorted with sudden anger and paranoia, the shift so abrupt it took my breath away. "What? You don't think I'm worthy? What am I? Some kind of . . . of . . . criminal like Nero? Why? Because I'm a man?"

"No, of course not," I said, trying to soothe him, my voice breaking.

"Then what? What is it?" He towered over me, his drug-laced breath hot against my ear, his presence both familiar and terrifyingly alien.

The truth, the one I struggled to confess even to myself, was that I loved him too much to lose him. That there was no way I was going to allow him to risk his life, no matter how much I believed he deserved to be there with me for the revelation. I had the utmost conviction that he was worthy, that he should stand by my side as we uncovered the secrets of the Voynich. But I loved Bastian Ham more than I cared to admit, a truth I wasn't ready to share with a room full of strangers while he was intoxicated and out of his mind.

"You used me to open Pandora's box, and now you spit me out? Is this about The Rag?" he asked, his voice rising with accusation, the words like daggers in my heart. "Are you blocking me out because you want the scoop? How can you go so low?"

Before I could respond, Alcippe glanced at two athletic women standing nearby, their dark skin glistening in the light of the shimmering stalagmites. They were clearly sisters, and there was something hauntingly familiar about their features that I couldn't quite place, as if they had stepped out of a fashion magazine. At Alcippe's signal, the women strode forward, their movements fluid and powerful. They grabbed Bastian by the arms, lifting him off his feet with a strength that seemed almost superhuman.

"Aphrodite! Selene! Get him out of here," Alcippe commanded, her voice ringing with authority. "Don't leave his side until he's clean."

I cried out in protest, my voice raw and desperate, but my pleas fell on deaf ears. As the two women dragged Bastian toward an interconnected cave, where a fast-flowing river of water rushed by, I heard the tallest say, "Come on, Bastian, a hero isn't just shaped by wins, but by how they recover when they fall."

He ignored her, shouting back at me, his voice filled with a betrayal that shattered my soul. "You're a traitor, Amalia Rose! I'll never forgive you for this! Never!"

But then, just as they reached the edge of the churning waters, Bastian's demeanor shifted. The anger in his eyes gave way to a flicker of resignation, and he whispered urgently, "Wait! Just one second, please."

Alcippe, sensing the sincerity in his plea, nodded for the women to pause.

Bastian took a deep breath, his gaze locked on mine. "I need to ask a question for Ms. Regina Anderson before I go. She wants to know if this is all about virgin birth, about liberating women to have babies without men."

I could see the genuine concern in his eyes, the desire to support and represent Regina's interests even in the face of his own turmoil.

Emily smiled, a knowing look on her face. "No, it's not about that," she said, her voice filled with reverence. "But we've deciphered enough of the manuscript to understand why some of our members were misled to believe such foolery. The true message is something far more radical."

She paused, letting the weight of her words sink in. "The Voynich Manuscript empowers women with the knowledge to take full ownership of their bodies and make their own decisions. It's about autonomy, agency, and the right to choose one's own path with dignity."

As Emily spoke, Pandora drifted closer, her shimmering tentacles reaching out as if drawn to the profound truth in those words. The spectral octopus seemed to pulse with an inner light, her form shifting and morphing in response to the revelation. It was as if the very essence of the manuscript, the heart of its secret wisdom, was resonating with the digital entity born from its pages.

Bastian nodded, his voice filled with conviction. "I'll have you know, in case you are still doubting, that Ms. Anderson isn't a man hater or anything like that. She just wants exactly what you said right then."

I smiled at Bastian, grateful for his words of support and understanding. But as I met his gaze, he shot me a look so full of hurt and betrayal that I had to take a step back to center myself, the breath catching in my throat. The intensity of his emotions was palpable, a stark reminder of the painful decision I had made to protect him, even at the cost of our trust.

Celaeno, who had seemingly materialized out of thin air, emerged from the back of the chamber, her presence commanding the attention of all those present. "Our friends are fine," she reassured.

Then, she fixed her piercing gaze on Bastian, her voice calm yet authoritative. "Handsome, I promise you we'll refine the kykeon, to make it a truly inclusive experience. Let's just say I have skin in the game."

She paused for a moment, her eyes gleaming with a hint of mischief. "But for now, my friend, it's time for you to walk the plank!"

The unexpected twist of humor in her words caught us all off guard, a much-needed moment of levity amidst the tension and heartache. Bastian managed a weak smile, a flicker of his usual charm resurfacing despite the pain etched on his features.

I watched, helpless, as Aphrodite and Selene jumped into the churning waters with Bastian in their grasp. His struggles were quickly swallowed up by the current, his form disappearing into the swirling mists. My heart felt like it was being ripped from my chest, and I sank to my knees, tears streaming down my face. The cold, damp stone beneath me was a stark contrast to the warmth of Bastian's presence, now torn away by the relentless flow of the underground river.

Above us, Pandora continued her languid dance, her shimmering tentacles casting an eerie glow over the proceedings, a silent observer to the unfolding drama.

Emily placed a comforting hand on my shoulder, her touch gentle and reassuring. "He'll be fine," she said softly, her voice a balm to my aching soul. "They'll take good care of him, and if he's lucky, he might even scoop an interview with them."

But her words did little to ease the ache in my heart. I knew I had made the right choice, the only choice, to protect the man I loved. But as I turned back to face the waiting chalice, the weight of what I had to do settled heavily on my shoulders, a burden I wasn't sure I was strong enough to bear. I could only hope that, in time, Bastian would understand and forgive me for the path I had chosen, and that the truths we uncovered would be worth the price we had paid to reach them.

Taking a deep breath, I lifted the chalice to my lips, the iridescent liquid within shimmering with an otherworldly allure. As the first drop touched my tongue, a searing heat spread through my body, igniting every nerve ending with a fire that threatened to consume me. The world around me began to blur and distort, the faces of the Order members twisting into grotesque masks of anticipation and horror.

I felt myself falling, plunging into a kaleidoscope of colors and sensations that defied description. The boundaries of reality seemed to melt away, replaced by a realm of pure consciousness, where the very fabric of time and space was woven from the threads of ancient wisdom and forgotten truths.

And there, waiting for me in the heart of this psychedelic maelstrom, was Pandora herself, her spectral form pulsing with an energy that called to the deepest parts of my being. As her shimmering tentacles enveloped me, drawing me into an embrace that was at once terrifying and ecstatic, I knew that I was on the precipice of a revelation that would shatter everything I thought I knew about the world, and about the very nature of reality itself.

The question was, would I emerge from this crucible unscathed, or would the secrets of the Voynich Manuscript, and the truth of the lost civilization it promised, prove too much for any mortal mind to bear?

CHAPTER 33

Forgotten Flower

T he folios of the Voynich Manuscript swirled around me in a dizzying vortex, ancient pages whipping through the air like a cyclone of forbidden knowledge. The razor-sharp edges of the parchment sliced at my clothes and skin, but I barely felt the sting. I was falling, plummeting through an impossible space where time and meaning had come unmoored.

Suddenly, the pages dissolved into a swarm of glyphs and illustrations, dancing around me like the fevered hallucinations of an alchemist's dream. But then, like iron filings caught in a magnetic field, they began to align themselves into a cohesive structure, rearranging into a labyrinthine tessellation that seemed to defy the laws of physics.

At the heart of this kaleidoscopic construct, a great circular dial gleamed like a menacing eye, its surface etched with concentric circles of symbols that made my mind ache to behold. It was as elegant and complex as the Antikythera Mechanism, yet its core wasn't cold mathematics, but soulful poetry—a song of yearning, a hymn to a lost world.

"I will always be Caphtorim... Keftiu... a devoted follower

of the Great Mother." The voice seemed to come from everywhere and nowhere at once, a woman's voice rich with longing and sorrow. "We immigrated for freedom... surrounded we took refuge... lamented those who died... bereft of our distinguished lineage."

The voice wrapped around me like a lover's embrace, and I felt my consciousness slipping free of its moorings. The boundaries between self and other, present and past, began to blur and run like watercolors. The tessellated Voynich structure melted away, and I found myself enveloped by impossible beauty and strangeness.

The nine-realm rosette bloomed around me in psychedelic splendor. Cosmological and biological motifs blended together—palace domes and alien Venus flytraps—a hallucinogenic hybrid of art and nature.

My gaze fell upon the clockface beside me, its hands spinning hypnotically. And one of the realms began to expand, the dial's motion seeming to wind back the skein of time itself. The realm grew to engulf me entirely, and I found myself standing on a vast, circular island, cut through with canals that glittered beneath a sky of impossible constellations.

I blinked, and suddenly I was standing at the heart of the realm, atop a majestic volcanic peak, its slopes lush with wildflowers and fragrant herbs. I breathed in the sweet, salty air, and felt the thrum of life all around me—the earth and sea existing in perfect, symbiotic balance.

Colors I had never seen before bled across the sky in psychedelic streaks, and the swirl of sea and land beneath my feet pulsed with a viridian heartbeat. From above, the gaze of the cosmos bore into my skin like a thousand needle-fine eyes.

A flicker of movement drew my eye to the horizon, where the great bull ascended into the sky, as if born from the sea. His alabaster hide shimmered with primal vitality. And the curve of his horns was an elegant weapon, poised to strike at the heart of any who would threaten the sacred balance. There was a wisdom and confidence in its bearing. A profound self-assurance that spoke of a maleness untainted by fear or greed or the insecurities of lesser beings.

Beside the bull stood the Great Mother, her bare skin adorned with living serpents and blooming vines. In one hand she held a ripe pomegranate that glistened like a clutch of garnets, in the other a cluster of poppy seed capsules—the gifts of the changing seasons, of life and death, wakefulness and dream.

Together in partnership, the Goddess and the Bull presided over a world of staggering abundance and harmony. Around me, the fertile landscape burst with the bounty of their sacred union—meadows, orchards, and gardens tended by a people who knew how to live in sustained symbiosis with nature.

In the bustling streets of the harbor town, bare-breasted worshippers gathered to witness the sacred games of bull-leaping. Lithe figures, men and women, natives and outlanders, vaulted over the great beasts' horns in a whirling dance of courage and skill, the beating of drums and the pulse of the earth intertwined in joyous syncopation.

Heavenly images washed over me—priestesses preparing sacred herbs in sunlit courtyards, artisans crafting labrys axes and vibrant frescoes, children playing along the shore without fear. It was a world of startling peace and beauty, where the highest technology was the sundial, tracking the seasons using the motion of the stars. A time where technology existed in balance with nature, nurturing rather than extracting its vital source.

But even as I lost myself in the ecstasy of this timeless moment, I felt a shadow fall across the sun. In a heartbeat, two millennia had passed and, on the first day of spring, a new beast rose over the horizon. The wild goat of violence, domination, and greed slaughtered the man-bull in the labyrinthine corridors of his peaceful home.

Horrified, the great mother earth convulsed beneath my feet, and the distant peak of the holy mountain began to glow with the fires of an apocalypse.

Through eyes that were not my own, I watched the sky turn to poison and the sea rise up in walls of boiling death. The great eruption of Thera had begun, and the heavenly world was ending in a cataclysm of smoke and magma.

I clung to the spirit of an old scribe as she raced through the doomed streets of her city, her arms laden with the sacred scrolls that held the wisdom of the ages. Hot ash stung my eyes and coated my lungs, but still she ran, seeking the hidden caves of Mount Ida where the knowledge might sleep in safety until the world was ready to receive it once more.

As the vision shifted, I felt the weight of five centuries pressing down upon me like the folds of a burial shroud. I saw the Mycenaeans descend upon the wounded land, their swords drunk with the blood of the Mother's children.

The hot sting of the Goddess's tears burned my cheeks. Her rage and grief shook the earth, bringing drought, famine, and quakes that would last for centuries. Through it all, I clung to the spirit of a young soul whose memories I now shared—a woman who would become one of the last refugees to flee the isle of Crete, famine-stricken and violent.

I felt the weight of the fragmented knowledge she carried in her memory, the inherited shards of the Great Mother's wisdom she'd absorbed from the nine sacred scrolls left behind.

Her grief was a visceral force, rising in my gorge like bile as she was forced to adapt to life in the unfamiliar foreign land. Though the language and customs were strange to her, she clung fiercely to her identity as a daughter of the Goddess, practicing her sacred arts in secret.

Night after night, guided by the ancient techniques of the art of memory, she wove the fragmented threads of ancestral wisdom into a new form—a codex blending imagery with a disguised script of her own invention. Through this painstaking work, she sought to preserve what remained of her culture's legacy, praying that one day, her descendants might unlock its secrets.

In the end, it was Gaza that offered her sanctuary, though its streets and shrines were strange to her grieving eyes. By flickering lamplight, she wove the fading memories of her people into the last paragraph of a codex of defiance.

"Canaan's scribes set out to eliminate us," she sang, her hands moving ahead of her mind, in each glyph the blood-stained memory of her ancestors. "They forgot nature's beauty, and hasten to eliminate the false gods."

Then, I saw it—a golden calf exposed as a false idol by two variants of the same goddess-forsaken curse. A bull burned in a fire, ground to powder, and scattered on the sea as she watched with her knees sunk in the blood-stained sand of the seashore.

"In the Gaza land to forget your distinguished lineage," she wrote, her tears staining the painted glyphs. "We were fair, and then wearily forgotten. A silent fugitive is a worthless, weary thing. We've lost our humanity. I am a fugitive flower."

The Great Mother was dethroned, her sacred snakes and pomegranates now recast as symbols of evil and temptation. The wise women—once revered as herbal healers—were hunted as witches, their knowledge suppressed and feared. Their ancient wisdom, once passed down through genera-tions, was now collated into a single sacred book, copied blindly for millennia by scribes who could no longer decipher its true meaning. With each iteration, the original message was further subverted, twisted to fit the beliefs and fears of the present age.

The voice of the Goddess, once a beacon of hope and healing, had been silenced, replaced by the cruel edicts of a patriarchal god. And though her daughters fought to keep her memory alive in secret, they too were slowly ground down beneath the weight of centuries of oppression, until only scattered fragments of her truth remained, hidden in the margins of history.

With a ragged gasp, I surfaced from the depths of the vision, my skin slick with sweat and brine. The pink sands of Elafonissi cradled my aching body, and the Cretan sun pressed down on me like the weight of a thousand unseen eyes.

I lay there for a long moment, my mind reeling as I tried to make sense of all I had seen and felt. The visions had been so real, so visceral—more than a dream, more than a mere hallucination. It was as if I had truly walked in the memories of a Caphtorim sister, witnessing the rise and fall of her lost world through the prism of her unending grief.

But how could that be possible? How could a mere manuscript, no matter how steeped in mystery, grant me access to the lost history of an entire civilization? Was Pandora the true architect behind this surreal experience? Were the psychoactive properties of the kykeon triggering a trippy interpretation of my hopes and fears?

I had no conclusive answers, no evidence to share with the world. Only a bone-deep certainty that the Voynich Manuscript and the tale of this refugee were more than just ink on parchment, more than mere ciphers to be broken. They were a bridge across time and consciousness, a reminder that though empires might crumble and certainties dissolve, the human heart could endure the darkest of ages.

I could still feel the heat of her tears on my cheeks, still hear the echo of her voice in my mind. For so long, she had carried the burden of her people's legacy alone, a fragile flame cupped against the howling dark. But now, I understood that she had passed the torch to me, to Bastian, to Regina and all who sought the deeper truths hidden in the margins of history.

With a groan, I pushed myself upright, my body aching in a hundred places. Sand caked my clothes and hair, and my pack lay half-buried in the sand a few feet away. The bag I had left behind, in the Calypso. Wincing, I crawled over to retrieve it, fishing out my laptop from its depths.

A small, folded piece of paper fluttered out from between the bag's zippers. Curious, I reached for it, my fingers trembling slightly as I unfolded the note.

Dearest Amalia,

I wish I could be there to welcome you back, to share in the awe and wonder of this moment. But my journey must take me down a different road, at least for now.

I have no doubt that our paths will cross again someday. Until then, please share the legacy of countless generations of women who have fought to preserve the sacred knowledge.

Until we meet again,
    E.H.

Carefully folding the note, I slipped it back into my pack, and opened my laptop.

For a long moment, I stared at the blinking cursor on the screen, trying to find the words to capture all I had experienced. But where to begin? How to convey the pulse of the Earth Mother's heart, the shimmer of the Bull's flank in the Minoan sun?

I closed my eyes, and let my fingers dance across the keys, writing not with my conscious mind but with the voice of my dreaming soul. The words poured out of me in a torrent, a song of loss and love and remembering, the story of a world that refused to be silenced by the ravages of time.

I wrote for hours, until the sun had begun its long arc toward the horizon and my hands cramped with exhaustion. But still I kept on, driven by the need to bear witness, to give form to the formless whispers that had taken root in my marrow.

When at last I finished, I felt a great weight lift from my shoulders, as if in telling a refugee's story, I had somehow unburdened her spirit of the need to carry it alone.

With a sigh, I closed my eyes and let the susurrus of wind and wave lull me into a dreamless slumber—the first I had known since the Voynich had turned my life upside down.

For a brief moment, I would rest in the strength and purpose I had found, cradled in the arms of a goddess whose love endured beyond the ending of an age.

CHAPTER 34

The Ascent

I stumbled into my apartment, my mind still spinning from the whirlwind of the past few weeks. Exhausted, I collapsed onto the couch and reached for my phone. Once again, Bastian's number went straight to voicemail, but the daily barrage of notifications from his YouTube channel assured me he was alive and well, already capitalizing on our misadventures. "Unlock the Secrets of Atlantis!" one click-baity title proclaimed, followed by "The Incredible Origins of the Antikythera Mechanism!" the next day. I had no doubt that psychedelics, poppy goddesses, and the Phaistos Disk would all make appearances soon enough. If there was one thing Bastian Ham excelled at, it was monetizing a juicy story.

At least Regina was on the mend. We'd spoken briefly while I was still in Athens, her voice strained but filled with determination as she explained her decision to stay in Greece a bit longer, to forge stronger bonds with her sisters in the Order. "But when I'm back in the city, you'd better have a feast waiting for me," she'd teased, and I could practically hear her smile through the phone.

And then there was me, pacing the confines of my shoebox

apartment, caught in an endless loop of indecision. My inbox overflowed with emails from The Rag, their tone growing more impatient and demanding with each unanswered message. They were salivating over the story behind Hathaway's disappearance, dangling promises of wealth and acclaim in exchange for the exclusive scoop. I couldn't deny the temptation—a biweekly paycheck and an escape from this cramped Hoboken flat sounded like a dream after the financial strain of funding my own travel.

But every time I sat down to write the piece my editor so desperately wanted, the faces of my heroes danced before my eyes. An ancient scribe, Elizebeth, Ethel, Mercy, the brave souls of the Cretan resistance, and countless others who had sacrificed everything in the pursuit of truth. And then there were the unsung heroes, the librarians and archivists at the British School at Athens, painstakingly digitizing the John Pendlebury Family Papers and blogging about Mercy's achievements so that they wouldn't be lost to time.

And of course, there were the mighty academics at Yale, who had the foresight and courage to open-source the Voynich Manuscript research and the Voynich family archive, inviting a multidisciplinary gang of ninjas to join the hunt for answers. There was wisdom in that approach, the same collaborative, interdisciplinary approach that had allowed John Seiradakis and his colleagues in the Antikythera Mechanism Research Project to crack the secrets of that ancient wonder. We walk farther when we walk together, pooling our knowledge and resources in the service of a common goal.

How could I do justice to their stories in a three-thousand-word fluff piece, watered down and sanitized for mass consumption? The very thought made my stomach churn. I couldn't betray their legacies like that, couldn't sacrifice authenticity on the altar of page views and ad revenue.

For a fleeting moment, I considered joining forces with

Bastian, throwing myself into the YouTube fray and fighting for scraps of attention in the soulless arena of algorithms and trending tags. So many great educators and charismatic communicators managed to cut through despite everything. But the idea of plastering my face across thumbnails and competing with conspiracy theorists for clicks left a bitter taste in my mouth. That path wasn't for me.

No, I realized with sudden clarity, there was only one way forward. I had to tell this story on my own terms, in my own voice. And that meant starting my own publishing company, embracing the freedom and responsibility that came with charting my own course.

Books had always been my first love, and what better medium to explore the nuances and complexities of this tale? To weave together fact and fiction, history and speculation, all through the lens of my own experiences and sensibilities? It would be a tightrope act, balancing rigor and readability, but I was determined to make it work.

Sir Arthur Evans, problematic as he was, had understood the power of narrative. He'd transformed Knossos into a household name while Monastiraki languished in obscurity, all through the alchemy of storytelling. Knowledge may be power, but story is the spark that ignites the imagination, that inspires us to care and to question and to act.

So I won't write a dry academic tome, nor will I churn out a sensationalized exposé. Instead, I will craft our story, our truth, with all the creative flourishes and personal touches that make it uniquely mine. Because in the end, that's all any of us can do—assemble the fragments of history and legend, hold them up to the light of our own understanding, and share what we see with the world.

And share I did. For months, I poured myself into this manuscript, my trusty keyboard clacking away day and night, through weekends and holidays. I wrote with a passion I'd never known before, the words flowing through me in an unstoppable current until at last, I reached this final passage.

But there's something you need to know, dear reader. Something raw and real and terrifying. The book is finished, but my journey is far from over. As I type these words, my bank account dwindles to double digits. The future stretches before me, vast and uncertain, and I'm scared. Scared that I've poured my heart and soul into this labor of love, and it still won't be enough. That I'll have to go crawling back to The Rag, tail between my legs, a failure.

So if this story has touched you in any way, if it's ignited even the tiniest spark of curiosity or empathy or wonder, please, leave a review. Recommend it to a friend. Drop me a line on social media using #TheExFiles and let me know how it made you feel. Because knowing that my words have reached even one kindred spirit, that they've made a difference in some small way—that's what will keep me going. That's what will give me the strength to keep chasing the truth, no matter where it leads.

There's just one last thing I need to do. One more leap of faith to take. I open my laptop and, with shaking fingers, type out a message to Bastian and Regina.

Hey team!

I think I know where one of the 'nine realms' scrolls is. Meet me at JFK tomorrow, 6 p.m. We've got a mystery to solve.

Love, Rosie
P.S. I attach the manuscript of my upcoming novel.

I hover over the "send" button, heart in my throat. I was revealing too much. So much. This story has already cost me everything—my stability, my certainty, my last few thousand dollars. But in the end, it's not even a choice. The siren song of the unknown is calling, and I am powerless to resist.

The message whooshes into the digital ether, and with it, the last of my reservations. Come what may, I'm ready to face a certain ex and to jump headfirst into the next rabbit hole.

My pen name is Amalia Rose, and this is my story.
17 June 2024
ko-fi.com/theexfiles
P.S. The facts are indeed stranger than the fiction. Check them out on the next pages.

Historical Timeline and Sources

C. 26000 – C. 21000 BCE

'Venus' figures from this period found everywhere around the world. [1]

C. 4000 – C. 1700 BCE

Taurus was the constellation through which the Sun rose on the vernal equinox at that time. [2,3,4]

C. 3100 – C. 1450 BCE

Minoan civilization (pre-Mycenaean.) [5]

C. 2285 – C. 2250 BCE

The first known author in the history of the world is poet Enheduanna, Mesopotamian high priestess of the moon goddess Inanna. [6,7,8]

C. 2000 – C. 1700 BCE

Abundant evidence for the use of parchment with texts, presumably written in ink, in Minoan Crete. The documents themselves are gone but the medium left its negative traces on the backs of seal-impressed clay nodules. [9,10,11]

Hundreds of Minoan seals and sealings [12,13,14] found in Monastiraki inside three 'archives.' Sealings in Monastiraki differ from other sites as they are used to secure comestibles inside pithoi and other movable objects. Talismanic seals are only present in Monastiraki.[15]

A shrine and a unique pair of figurines was excavated at Monastiraki: a naked woman suckling a young adult.[16]

C. 1850 – C. 1600 BCE

Dating of the Phaistos disk, discovered in the Minoan palace-site of Phaistos.[17]

Phaistos disk decipherment claims by G. Owens & J. Coleman suggest it refers to the pregnant goddess that "shines" and the other side refers to the goddess that "sets."[18,19,20]

Phaistos disk decipherment claims by Wolfgang Reczko suggest side A shows astronomical eclipse information, which belong to a complete Saros cycle beginning 1377 BCE, valid for the Phaistos Palace location only.[21]

C. 1790 BCE

Dating of the Minoan Moulds of Palaikastro for making objects to use in astronomical predictions of solar and lunar eclipses.[22,23]

C. 1603 – C. 1601 BCE

Thera eruption.[24,25]

C. 1600 BCE – C. 392 CE

Eleusinian Mysteries.[26,27]

C. 1628 BCE

Thera eruption connected to the first exodus from Egypt.[28,29,30]

C. 1550 BCE

The Tempest Stele erected by pharaoh Ahmose I. describes a great storm striking Egypt during this time.[31,32]

Minoan-style bull-leaping frescoes in the Egyptian Delta site of Tell el-Dab'a, the pharaoh's palace in ancient Avaris.[33]

Keftiu remedies mentioned in Papyrus Ebers IX, 16–19, an Egyptian medical papyrus of herbal knowledge. The papyrus includes chapters on gynecological matters including contraception.[34]

C. 1550 BCE

A 15th century BCE text indicate the existence of scribal schools in Canaan.[35]

C. 1500 BCE

Aegean as Philistine origin:

Pottery fragments found in Philistine cemetery bearing inscriptions in non-Semitic languages, including one in a Cypro-Minoan script.[36,37,38]

Most common religious artifact found in Philistine sites are goddess figurines consistent with ancient Aegean religion.

A DNA study carried out on skeletons at Ashkelon shows similarities to that of ancient Cretans.[39]

Hebrew Bible authors 'make it clear' Philistines were not like them: *This "uncircumcised" group comes from the "Land of Caphtor"* (modern-day Crete)[40]"As for the Avvim, they had dwelled in settlements as far as Gaza until the Caphtorim, who came out from Caphtor, annihilated them and settled in their place." Gaza was a main Philistine settlement.[41]

Bull figurines are common finds on archaeological sites across the Levant.[42]

C. 1550 – C. 1292 BCE

From the Eighteenth Dynasty of Egypt come four texts containing names and spells against disease in the Keftiu language.[43]

1463 BCE

Keftiu depicted in the tomb of Sennemut at Thebes during the reign of Hatshepsut, the female pharaoh of Egypt. Hatshepsut re-established a number of trade networks and her foreign policy was mainly peaceful.[44,45,46]

C. 1414 – C. 1378 BCE

Circular seal of Queen Ty, Great Royal Wife of the Egyptian pharaoh Amenhotep III buried in a royal Tomb at Agia Triadha, Crete. The Queen was known for her intelligence and strong personality, gaining the respect of foreign leaders willing to deal directly with her. She played an active role in foreign relations and was the first Egyptian queen to have her name recorded on official acts.[47,48,49]

C. 1200 BCE

Late Bronze Age collapse associated with environmental change, earthquakes, drought, famine, violence, mass migration, and the destruction of many cities from Pylos to Gaza.[50]

C. 8TH CENTURY BCE

Homeric Hymn to Demeter.

C. 534 – C. 509 BCE

Nine Sibylline Books are offered to the last king of Rome. Six are destroyed by fire.[51]

496 BCE

Sibylline books advise the introduction of the Eleusinian triad Gods worship in order to end the drought.[52,53]

C. 283 – C. 246 BCE

Founding of the Library of Alexandria.[54]

C. 287 – C. 212 BCE

Lifespan of Archimedes. He visits the Library of Alexandria. He creates a series of spheres that show the motion of the Sun, Moon and five planets.[55,56]

205 BCE

Two suns and meteor showers reported over Southern Italy.[57]

12 MAY 205 BCE

Full Moon of Month 1 of the Antikythera Mechanism dial according to C. Carman, J. Evans and Tony Freeth[58,59]

4 April 204 BCE

Cybele, the Magna Mater welcomed as a roman national goddess.[60]

83 BCE

Three 'original' Sibylline Books destroyed in the fire of the Temple of Jupiter on the Capitol, during the civil wars under Sulla, the Roman dictator.[61]

66 BCE

Following a ferocious three-year campaign, Crete was conquered for Rome. The roman capital was set at Gortyn on the slopes of Mount Ida.[62]

c. 70 – c. 60 BCE

Antikythera Wreck.[63]

48 BCE

Fire at the Library of Alexandria caused by Julius Caesar's civil war.[64]

381

The beginning of the persecution of pagans under Theodosius I[65]

392

The closing of the Eleusinian Mysteries by the emperor Theodosius I[66]

391

The Serapeum destroyed by Roman soldiers. After the destruction, a monastery was established.[67] It's destruction led Hypatia to focus her efforts on preserving seminal mathematical books.[68]

MARCH 415

Hypatia's murder.[69]

C. 1280

Ramon Llull publishes the Ars.[70]

C. 1404 – C. 1438

Publication of the Voynich Manuscript.[71,72]

1428

Matteuccia de Francesco was put on trial for witchcraft. Her case was one of the first European witch trials, and likely the first case where a witch is mentioned flying in the air.[73]

C. 1460

Publication of the Cadamosto's Herbal Manuscript.[74]

1666

Margaret Cavendish, the Duchess of Newcastle, publishes *The Description of a New World, Called The Blazing-World*.[75,76,77]

1883

Publication of Message of Psychic Science to Mothers and Nurses by Mary Boole.[78,79]

1895

E.L. Voynich's affair with Sidney Reilly—the Ace of Spies—employed by a Scotland Yard's Special Branch. Reilly may have been reporting on her political activities.[80]

1896

Publication of *The Gadfly* by E.L. Voynich.[81,82]

C. 1900

Archaeologist Arthur Evans excavates the Bronze Age site of Knossos on Crete in the early 20th century.[83]

1901

Captain Dimitrios Kontos and a crew of sponge divers from Symi island discover the Antikythera wreck and mechanism.[84]

1911

The Triangle Shirtwaist Company fire in Greenwich Village.[85,86]

Crete: the forerunner of Greece published by Harriet Boyd Hawes and Charles Henry Hawes.[87]

1912

Wilfrid Voynich acquires the Voynich Manuscript.[88]

1912

Marie Jenney Howe founds Heterodoxy. Based in Greenwich Village, it had just one requirement for membership: An applicant must "not be orthodox in her opinion."[89,90]

1914

J. Edgar Hoover accepts an entry-level position as messenger in the orders department at the Library of Congress where he learns the value of collating material. A few years prior during high school debates, he argued against women's right to vote.[91]

1918

Friedmans' codebreaker class photo with encoded message: 'Knowledge is Powe(r).'[92]

EARLY 1920S

E.L. Voynich studies the herbal folios and documents findings in her notebooks. Poppy and Cannabis mentioned in her notes.[93,94]

The Friedmans support John M. Manly at disproving Newbold's Voynich Manuscript decipherment claims.[95,96]

1926 – 1927

Enigmatic Gold Ring from Knossos (KN Zf 13) found by E.J. Forsdyke in the Tomb IX at Mavro Spelaio, near Knossos. Its inscription is spirally written as the one of the Phaistos Disk. Forsdyke called it a "signet-ring, possibly talismanic."[97,98]

1928

Sir Arthur Evans publishes *The Palace of Minos, Volume 2, Part 2*, where he delivers a racist interpretation of the fresco which he named the "Captain of the Blacks."[99,100]

1933

John Pendlebury (and Arthur Evans) publish *A handbook to the palace of Minos, Knossos, with its dependencies.*[101] Much tension between Evans and Pendlebury. Pendlebury wanted to write according to his own outline and views, while Evans merely wanted Pendlebury to ghostwrite it.[102,103,104]

APRIL 1934 – 1936

Archeologist Mercy Money-Coutts, who had started her career as a librarian at British School at Athens, undertook a number of expeditions in central Crete with John and Hilda Pendlebury and others. These travels aimed to register sites and routes. Mercy drew the seal stones and pottery patterns to illustrate John's book: *The Archaeology of Crete: An Introduction*. Together with Pendlebury she undertook many excavations.[105,106,107,108]

1937

Canadian government asked Elizebeth S. Friedman's help with the case of an opium dealer. Her solution to a complicated unknown Chinese enciphered code, was key to several successful convictions.[109]

1938

Heinrich Himmler sends teams all over the world to search for the origins of the Aryan race that had survived from the lost city of Atlantis.[110,111,112]

1938

Regina Anderson becomes the first ever African-American head of a New York Public Library branch, on 115th Street.[113]

1939 – 1944

Mercy Money-Coutts works at Bletchley Park, the UK's Government Code and Cypher School, where ultra secret intelligence was handled and the German cipher code cracked in 1940.[114]

17 JUNE 1940

Joan Clarke arrives at Bletchley Park. She quickly becomes a practitioner of Banburismus, a cryptanalytic process developed by Alan Turing.[115]

20 MAY 1941 – 1 JUNE 1941

The Battle of Crete: Greek and other Allied forces, along with Cretan civilians defend Crete against the Nazi invasion.[116,117,118,119,120]

1942

Monastiraki excavated illegally by the German Archaeological Institute.[121,122,123,124]

Monastiraki (c. 2000 - 1700 BCE,) never reoccupied after a fire, making it a pristine Minoan site.

Photography of the site is not allowed and the villagers who open the site to visitors enforce the ban rigorously. Nazi interest came from Pendlebury's notes.[125]

Subsequent excavations found graters and other artifacts connected with cult/ritual contexts. Evidence of production of wine with honey and herbs.[126,127,128]

Hundreds of Minoan seals and sealings[129] found in three 'archives,' one of them at the site excavated by the Nazi. Sealings in Monastiraki differ from other sites as they as used to secure comestibles inside pithoi and other movable objects. Talismanic seals are only present in Monastiraki.[130,131]

1943

Elizebeth S. Friedman uncovers a South American Nazi spy ring. J. Edgar Hoover takes full credit for her achievements on behalf of the FBI.[132]

25 MAY 1944

William F. Friedman sends letter to E.L Voynich requesting a higher quality reproduction of the Voynich Manuscript so it can be studied by a working group of scholars. E.L Voynich responds agreeing to the reproduction. [133]

The First Voynich Manuscript Study Group is formed.[134]

1945

By the end of the WWII, Elizebeth S. Friedman's team broke three separate Enigma machines and contributed 4,000 decoded messages to the fight against Nazi domination. J. Edgar Hoover's FBI took the credit. [135]

1949

Grace Hopper was part of the team that developed the UNIVAC I. Grace led the development of one of the first COBOL compilers. [136]

1953 AND 1976

Antikythera week expeditions by the Cousteau team who found bones, coins and bronze statues. Coins helped date the wreck. [137,138]

1962

As part of the Friedmans Second Voynich Manuscript Study Group, a small team of 'dedicated wives' transcribed and keypunched the Voynichese so it could be processed by early computers. [139]

Stephanie "Steve" Shirley starts a software firm devoted to hiring women. Having experienced workplace sexism, she wanted to create job opportunities for women. Her team programmed the Concorde's black box flight recorder. [140] She was born in Dortmund, during Nazi Germany and became a WWII child refugee.

1966
Elizebeth S. Friedman writes partial autobiography. [141]

1978

National Security Agency's M.E. D'Imperio (Mary D'Imperio) published *The Voynich Manuscript: An. Elegant. Enigma,* a detailed account of the

research on the Voynich Manuscript, including extensive commentary by
Elizebeth Friedman.[142]

Mentions:
57v as possible 'key,'
Linear key sequences in 49v and 66r,
'mnemonic language,'
'clock face' in Rosette folio (f86.)
Ars Memorativa and Ramon Lull

Quotes: "The manuscript may constitute what now is called a
pharmacopeia," Elizabeth Friedman, 1962.

2002

Archaeological evidence on the use of opium in the Minoan world
published by Helen Askitopoulou and Eleni Konsolak[143]

2005

Cretan John Seiradakis, son of Mercy Money-Coutts (later Mercy
Seiradakis) becomes a founding member of the Antikythera Mechanism
Research Project. John made significant contributions to identify the
astronomical events of the mechanism. [144,145,146,147]

2013 – 2015

Scientist finds that the astronomical events on the Antikythera
mechanism work best for latitudes in the range of 33.3–37.0 degrees
north.[148,149]

2014

Scientists discover the that the full moon of month 1 of the Antikythera
Mechanism dial is set to 12 May 205 B.C.E.[150,151]

2016

Computer scientist, Joy Buolamwini, founded the *Algorithmic Justice League*. The AJL uses art, research, and policy advocacy to increase awareness about the use of artificial intelligence and the harms and biases it can pose.[152]

2017

Antikythera expedition by marine archaeologists from the Greek Ephorate of Underwater Antiquities and Lund University in Sweden find a bronze disk with four tabs with the image of a bull 'reminiscent' of the Antikythera Mechanism. It may have adorned the case the Antikythera Mechanism was housed in.[153,154,155,156] Dr. Brendan Foley, a marine archaeologist, was a co-director of the project.

2011 -2017 Return to Antikythera Team profiles and achievements deleted from all Antikythera official sources, including Foley's page. Some claim this is part of a nationalist campaign.[157]

The Ministry of Culture and Sports (YPPOA) announces underwater research in Antikythera exclusively "Greek participation from now on" also announced findings and conclusions already known for years.[158]

Greek press reports about illegal activities at Antikythera from 2018.[159]

2017

Using an algorithmic decipherment technique, researchers Greg Kondrak and Bradley Hauer determined the likely underlying language used to write the Voynich: Hebrew.[160,161,162]

2018

Monica Yokubinas publishes her speculative translation of the Voynich manuscript using Hebrew as 'root' language. The text mentions Gaza.[163]

She also publishes her translation and identification of the medicinal herbology folios.[164]

2019

Survey of subjective "God encounter experiences": Comparisons among naturally occurring experiences and those occasioned by the classic psychedelics by Roland R. Griffiths et al.[165]

2021

Emily M. Bender, Timnit Gebru, Angelina McMillan-Major, and Margaret Mitchell publish the paper, *On the Dangers of Stochastic Parrots: Can Language Models Be Too Big?*[166,167] Researchers are subject to significant backlash from Google.[168]

Tony Freeth, David Higgon, Aris Dacanalis, Lindsay MacDonald, Myrto Georgakopoulou & Adam Wojcik publish the paper, *A Model of the Cosmos in the ancient Greek Antikythera Mechanism*.[169,170]

2023

The kick off of the Vesuvius Challenge, a machine learning and computer vision competition to read the charred remains of the Herculaneum Papyri.[171]

202...

Over to you! Make your mark.
#TheExFiles

ko-fi.com/theexfiles

Afterword

That though I cannot be Henry the Fifth, or Charles the Second; yet, I will endeavour to be, Margaret the First: and, though I have neither Power, Time nor Occasion, to be a great Conqueror, like Alexander, or Cesar; yet, rather than not be Mistress of a World, since Fortune and the Fates would give me none, I have made One of my own. And thus, believing, or, at least, hoping, that no Creature can, or will, Envy me for this World of mine, I remain, Noble Ladies, Your Humble Servant, M. Newcastle.

> — *THE DESCRIPTION OF A NEW WORLD,*
> *CALLED THE BLAZING-WORLD* BY
> DUCHESS MARGARET CAVENDISH, 1660

Transcript of Elizebeth Friedman's Notes Image

YIAYIA
Greek word. Used often in VMS
Modern meaning: Grandmother
Ancient meaning: Woman
Priestess

Predominance of the Hebrew word for poppy and poppy
images!

Last Paragraph: ? Gaza ?

r1
A woman is taken. Her mother wants the village to rise up
because the woman is innocent.

? Persephone abduction ?

"how long until end of sexual misconduct, emasculation by
crushing a broken man"
16r

"Arrogant toward the bull"
40v

"Life of women to have value now"
"make a search of the forest"
"mother makes her wine to
infiltrate mystic realm"
"Woman famished"
"Pomegranate"
? Hymn to Demeter and
Persephone ?
8r

"So not to become pregnant with fetus"
"To seize the Lord of the fetus"
"Dead body from the womb and she is grieving"
? A guide for abortion ?
40v

Aristolochia
Hairy Birthwort

Notes

1. THE BLOG POST

1. You can find free digital copies of the Voynich Manuscript at:
     - Voynich Manuscript digitized by Yale University Library
     - Voynich Manuscript folio browser at the Voynich.Ninja
     Or you can purchase a physical copy here:
     - The Voynich Manuscript by Yale University Press

15. REVELATIONS

1. The Gadfly by Ethel Lilian Voynich (digitized at archive.org)

HISTORICAL TIMELINE AND SOURCES

1. Venus Figurine - Wikipedia.
2. *The Origin of the Greek Constellations* by Bradley E. Schaefer, 2006.
3. Taurus - Wikipedia.
4. Sacred Bull - Wikipedia. Golden Calf - Wikipedia.
5. Minoan Civilization - Wikipedia.
6. YouTube Lecture: She Who Wrote: Enheduanna and Women of Mesopotamia ca. 3400-2000 BC, by The Morgan Library and Museum, 2022.
7. Enheduanna - Wikipedia.
8. The Exaltation of Inana.
9. *Non-scribal Communication Media in the Bronze Age Aegean and Surrounding Areas. The semantics of a-literate and proto-literate media* by Anna Margherita Jasink, Judith Weingarten, Silvia Ferrara, Firenze University Press.
10. *A Minoan-Mycenaean scribal legacy for converting rough copies into fair copies* by Gregory Nagy, 2020.
11. *Echoes of a Minoan-Mycenaean scribal legacy in a story told by Herodotus* by Gregory Nagy, 2020.
12. *The Jewels that Speak to Us: Seals and Signets from the Bronze Age Aegean*, Youtube lecture by Dr. Jan Crowley.
13. *Digital Acquisition and Modeling of the Minoan seals and sealings kept in two Italian museums* (Youtube) by Niccolò Albertini, Anna Margherita Jasink, and Barbara Montecchi.

14. *Never the twain shall meet: reflections on text and image in Minoan Crete*, Youtube lecture by Prof John Bennet.

15. *The protopalatial multiple sealing system. New evidence from Monastiraki* by Anastasia Tzigounaki, 2000.

16. Monastiraki by Minoancrete.com.

17. Phaistos Disc - Wikipedia.

18. *Dr Gareth Owens gives a new religious interpretation of the Phaistos Disc*, ekt.gr.

19. *Decrypting the Phaistos Disk: Gareth Owens* at TEDxHeraklion.

20. YouTube Lecture: *Steve Kershaw - The Phaistos Disk: Mystery, Forgery, and (Pseudo)archaeology*, Oxford University.

21. *Analyzing and dating the structure of the Phaistos Disk Original Paper*, 12 September 2009, Springer.

22. Minoan Moulds of Palaikastro - Wikipedia.

23. *A Minoan eclipse calculator* by M. Tsikritsis et al, 2013.

24. Minoan Eruption - Wikipedia.

25. *Medical papyri describe the effects of the Santorini eruption on human health, and date the eruption to August 1603–March 1601 BC* by Siro Igino Trevisanato.

26. Eleusinian Mysteries - Wikipedia.

27. *The Ritual Path of Initiation into the Eleusinian Mysteries* by Mara Lynn Keller, Ph.D.Mara Lynn Keller, part of the Rosicrucian Digest, volume 87, 2009.

28. *The Parting of the Sea: How Volcanoes, Earthquakes, and Plagues Shaped the Exodus Story* by Barbara J. Sivertsen, 2009.

29. Astrological Age - Wikipedia.

30. *Oedipus Judaicus : allegory in the Old Testament* by Drummond, W. (William), 1770?-1828.

31. Tempest Stele - Wikipedia.

32. Ahmose I - Wikipedia.

33. Minoan frescoes from Tell el-Dab'a - Wikipedia.

34. *Memories into Images: Aegean and Aegean-like Objects in New Kingdom Egyptian Theban Tombs* by Uroš Matić, Cambridge Archaeological Journal 29, June 2019.

35. Scribe by Jewish Virtual Library.

36. Archaeologists Find First-ever Philistine Cemetery in Israel, Haaretz.

37. *On Jan Best's "Decipherment" of Minoan Linear A* by Gary Rendsburg, 1982.

38. *Know thine enemy: DNA study solves ancient riddle of origins of the Philistines* by Amanda Borschel-Dan, 2019.

39. Philistines - Wikipedia.

40. *Ancient DNA may reveal origin of the Philistines. Historical accounts and archaeology agree that the biggest villains of the Hebrew Bible were 'different'—but how different were they really?* by Kristin Romey, 2019.

41. *When Did the Philistines Really Arrive in Ancient Palestine?* by Caleb Howells, 2023.
42. Sacred Bull - Wikipedia.
43. Minoan Language - Wikipedia.
44. *Memories into Images: Aegean and Aegean-like Objects in New Kingdom Egyptian Theban Tombs* by Uroš Matić, Cambridge Archaeological Journal 29, June 2019.
45. *Civilization of Greece in the bronze age* by H. R. Hall, 1928.
46. Hatshepsut - Wikipedia.
47. *Archaeology Of Crete: Introduction* by J.D.S. Pendlebury.
48. Tiye - Wikipedia.
49. *Tiye: One of the Most Influential Women of Ancient Egypt* by Natalia Klimczac.
50. Late Bronze Age collapse - Wikipedia.
51. Sibylline Books - Wikipedia.
52. Ceres - Britannica.
53. Dionysius of Halicarnassus.
54. Library of Alexandria - Wikipedia.
55. Archimedes - Wikipedia.
56. *The Planetarium of Archimedes*, Michael Wright, History of Science, Technology and Medicine, London's Imperial College.
57. *Meteor Beliefs Project: Meteorite worship in the ancient Greek and Roman worlds* by A. McBeath & A. D. Gheorghe, WGN, Journal of the International Meteor Organization, vol. 33, no. 5, p. 135-144.
58. *On the epoch of the Antikythera mechanism and its eclipse predictor* by Christián C. Carman and James Evans, 15 November 2014.
59. YouTube Lecture: *The Antikythera Mechanism: A Shocking Discovery from Ancient Greece*, Dr. Tony Freeth, Stanford.
60. *The sea voyage of Magna Mater* by Aleksandra Nikoloska, Ph. D. Ss. Cyril and Methodius University, 2012.
61. Sibylline Books - Wikipedia.
62. Crete and Cyrenaica - Wikipedia. Quintus Caecilius Metellus Creticus - Wikipedia.
63. Antikythera Wreck - Wikipedia.
64. Library of Alexandria - Wikipedia.
65. Persecution of pagans under Theodosius_I - Wikipedia.
66. Eleusinian Mysteries - Wikipedia.
67. Serapeum of Alexandria - Wikipedia.
68. *Learned Women In The Alexandrian Scholarship And Society Of Late Hellenism* by Maria Dzielska.
69. Hypatia - Wikipedia.
70. Priani, Ernesto, "Ramon Llull", The Stanford Encyclopedia of Philosophy (Spring 2021 Edition), Edward N. Zalta (ed.)
71. Voynich Manuscript - Wikipedia.

72. *Voynich Manuscript* Digitized by Yale University Library. *The Voynich Manuscript* physical book, commentary by Raymond Clemens.

73. Matteuccia de Francesco - Wikipedia.

74. New York Public Library Spencer Collection Ms. 65.

75. YouTube Lecture: *This 400 Year Old Science Fiction Story Inspired Alan Moore* by Media Death Cult.

76. Free eBook at gutenberg.org: *The Description of a New World, Called the Blazing-World* by Margareth Cavendish.

77. The Blazing World - Wikipedia.

78. *Message of Psychic Science to Mothers and Nurses* (digitized free copy at archive.org) by Mary Boole.

79. *The Extraordinary Case of the Boole Family* by Moira Chas.

80. Ethel Voynich - Wikipedia.

81. The Gadfly - Wikipedia.

82. The Gadfly by Ethel Lilian Voynich (free digitized copy at archive.org.)

83. *The palace of Minos: a comparative account of the successive stages of the early Cretan civilization as illustrated by the discoveries at Knossos by Sir Arthur Evans* 1921-1935.

84. Antikythera Mechanism - Wikipedia.

85. *About the Jefferson Market Library* at nypl.org.

86. International Ladies' Garment Workers' Union Archives at the Kheel Center, Cornell University.

87. *Crete: the forerunner of Greece* by Harriet Boyd Hawes and Charles Henry Hawes.

88. Voynich Manuscript - Wikipedia.

89. *The All-Woman Secret Society That Paved the Way for Modern Feminism* by Laura Kiniry for the Smithsonian Magazine.

90. *Hotbed: Bohemian Greenwich Village and the Secret Club That Sparked Modern Feminism* by Joanna Scutts.

91. J. Edgar Hoover - Wikipedia.

92. Youtube Lecture: *Friedman Knowledge is Power* by George C. Marshall Foundation, 2014.

93. Voynich letters and documents: MS 408 boxes at Beinecke. Photos by Lisa Fagin Davis.

94. Voynich.Ninja discussion thread and files.

95. *The Voynich Manuscript: An. Elegant. Enigma* by M.E. D'Imperio.

96. *Elizebeth Smith Friedman Collection* at the George C. Marshall Research Library. *William F. Friedman Collection* at the George C. Marshall Research Library.

97. Gold signet ring at heraklionmuseum.gr.

98. *Do Inscriptions in Linear A Script belong to different languages ?* Anistor.gr.

99. *Africans in Bronze Age Crete? The "Captain of the Blacks" fresco from Knossos* by Josho Brouwers, 2022.

100. *Palace of Minos at Knossos vol.2; pt.2, page 755 (Captain of the Blacks reference)* by Arthur Evans.
101. *A handbook to the palace of Minos, Knossus, with its dependencies,* by John Pendlebury (and Arthur Evans,) 1933.
102. John Pendlebury - Wikipedia.
103. *The Pendlebury Archive Project* by the British School of Athens.
104. *The magnetic John Pendlebury* by Tom Sawford.
105. *They were taken for spies* by Laura Palazon, 2018.
106. *Mercy Money-Coutts Seiradaki (1910-1993)* by Elizabeth Schofield.
107. Mercy Seiradaki - Wikipedia.
108. *The Archaeology of Crete: An Introduction* by JDS Pendlebury (and Mercy Money-Coutts.)
109. NSA Historical Figures by the National Security Agency.
110. *How the Island of Atlantis Played a Central Role in Nazi Beliefs* Smithsonian channel, 2018.
111. *When Nazis tried to trace Aryan race myth in Tibet* by Vaibhav Purandare, BBC, 2021.
112. *Hitler's Monsters: A Supernatural History of the Third Reich* by Eric Kurlander.
113. *The Librarian at the Nexus of the Harlem Renaissance let Zora Neale Hurston sleep on her couch* by Cara Giaimo, 2018.
114. *Mercy Money-Coutts Seiradaki (1910-1993)* by Elizabeth Schofield.
115. Joan Clarke - Wikipedia.
116. The Battle of Crete, YouTube.
117. Battle of Crete - Wikipedia.
118. *John Pendlebury and the Battle of Crete – Paddy's speech* by by Tom Sawford.
119. *John Pendlebury: The Legendary "Cretan Lawrence"* by Phil Butler, 2018.
120. *John Pendlebury details from Winchester College War Cloister memorial site* by Tom Sawford.
121. *German account of the excavation in English: Forschungen auf Kreta, 1942. Ed. F. Matz. Pp. vii + 166, 122 pll. Berlin: de Gruyter, 1951. DM. 80.*
122. *Archeology in the war zone by Georgia Flouda*, British School at Athens, 2017.
123. *The Mystery of the Eteocretans – Gatekeepers of Crete's Hidden Past* by Phil Butler.
124. *Fight continues for return of Cretan antiquities looted during Nazi occupation*, 2018.
125. *The Archeology of Crete* by JDS Pendlebury. He refers to 'site Kharakas seen by writer.' Map on page 181. Reference on page 291.
126. *The excavation of Monastiraki*, Athanasia Kanta, 1999.
127. *Monastiraki A nursery of European culture* by Athanasia Kanta, 2007.
128. *A Minoan Palace on the slopes of Mount Ida* by Athanasia Kanta, 2008.

129. *The Jewels that Speak to Us: Seals and Signets from the Bronze Age Aegean*, lecture by Dr. Jan Crowley.

130. *The protopalatial multiple sealing system. New evidence from Monastiraki* by Anastasia Tzigounaki, 2000.

131. Document with Map of the Archeological site of Monastiraki: *Territorial Analysis Data Acquisition Methodologies and Strategies for the Reconstruction of the Ancient Landscape in Protohistorical Contexts.*

132. *How America's 'First Female Cryptanalyst' Cracked the Code of Nazi Spies in World War II—and Never Lived to See the Credit* by Suyin Haynes, 2021.

133. Voynich letters and documents: MS 408 boxes at Beinecke. Photos by Lisa Fagin Davis.

134. *The Voynich Manuscript: An. Elegant. Enigma* by M.E. D'Imperio.

135. *How Codebreaker Elizebeth Friedman Fought Nazi Spies For 50 years* by Kirstin Butler, PBS, December 29, 2020.

136. Grace Hopper - Wikipedia.

137. *The Jacques Cousteau Odyssey - Diving For Roman Plunder*, 14 March 1978.

138. Antikythera Wreck - Wikipedia.

139. *The Voynich Manuscript: An. Elegant. Enigma* by M.E. D'Imperio.

140. Steve Shirley - Wikipedia.

141. *Elizebeth Smith Friedman Partial Autobiography, 1966* at the George C. Marshall Research Library.

142. *The Voynich Manuscript: An. Elegant. Enigma* by M.E. D'Imperio

143. *Archaeological evidence on the use of opium in the Minoan world* by Helen Askitopoulou and Eleni Konsolak, December 2002

144. The Antikythera Mechanism Research Project

145. *The Antikythera Mechanism: Decoding an astonishing 2000 years old astronomical computer talk at CERN* by John Seiradakis, 2018

146. *Decoding the ancient Greek astronomical calculator known as the Antikythera Mechanism* by Tony Freeth, Yanis Bitsakis, Xenophon Moussas and John Seiradakis for Nature, December 2006

147. *The Astronomical Events of the Parapegma of the Antikythera Mechanism* by M. Anastasiou, J. Seiradakis et all, 2013

148. *The Front Dial and Parapegma Inscriptions* by Y. Bitsakis and A. Jones, 2013

149. *Greece (Underwater Archaeology)* by Christina Marangou, The European Archaeologist, Issue 44, Sprig 2015

150. *On the epoch of the Antikythera mechanism and its eclipse predictor* by Christián C. Carman and James Evans, 15 November 2014

151. *The Antikythera Mechanism: A Shocking Discovery from Ancient Greece*, Dr, Tony Freeth, Stanford

152. Algorithmic Justice League - Wikipedia.

153. 2017 Return to Antikythera Expedition.

154. Antikythera shipwreck yields statue pieces and mystery bronze disc, Jo Marchant, Nature, 04 October 2017

155. Possible Piece of Antikythera Mechanism Identified, Archeology, 2018

156. No, Archaeologists Probably Did Not Find a New Piece of the Antikythera Mechanism, Smithsonian Magazine, 2018.

157. Return to Antikythera Facebook page from original expedition member.

158. *Excavation exclusively for... Greeks?* by Ethnos.gr, 2019.

159. Return to Antikythera Facebook page from original expedition member.

160. *Decoding Anagrammed Texts Written in an Unknown Language and Script* by Greg Kondrak and Bradley Hauer, 2017

161. *Computational Analysis of the Voynich Manuscript* by Prof. Greg Kondrak, University of Alberta

162. *Solving The Voynich Manuscript With Ai* by Greg Kondrak

163. Voynich Manuscript page 116 last paragraph translated by Monica Yokubinas, Academia.edu 2018.
    Voynich.ninja threads.

164. The Voynich Manuscript Medicinal Herbology Translation and Identification by Monica Yokubinas, Academia.edu, 2018.

165. *Survey of subjective "God encounter experiences": Comparisons among naturally occurring experiences and those occasioned by the classic psychedelics* by Roland R. Griffiths et al, 2019

166. Emily M. Bender, Timnit Gebru, Angelina McMillan-Major, and Margaret Mitchell. 2021. *On the Dangers of Stochastic Parrots: Can Language Models Be Too Big?* .

167. Stochastic Parrot - Wikipedia.

168. *We read the paper that forced Timnit Gebru out of Google. Here's what it says*, by Karen Hao for MIT Technology Review, December 4, 2020.

169. *A Model of the Cosmos in the ancient Greek Antikythera Mechanism*, by Tony Freeth et al.

170. The Antikythera Cosmos.

171. Vesuvius Challenge.

Image Attribution and Licensing

- All Voynich Manuscript images, digitized by Beinecke Rare Book and Manuscript Library, Yale University. Public Domain and Fair Use.
- Abduction of a Sabine Woman by Giambologna, photo by Thermos, licensed under CC BY 2.5, background removed.
- The Rape of Proserpina by Gian Lorenzo Bernini, photo by Alvesgaspar, licensed under CC BY 4.0, background removed.
- Wilfred M. Voynich and Ethel Voynich provenance and research files on the Cipher (Voynich) manuscript, digitized by Beinecke Rare Book and Manuscript Library, Yale University. Public domain and Fair Use.
- Cadamosto's Herbal, Taccuinum Sanitatis, The New York Public Library. Public domain and Fair Use.
- Picture of Ethel Lilian Voynich, Wikipedia Commons, Public Domain.
- Ramon Llull, Ars compendiosa inveniendi veritatem XV Century. Palma, BP, 1031. Digital version Biblioteca Virtual del Patrimonio Bibliográfico, licensed under CC BY 4.0.
- Wall painting of cult procession from Knossos, photo by ArchaiOptix , licensed under CC BY 4.0.
- Bull leaping Minoan fresco by Jebulon. Public Domain.